MW01243457

MY KINDA
forever

Summer Sisters - Book 6

LACEY BLACK

My Kinda Forever

Summer Sisters Book 6

Index

Also by Lacey Black

Rivers Edge series
Trust Me, Rivers Edge book 1 (Maddox and Avery) – FREE at all retailers
> ~ *#1 Bestseller in Contemporary Romance & #3 in overall free e-books*
> ~ *#2 Bestseller in overall free e-books on another retailer*

Fight Me, Rivers Edge book 2 (Jake and Erin)
Expect Me, Rivers Edge book 3 (Travis and Josselyn)
Promise Me: A Novella, Rivers Edge book 3.5 (Jase and Holly)
Protect Me, Rivers Edge book 4 (Nate and Lia)
Boss Me, Rivers Edge book 5 (Will and Carmen)
Trust Us: A Rivers Edge Christmas Novella (Maddox and Avery)
> ~ *This novella was originally part of the Christmas Miracles Anthology*

BOX SET – contains all 5 novels, 2 novellas, and a BONUS short story

Bound Together series
Submerged, Bound Together book 1 (Blake and Carly)
> ~ *An International Bestseller*

Profited, Bound Together book 2 (Reid and Dani)
> ~*A Bestseller, reaching Top 100 on 2 e-retailers*

Entwined, Bound Together book 3 (Luke and Sidney)

Summer Sisters series
My Kinda Kisses, Summer Sisters book 1 (Jaime and Ryan)
> ~*A Bestseller, reaching Top 100 on 2 e-retailers*

My Kinda Night, Summer Sisters book 2 (Payton and Dean)
My Kinda Song, Summer Sisters book 3 (Abby and Levi)
My Kinda Mess, Summer Sisters book 4 (Lexi and Linkin)
My Kinda Player, Summer Sisters book 5 (AJ and Sawyer)

Lacey Black

My Kinda Player, Summer Sisters book 6 (Meghan and Nick)

Standalone
Music Notes, a sexy contemporary romance standalone
A Place To Call Home, a novella

*Coming Soon from Lacey Black
My Kinda Wedding, a Summer Sisters Novella
Book 1 in the Rockland Falls series, a new contemporary series

Dedication

To my readers – to everyone who stuck with me
and saw this storyline through. I know it wasn't easy,
but I hope it was worth the ride.
I promised you a happily ever after –
This one's for you!

Lacey Black

Chapter One

Meghan

It's a Summer sister tradition that on the first Saturday of each month, the six of us get together. We take turns picking the location or activity, anything from margaritas and a movie to wine and painting classes at the small gallery uptown. One thing, though, is as certain as the sun rising over the Chesapeake Bay every morning: there will be alcohol involved.

Always.

Well, except tonight.

See? I'm already a liar and I've only barely begun my story.

Tonight, we're doing string art in the back room of Lucky's Bar, and even though we're spending a sisters' night at a bar, no one is partaking in alcoholic beverages. Not because we don't want to, but because one-third of our group is very pregnant, and while both Lexi and Jaime have continuously proclaimed to be fine with watching everyone else drink, we've decided to stand united and go alcohol-free.

It's actually not the first time. In fact, a few months ago, when we were making chocolates for Valentine's Day, we didn't drink. It just depends on who's organizing our group activity and where it's located.

This month was my turn. It's hard to find activities that aren't repeated too often, but also find something that we can all agree on. Me? I prefer the crafty, creative nights, which is why we're tapping tiny nails into a piece of treated wood so we can run string from nail to nail, displaying the design of a colorful flower.

And that's why Lexi is grumbling on the opposite side of the table. She doesn't have the patience for crafts. Actually, she doesn't have much patience for anything.

"I've hit my fingers at least four times already. My fingers were already fat and swollen," our youngest sister complains as she gently taps the nail with her small hammer.

"We need to get that baby out of you. You're so moody," AJ says as she gingerly taps her final tiny nail into her board.

"I know," Lexi agrees. "I still have just over two months to go. I'm just so exhausted all the time."

"It's probably because you're chasing twins around the house," Abby adds, referring to Lexi's seven-month-old twin sons.

"Well, only one is actually mobile. Hudson army crawls all over the house like no one's business, and little Hemi is content just sitting and watching him go. He doesn't actually have to do much of anything because Hudson gets everything for him."

"Sounds like you and Abby," Payton, our oldest sister, chimes in.

"Truth. Lexi didn't walk until she was well over a year old because Abby ran around and did everything for her," Jaime adds.

"Didn't Lexi *not* walk until closer to a year and a half?" I ask, knowing that it's a sore spot with our youngest sister. She hates to be reminded that she was lacking in something, even if that something took place while she was still pooping her diaper and drooling down her chin.

"Zip it! Why do we always bring this up? It's not like I could change it. I was a late bloomer!" Lexi proclaims, her pregnant belly bouncing as she tries not to laugh.

"Almost as late as Abby. When did you finally get boobs?" AJ asks Lexi's twin without looking up from her art.

"Shut up!" Abby screeches, drawing the attention of the table beside us. "It's not my fault my boobs didn't come until I was twenty!"

We all laugh at her exasperation, while she grumbles under her breath about mean and disrespectful sisters.

We should probably go over my family tree, right? Hang on tight. It's a doozy.

First, there's Payton. She's the oldest Summer sister and proud owner of Blossoms and Blooms, the local floral and gift shop in downtown Jupiter Bay. Payton is married to Dean McIntire, an accountant–*her* accountant, actually. Long, dirty story there. Dean has a daughter, Brielle, from a previous relationship and was a single dad and sole provider until his relationship with my sister. Payton was diagnosed with PCOS years ago and has been struggling with infertility issues. She completed her sixth and final month of Clomid, and has yet to announce what steps they'll take next, if any, to conceive.

Jaime is next in line as second oldest. She works at Addie's Place, a local not-for-profit that helps provide afterschool care and assistance for those families who may not be able to afford it. She helps with homework, organizes movies and playtime, and just hangs out with young kids in a mentor kinda way. It's a wonderful program, one she's helping grow to include more services. She's married to Ryan Elson, a local contractor, and together, they're expecting their first baby mid-June.

AJ, or Alison Jane, is third, and is getting married at the end of July. She's a math teacher at the grade school and met her fiancé when they almost slept together one night before realizing they were actually coworkers. Funny story; I'll tell you about it sometime. Sawyer Randall is a former Major League Baseball third baseman, who played ten years for the Rangers, which only elevates his hotness factor with the locals.

I'm next in the order of Summer girls, but we'll skip me for now.

Finally, rounding out our group at number five and six are the twins, Abigail and Alexis.

Abby is our closet sex-fanatic, working as an editor for a large publisher from New York. She reads smutty, dirty books all day before welcoming home her firefighter and EMT boyfriend, Levi Morgan. They live together (with their supposed "unused" sex swing) and have been hinting about buying a house. I foresee a ring on her finger and another wedding on the horizon very soon.

Finishing off the six Summer sisters is Lexi. By day, she's a beautician in one of the most popular hair salons in town, with a clientele list longer than my arm. By night, she's chasing babies around her cute little house with her eight-pack of abs husband, Linkin. He's a mechanic at a restoration shop and dotes on her so much that it's almost sickening. They welcomed their twin sons, Hudson and Hemi last September, and quickly learned how fertile a woman can be after being deprived of sex post-delivery. Their third child is due mid-July. Yep, three babies ten-months apart.

Should be fun.

The six of us live in Jupiter Bay, Virginia, a small coastal town along the Chesapeake Bay that fills with tourists during the summer months. Our father, Brian, still lives in the home we all grew up in, but one person has been noticeably absent since I was eleven years old. Our mom, Trisha, passed away from ovarian cancer, leaving behind her husband and six young daughters. It was a difficult time, but not the most heartbreaking I've endured, unfortunately.

As horrific as it was to have a parent die at such a young age, we were never alone. Our mom's parents, Emma and Orval, moved in to help. Dad is a pilot and would often work long hours, which left six girls in need of care. That's why our grandparents stepped up and played a pivotal role in our lives. They were there when we all needed them most, which was a huge relief to our dad. Of course, what he couldn't have been prepared for was the inappropriate amount of groping and PDA that was to follow their arrival in our home.

And age hasn't slowed them down one bit.

Well into their eighties, and they're still as frisky and ornery as ever.

We're a close family who has shared our fair share of heartache; something I know all too well, but also something I'm not going to dwell on tonight. I'm actually having a good night, laughing and joking with my sisters. The last thing I need is to feel the return of the heavy weight settling into my chest.

"I don't understand this," Payton whispers as she tries to wind her turquoise string around her nails in the pattern displayed on the paper in front of her.

"Your string is knotting," I instruct, reaching across the table and taking her balled-up mess. "You need to keep it wound around the cardboard so it doesn't tangle," I add, rewrapping it around the small piece of cardboard.

"Any name ideas, Jaime?" Abby asks as she continues to wrap her string, a bright pink flower taking shape.

"We can't agree on anything for a girl. I really like Faith," she says with a wide smile as she rubs her belly.

"That's adorable," I reply, handing back the straightened out string to my oldest sister.

"I love it. He doesn't like the name?" Payton asks, jumping right back in to stringing her flower.

"He likes Jasmine. Jasmine! She'll either be a Disney Princess or a stripper!" Jaime proclaims loudly, making us all giggle. "I can't name my daughter Jasmine, guys. Everywhere she goes I'll hear the *Aladdin* soundtrack."

"Well, that's better than the soundtrack to *Independence Day*," AJ offers with a laugh, referring to Will Smith's girlfriend in the movie, who was a stripper named Jasmine.

"Seriously. Who names their daughter Jasmine?" Jaime huffs.

"It's not a bad name," I insist, finishing up my flower in record time.

Jaime exhales and winces. "This baby uses my kidneys as punching bags. And no, it's not a bad name. I suppose it could even be a perfectly acceptable name, you know, if you were a burlesque dancer."

"What about boy names?" Abby asks, completing her flower as well.

"Actually, that's the one name we've settled on."

"Oh? Spill!" AJ insists.

"Henry."

"What? No! You can't name your baby Henry. We're using Henry!" Lexi declares, her string art all but forgotten.

"You know you're having a boy?" I ask, quickly loving the idea of having another nephew.

Lexi stumbles. "Well, no, actually, we don't know, but we decided on Henry. We have H names."

"You're calling dibs on the name because it begins with an H?" Jaime asks, exasperated.

"Yes. Pick a new name," Lexi insists.

"No. You pick a new name," Jaime argues.

"Why are you being so difficult?" Lexi inquires, glaring at our sister.

"I'm being difficult? Why don't you just pick a new name? There are dozens of other H names to choose from. Why not Herbert or…Harry?"

"We like Henry," Lexi growls.

"Well, so do we." Jaime sits back and crosses her arms over her chest. "I guess whoever has their baby first will get the name." To settle her point, she arches her eyebrows and gives Lexi a victorious smirk.

Lexi gasps. "You wouldn't!"

"Not my fault I'm due before you."

"Ladies, ladies, ladies, do we have to argue over a name? I mean, what if you both have girls? Then this dispute is a moot point," Payton reasons.

"This is just like when we were little," AJ whispers to me. "Only this time, I hope someone's underwear doesn't end up on the front lawn." We both giggle as memories flood my mind. Back when we were in junior high, Jaime and Lexi got into a fight over God knows what, which resulted in Lexi throwing all of Jaime's underwear on the front lawn moments before a bunch of her classmates were due to come over. Little did they know they were going to see a fireworks show (which may have involved Jaime's panties hanging from the tree like party lights).

"Or hanging from the chandelier?" I tease AJ, referring to the time her thong ended up hanging from the light fixture at Sawyer's house. It was there for weeks.

"Bitch," she teases, feigns indignity, which makes me laugh because I know she really doesn't mean to call me the name.

It feels damn good to laugh and carry on with my sisters. Like the days, some nights are better than others, and I'm thankful that tonight is a good one.

It's been more than two years since my life changed forever.

Pushing invading thoughts of Josh and the night he was taken from me out of my mind, I turn back to my project. I've become a master at distraction, and tonight is no different. I've learned that if you keep yourself busy, you have less of a chance of those pesky little what ifs creeping into your mind.

What ifs that I won't allow to ruin another night with my sisters.

So I take a page from my own playbook, push it all to the back of my mind, plaster on my smile, and pretend like I'm fine and didn't die alongside my fiancé that cold and rainy night more than two years ago.

It's worked for me for this long.

It'll work for me tonight.

At least until I go home.

Alone.

* * *

Ryan and Jaime drop me off on their way to grab French fries. When Jaime has a craving, it's always salty. Honestly, I think it's just an excuse to try road-head. Those two get busy in vehicles more than anyone I know. And considering who my grandparents are, that's saying something.

I chickened out on telling them my news.

As I make my way into the cute little house that was once so full of life and love, I wonder (for the ten millionth time) if I'm making a mistake. Am I ready for this? My heart starts to gallop in my chest at the thought. A date. But it doesn't have to be a big deal. I mean, we're just two former classmates enjoying a meal together, right?

Wrong.

This is so much bigger than that.

It's acknowledgment that Josh isn't coming back.

It's my first real taste of acceptance that he's gone.

I twist the ring on my left ring finger, the one I can't seem to take off, and take a deep breath. As I glance around the house we used to share, I spy so much of him still in the place. His worn pair of tennis shoes are still on the floor by the front closet. The throw he bought as one of our first purchases for the new house is on the couch. His favorite coffee mug is still in the cabinet, as if waiting for him to wake up, fill it, and enjoy that first cup of coffee of the day.

But none of that is going to happen again.

That's why I need this date.

It's been two years.

As scary as it is, and believe me, it's terrifying, I need this. I may not be completely ready, but there's only one way to find out, right? So next Saturday, I'll meet Adam Sullivan at the Mexican restaurant uptown, catch up on the last ten years of our lives, and see where it goes. I'm not anticipating it going much further, honestly, and the thought of a goodnight kiss makes me want to hurl. Not because kissing Adam wouldn't be nice. I'm sure it would be.

Because it's not Josh.

And I swore I'd never kiss another.

Never love another.

The familiar anger sweeps through my blood. Anger at a young driver who decided to drink and get behind the wheel. Anger at the weather that made it difficult to drive safely. Anger at time I can't have back. Anger at the man I loved with my entire being for leaving me alone and afraid.

And I am.

Completely alone and wholly afraid.

Resentment and fear seem to be all I have anymore, and as the all too familiar sensations slam into my body, I do what I do best: hide it. Push it aside. Sweep it under the rug. Grab my cleaning supplies and scrub the bathroom until you could eat filet mignon off my floor with a freaking plastic fork.

By the time I'm finished, my bathroom is spotless and I'm completely exhausted. But do you know what I'm not doing? Thinking about Josh. I'm not lost in the sea of despair, being pulled under by powerful and unforgiving memories.

I'm too tired to think, and that's when I know it's finally time for bed. I may not get much sleep before his memory visits me, but at least I know I'll be able to steal a few hours before he arrives.

And he will.

Like clockwork most nights, I'll be seeing Josh Harrison in my dreams.

Chapter Two

Nick

"All right, Tanner, you're all fixed up. I was able to get rid of the cavity and fill it in. Did Meghan talk to you about better brushing?" I ask the nine-year-old who's lying in the reclined chair before me.

The boy nods his head profusely, and out of the corner of my eye, I don't miss the smile that plays on Meghan's lips.

Very sexy and totally kissable lips.

I mentally shake that completely inappropriate and unprofessional thought out of my head and give the boy my full attention. "You'll be numb for about another hour. It should be completely gone by dinner," I tell him, glancing up and noticing the mid-afternoon time.

"Tank you," he replies, his mouth barely moving.

"You're welcome. We'll see you back in six months, okay? If you do better at brushing, we can add you to our no cavity club. You'll even get a free pizza certificate," I tell him as I pull the latex gloves from my hands.

"I wike pizza!"

"I figured," I reply with a laugh. "But you need to make sure you're brushing really good, hitting all of your teeth, and you have to remember to floss. Even those pesky ones in the back." Standing up, I smile down at the boy and hold out my fist for the expected fist bump. "You did good. I'll see you soon, Tanner."

No sooner do I step into the hallway of my dental practice does Patty, our receptionist, flag me down. "Mrs. Ellis is on the phone. She says that tooth just fell out again," she says as she rolls her eyes.

"Teeth don't generally just fall out of your dentures unless you've done something to knock them out," I say aloud to no one in particular.

"I'm aware, Dr. Adams," she replies with a smile.

"Who do we have left?" I ask, glancing up at the clock again. Three o'clock.

"Two regular cleanings. We've been on schedule all day," she says with a pleased look.

"Excellent," I reply with a matching grin as I step into my office.

"Oh, but your four o'clock," she starts but stops, causing me to turn around. Patty clears her throat before she confirms my final appointment of the day. "It's Collette."

"Oh goodie," I mumble, choosing not to use the colorful language I normally say when referring to my ex, but resorting to Meghan's standard response when she can't curse.

Before my office door closes, Patty hollers, "Mrs. Ellis is on line two!"

Looks like I'll be dealing with Mrs. Ellis and Collette today.

Awesome.

I spend the next forty minutes working at my desk, finishing up a few things, until I'm paged to Meghan's room. My heart starts to race as I get up and make my way down the hall. Plastering on my best professional face, I step through the doorway. Meghan is there, standing at the small counter and writing in the chart. Her long, brown hair is pulled back in a messy ponytail that looks like someone might have just tangled his fingers in it.

Okay, so I might be that someone. It is my fantasy, after all.

Clearing dirty images of my dental hygienist from my mind, I turn my attention to the old woman lying in the chair. "Ahh, Mrs. Huxley. How are the tulips blooming this year?" I ask as I slide my hands into a pair of latex gloves.

"Wonderful, Dr. Adams. My entire garden is full of bright colors," the elderly woman gushes. "My lilac bush is in full bloom, as well, and my entire garden smells so heavenly."

Smiling, I glance over at Meghan to find her with a sly grin aimed directly at me. "Well, Mrs. Huxley, let's see if we can't get you back in your garden before dinner. Meg, how did Mrs. Huxley's cleaning go?" I ask, slipping the paper facemask over my mouth.

"Perfect. Her x-ray images are on the screen for your review," she replies, handing me the mirror.

I glance around inside my former high school English teacher's mouth, making note of changes from her last appointment. As I turn to Meghan, I start, "Can you hand me–" but am cut off by the periodontal probe being placed in my hand.

"Thanks."

She doesn't reply, just makes the notes in the chart as I speak. We're a great team. The best, actually.

When I moved back home to Jupiter Bay to work under Dr. Zastrow, it was with the option to buy the practice when he was ready to retire. That was three years ago. Last year, the good doctor decided to finally move away and relocate to Florida, where the golf courses were calling his name.

Meghan was a new hire straight out of college. She was young, energetic, and with a deep-rooted love for good oral health. She's been here for six years now, and really has become a key part of the team. She makes my day a hell of a lot better, that's for sure, and I'm not just talking about the hard work and dedication she has to her job.

"Time to stick out your tongue," I instruct my former teacher as the gauze is placed in my hand. With a quick screening for oral cancer, I complete her appointment. "Everything looks great."

"Everything feels great. I love it when Meghan cleans my teeth," she says as I help her sit from the reclined position.

"She's the best," I agree, winking at Meghan, who glances up from her notes and gives me another smile. "Come on, Mrs. Huxley, I'll walk you up to Patty. She'll make your next appointment."

I leave Meghan behind to get ready for the next patient, dreading the arrival of my ex. Why she hasn't transferred to the other dental practice in town is beyond me. Probably so she can keep fucking with me, waving my damn cat (albeit former feline) in my face in her fucked-up game of tug of war.

I miss that damn cat.

"Here you are, Mrs. Huxley. Patty will get you set up with your next appointment. We'll see you in six months," I say politely, shaking my former teacher's hand.

"You're such a doll, Nick. When are you gonna settle down and give your mama grandkids?" she asks innocently.

As I'm getting ready to reply, movement behind her catches my attention, and I realize Collette is sitting in the waiting room. She surely heard the question, but I choose to ignore her. "I'm sure she's very anxious. I just haven't found the right woman yet," I reply with a warm grin, feeling slightly vindicated that my ex heard me. Without waiting for her to reply, I wave my goodbyes and turn back the way I came.

"Nick, wait." Stopping dead in my tracks, I slowly turn and face Collette. She's quiet for a few moments, allowing her eyes to peruse my body, before returning them to my face. I get no satisfaction that she may have been checking me out. "How have you been?"

"Fine." My one-word answer is curt, but to the point. I'm not about to elaborate on my life post break-up.

"Good, good," she says, flashing her bright pearly-white smile and twisting her long blonde hair around her finger. "I was worried about you."

Raising my eyebrow, I reply, "It's been nine months, Collette."

"I know, but it was devastating for you when we broke up." Her voice rises slightly, taking on a whiny, singsong tone. Did I ever find that attractive before?

"I was devastated that you cleaned out my house while I was gone to work. And you took my fucking cat," I reply, teetering on the verge of anger.

"We got Cosmo together!" she bellows, her own voice rising to meet mine.

Glancing around, I quickly notice both Patty and Mrs. Huxley are both watching the show. "I'm sure Meghan is ready for you. Come on back," I say politely, even though I'd rather kick her spoiled, pampered ass out onto the sidewalk.

We're both quiet as I lead her down the hall. As I step into the small room where my dental hygienist works, I catch Meghan's attention. "Hey, how was–" she starts, but stops when Collette steps out from behind me.

"Hi, Meghan. How are things?" she asks as she deposits her purse on the chair in the corner.

"Things are…fine," she stammers with a smile (a fake one that she flashes too damn much lately). She glances my way with a questioning look in her deep green eyes, before mouthing "what the fuck?" to me.

"Your four o'clock," I say with a shrug, knowing Collette's presence in the office is as annoying to Meghan as it is to me. Meg was definitely Team Nick when the break-up happened, even going as far as to help me pick out all new furniture for my house. You know, the furnishings my *ex* took with her when she left?

"Oh, goodie," she mumbles as she reaches for her gloves. "Have a seat, Collette, and we'll get started in a moment." Meghan reaches for my arm, wrapping her firm little fingers around my forearm. "A word?" she whispers pleasantly.

Following her into the hallway, I'm rewarded with a big whiff of her summery scent as she steps close, practically against my side. "Am I going to get fired if I accidentally pull a tooth?" she whispers.

Chuckling, I match her stance, leaning down just enough that my mouth is dangerously close to her ear. "Never. I mean, accidents happen."

"Good to know," she says with a deep exhale as she stands to her full five-foot, six inch height. I know this because the top of her head hits directly below my chin.

"Just try not to make her bleed too much," I add humorously.

"I make no promises," she huffs. "I mean, if she accidentally bleeds out on the chair, then we can sneak over and get Cosmo."

That makes me laugh. After Collette and I broke up and she moved from my house, it was the fact that she took Cosmo, claiming him to be hers, that pissed Meghan off the most. She knows damn well that I fed, watered, and changed the litter box of our two-year-old gray and white cat.

"Your vindictive side is inspiring, Megs. Call me when you're ready for me," I say as I turn to head toward my office.

"Oh, hell no, Dr. Adams. If I have to deal with her, so do you," she sasses as she grabs my arms and pulls me back. 'She's freakishly strong,' I think to myself, which is quickly followed by, 'Stop thinking about your dental hygienist in any other manner than professional.'

"I can hear you," Collette says in an annoyed tone, from the room behind me, which makes both Meghan and me laugh quietly.

"Come on. Inside," she giggles, pushing me into the small cleaning room.

When I step back into the room, Collette is glaring daggers at me. "I'm just going to…assist." I throw her an unapologetic grin before stepping over to the counter and grabbing Collette's chart, flipping open the file and glancing down at the information from her last appointment. It was a year ago.

"You need updated X-rays," I say aloud before looking over my shoulder. Meghan is already there, the lead bib fitted across Collette's chest, and the paper placed in her mouth for bitewing X-rays.

"On it," Meghan says with a wink. "Care to step out?"

It takes only a few minutes for Meghan to take the images we need, readjusting the paper and the machine between each one. I watch her work effortlessly, getting everything done and in a timely manner. It's probably so she can get rid of my cat stealing ex that much quicker.

When she completes the X-rays, we both slip back into the room, and Meghan gets to work. Occasionally, she asks me to add notes in the chart, but for the most part, everyone is quiet. There's no small talk that usually takes place during appointments. In fact, it's an uncomfortable silence; one that speaks of untold secrets and strong dislike. It makes me adjust the tie at my neck in an attempt to suck in a few extra breaths of air.

"It's okay, Patty dear. I'll only be a minute," we hear coming from the front office. Meghan and I glance at each other at the exact same moment and know what's about to happen next.

"Meggy Pie, are you here?" her Grandma bellows down the hall, moments before popping her head in the doorway. "Oh! There you are!"

"Yep, here I am. Working," Meghan replies sarcastically without looking up from her task inside Collette's mouth.

"I was just in the area," Emma says with a bright smile. "We were out of KY."

I choke on air. "KY?" I ask, giving my full attention to the old woman before me.

"Oh, yes. I've developed a liking for the one that also warms your–"

"*Why* are you here again?" Meghan interrupts loudly.

"To invite you to dinner tomorrow evening. That is, if you're not doing the good doctor tomorrow after work," Emma says, followed by collective gasps.

"What?" Meghan gasps.

"What?" Emma asks innocently.

"You just said I was...*doing*... Nick," Meghan says, mortified.

"No I didn't," Emma insists, even though we all clearly heard her. "I said if you weren't doing anything *with* the good doctor tomorrow night," Emma adds, an ornery, evil glint in her light green eyes. "Your mind is always in the gutter." Emma glances down, as if noticing the patient for the first time. "Oh! Is that Collette Cartwright? I'm surprised to see you, dear. You let your ex near your mouth with his tool?"

Now I really am choking on air.

Quickly, I realize I'm not the only one who took her seemingly innocent statement and turned it into a porno. Meghan's face is beet red, and Collette looks completely mortified. And Emma? Well, if the grin on her face is any indication, I'd say her "seemingly innocent" statement was anything but.

"I'm sorry Grandma, but I have book club tomorrow," Meghan says, getting back to work on finishing Collette's cleaning.

"Book Club? Have they added erotica to their reading list yet? Irma Daniels keeps trying to get me to join her little club, but I just can't read without the good stuff," Emma says, waving her hand dismissively. Turning to me, she adds, "It's like having to read *Playboy* without the pictures. Boring," she sings.

"Anyway, I should go. If you'd rather go read and discuss books where the hero and heroine don't even dip the pen in the inkwell, then you just go right ahead. Grandpa and I will be at home, giving the dog a bone," she says with a wave goodbye.

"But, you don't have a dog," Meghan refutes.

"I know," she grins widely and winks before walking out of the room.

"Did that just happen?" Meghan asks, her wide green eyes locked firmly on mine.

"'Fraid so, Meggy Pie," I tease, unable to stop the laugh. She hates it when I call her that. "Let's get this appointment finished so we can get on with our nightlife."

* * *

That night, while the sun sinks behind the trees, casting shadows on my living room, I sit at the kitchen table with my sister, Natalie, and her husband, Stuart, as they continue to make googly eyes at each other, like I'm not even in the room.

"Stop it," I tell them in a firm big brother voice.

"What?" Nat asks, a mischievous smile cresting her face. Then I notice her lower body move and Stuart slightly jump in his seat.

"Are you playing footsy under the table? Please don't make me look. I'll have nightmares."

"You definitely don't want to look," Nat teases.

"Jesus," I grumble, rubbing my temples, as if fretting a headache. "You two are too much. How long does the honeymoon phase last again?"

"Forever. It's never going to end," Natalie replies, taking a sip of her wine.

"Lies. It'll end," I retort, taking a pull from my own beer bottle.

"Don't transfer your relationship woes and troubles on us, big brother. Stuart and I are perfectly content and happy in our own little marriage sex bubble," my horrible sister adds with a shrug.

"Don't say sex."

"Sex, sex, sex, sex…" she trails off, an evil smirk on her face.

"Gross," I grumble lightheartedly and turn to my brother-in-law. "Can't you control her?"

Stuart smiles. "Why would I want to? She's so much more fun when she's out of control," he adds, making my chicken breast and baked potato threaten to make a reappearance.

"For fuck's sake, you two," I chastise to a chorus of laughter. "Now you sound like Meghan's grandparents."

Natalie gets up and starts to clear the dirty dishes. I try to stop her, but she waves me off. "How are Orval and Emma? I haven't seen much of them since the infamous Viagra brownies incident. That was, what, almost two years ago?"

That brings a smile to my face. I remember hearing all about the time Orval laced homemade brownies with the erectile dysfunction drug and proceeded to give them to the guys at Jaime and Ryan's joint bachelor/bachelorette party. "Emma stopped by today when Collette was in the chair."

"Wait, your ex still comes to you for dental work?" Stuart asks, his eyebrows arched.

"Apparently. It was a pleasant surprise at the end of my workday."

"You should have accidentally pulled all of her teeth," Natalie sneers an unhappy look.

"Now you sound like Meghan," I point out, recalling her saying the exact same thing earlier.

"Ohh, Meghan," she coos in a singsong voice.

"Stop it," I chastise, knowing exactly where she's going with this. It's the same place she goes every chance she gets.

"How is your Meggy?" Natalie places her chin in her palms and gives me one of those dreamy, far-off looks.

I roll my eyes. "She's not *my* Meggy. She's my employee."

"Keep tellin' yourself that, big brother." My annoying little sister grins at me, which results in very maturely sticking my tongue out at her.

"Meghan is…" How to explain it. She's miserable, but tries to hide it. She's sad and doesn't know what to do with herself, so she keeps herself so overly busy that she barely has time to breathe. But I suppose that's the point, right? Then she's not forced to think about the love she lost and the life she'll never have with him. "She's doing fine."

That's all I got, because even though she's anything but fine, it's not my place to tell her secrets or talk about her. I see everything she tries to hide from the world, including me. She paints on her pretty smile and pretends.

And it kills me.

Because her smiles aren't real. They haven't been for more than two years.

Her laughter is hollow.

Her eyes don't sparkle like emeralds anymore.

She's just going through the motions.

I hate it.

"I couldn't imagine going through what she has. I mean to lose your fiancé? No way. You might as well throw me in the hole with him," Natalie says, reaching over and grabbing Stuart's hand.

"She'll get there." I really do think that. She's getting closer, but she's not quite there yet. One day, she'll move on and let love in again. Oh, I'm sure it's terrifying as hell, but if anyone is strong enough to do it, it's Meghan.

As for me? I'm still scared as hell that the next woman I fall for is going to steal my furniture again. I mean, who does that shit, anyway? My ex, that's who. I've always been attracted to the crazy ones. Cat stealers.

I've been feeling the itch to get back on the horse for a few weeks now. I think that's why I've suddenly started to see Meghan in a new light. One that bosses and friends shouldn't take notice of, that's for sure. It's a lawsuit waiting to happen.

Instead, I try to focus on other women around me. A single mom of one of my Little Dragons, an hour-long class, one day a week, for five to eight year olds who are just learning karate. The barista at the coffee shop uptown. Hell, even the divorcee who cuts my hair. Anyone besides my brunette employee with emerald eyes, a dazzling smile, and a quick wit that makes me laugh.

But no patients.

Never another patient.

Or employee.

New rule.

Actually, old rule, but one I'm highlighting and bolding in the next edition of the employee handbook.

It's time to try the whole dating thing again. Dinner. Maybe a movie. Hopefully, a little kissing. It's been a while, but I think I remember how to do this. It's like riding a bike, right?

Find a date.

Enjoy said date.

How hard can it be?

Chapter Three

Meghan

There are fourteen of us in Irma Daniels' living room sipping wine or lemonade and discussing the latest John Greer book on a Thursday night. My attention isn't one hundred percent there, especially after Grandma's comment about reading smutty books. What would happen if my next pick was something a bit racier? Would they freak out if I suggested E L James or Sylvia Day? At twenty-eight, I'm the youngest woman in the room.

By a good twenty years.

I haven't even reached my prime yet. Hell, most of these women have been married for as long as I've been alive. You'd think they'd be all about reading a few kinky words to spice up their marriage.

Married book clubbers outweigh the non-married ones. With nine wearing a ring on their finger, only three are singles, two of which are widows. I consider myself a widow, even though Josh and I were never married. We had plans though, and a diamond on my finger, so I believe that puts me in the same class as Cindy Jones, the nice woman whose husband died a few years ago from a heart attack.

After we discuss the book, which I barely participated in, everyone congregates to the dining room, where the appetizers and desserts we all brought are laid out. I pile some crab dip and cream cheese bars on my plate and head over to the corner of the room. Everyone is discussing the newest coffee shop to open uptown, anxious to find out all of the gossip on the young family who recently relocated to Jupiter Bay and opened the business.

"Hey, you've been quiet tonight," Cindy says as she comes over to sit beside me along the back wall.

"Yeah, sorry. I've been a little sidetracked tonight."

"No worries here. I had a hard time getting into the book myself, which is why I didn't have much to say. Sometimes, I just don't want those gut-clenching, tear-jerking stories that make me bawl my eyes out from start to finish. Sometimes, I just want to read something that will make me laugh until I cry."

Yes. This.

Exactly.

"No, I totally get it," I tell her with a smile.

"Personally," she starts, bending down and whispering so only I can hear, "I'd love to read something a bit...dirtier."

I glance her way, a wicked little glimmer lighting her blue eyes. "Me too."

Cindy laughs and holds up her hand for a high-five. "It's settled. Next time it's yours or my pick, we're totally choosing smut."

Laughing, I turn my body so that our knees are a bit closer. "Deal."

We both continue to eat our food, watching the speculation and conversations of the other attendees around the table. Someone actually just suggested that the young couple moved to Jupiter Bay because the husband has an illegitimate kid with one of the young single women in town.

Clearly, they read too much fiction.

"How's your dad?" Cindy asks casually.

But my radar perks up.

"He's fine," I answer, looking her way and watching her body language. She's completely relaxed. Casual. Nothing that says she's being nosy, or worse, looking for a date.

Not that dating my dad would be bad. Actually, it would be the complete opposite, and the more I think about it, Cindy would be a great woman for him to date. But am I ready to see my dad date?

I come to my answer immediately, and realize I mean it a thousand percent.

Yes.

As far as I know, Dad hasn't dated since Mom passed away. It's been years – more than sixteen years, actually – and I've never seen him so much as glance toward another woman.

That thought truly makes me a little sad. Even though I completely understand it – the prospect of dating again makes me a little queasy – I don't want that for the patriarch of our family. I want him happy, smiling, and if love is in the cards for him again, I want that too, and I believe my sisters would all feel the same way.

"Can I ask you something?" My voice is quiet as I glance around the room to see if anyone is paying us any attention.

"Of course," Cindy replies, giving me her full attention.

Before I can chicken out, I ask, "Would you be interested in getting coffee sometime Saturday? I have plans later that night, but I'd love to, maybe, talk to you again. More privately." It's as if she knows what I'm getting at. Hell, do I even know what I'm getting at? All I know is that I enjoy chatting with this woman the few times we've spoken during book club, and maybe, just maybe, it would be nice to talk to someone who has been where I am.

Someone who has lost the one she loved.

"I'd love to," Cindy replies instantly, a warm smile on her face. "Name the place and pick the time. I'll be there."

"Say, eleven? At the new place on Main Street, Hendricks?"

"That sounds wonderful. We can grab a sandwich, too. I've heard amazing things about their lunches."

"Perfect," I say, relaxing in my chair a bit, the tension ebbing from my shoulders almost immediately.

After chatting for a few more minutes, everyone starts to gather their belongings to head home. Cindy makes sure to give me a quick hug, letting me know she's looking forward to meeting me for coffee on Saturday, and reminding me that our next book club pick is going to be smutty.

The smuttier, the better.

Grandma would be so proud.

* * *

When I pull into my driveway, my phone lights up with a text. Dr. Adams. Or Nick, as he's repeatedly asked me to call him. It was difficult at first, but over the last few years, I've definitely developed more of a friendship with my boss than just a standard eight-to-five work relationship.

In fact, he's kinda become "my person" when I need a friend or am feeling exceptionally low. He's attended family gatherings, as well as rescued me when the memories of Josh start to swallow me whole. Nick is a good friend, and besides my sisters, I don't really have too many of those.

Josh was my life, my everything.

My best friend.

Now isn't the time to let his memory grab me and pull me under. While sitting in the driver's seat, I swipe my finger across the screen and pull up Nick's text message.

Nick: *What was it tonight? War & Peace? The Diary of Anne Frank?*

Me: *You would be wrong on both accounts. We read those last year.* *emoji sticking its tongue out*

Nick: *Damn. I always miss the good ones. So what was it? 50 Shades?*

Me: *You're picturing Irma Daniels reading it, aren't you?*

Nick: *I just threw up in my mouth.* *vomiting emoji*

Me: *laughing emoji*

Nick: *I should fire you for that.*

Me: *You wouldn't dare. You need me.*

His bubbles appear, but then disappear without text, like he started to write and then deleted it. Finally, after a few long, drawn-out seconds of anticipation, he finally replies.

Nick: *Truth. I do.*

Me: *Whatcha doing? I'm sure you're not actually sitting around, wondering about what book we read this week at book club.*

Nick: *Another thrilling Thursday night for me. On my way home from helping Rhenn with a class. I'm starving. Probably stopping at the burger place on Main for a big, juicy to-go order.*

Me: *They have the BEST milkshakes.*

Nick: *You've mentioned. Strawberry, right?*

Me: *Yep. They use real strawberries. Like the real thing, Nick. Not syrup. This is a big deal, my friend.*

Nick: *It most certainly is. Strawberry syrup is a crime against ice cream, Meghan.*

Me: *fist bump gif*

Nick: *I'm getting ready to pull out of the lot. Glad you made it home safely.*

Me: *It's Jupiter Bay. What could have possibly happened to me?*

But as soon as I send the message, I know the answer. Plenty can happen, especially when behind the wheel.

Nick: *Don't make me answer that. I'll see you soon.*

Me: *Tomorrow morning.*

Nick: *smirky emoji*

Me: *Good night*

I drop my phone into my purse and grab my bag before making my way toward the house. The light above the kitchen sink gives off just enough light that I don't trip over the extra pair of shoes I kicked haphazardly by the door. Setting the bag down on the table, I pull off my shoes and head toward our bedroom to change into pajamas.

Wait. My bedroom.

I know it. It's still a struggle to accept it.

Just after throwing on a pair of old flannel shorts that are way too short and one of Josh's t-shirts, the doorbell rings. It's well after nine, which tells me it must be one of my sisters. They're the only ones who would drop by unexpectedly after nine o'clock on a weeknight.

Though, when was the last time one of them just happened to drop by? All of my sisters have significant others now. They have families. Busy lives.

I don't even have time to grab a robe before the knocking starts. Yep, it must be one of my sisters. They all have the patience of...well, something that doesn't have a lot of patience. "I'm coming," I holler as I round the corner from the bedroom and run to the front door. When I check the peephole, I'm shocked at the face staring back at me.

Not one of my sisters at all.

Nick.

I disengage the lock and slowly open the door, carefully concealing my too-short shorts and the fact that I'm braless beneath the shirt. "Hey, everything all right?" I ask, worried that something is wrong.

"Everything's fine. I just happened to have an extra milkshake, and since I was in the area, I thought I'd see if you wanted it." He gives me an innocent smile, but I'm on to his game, as he waves it in my face. Not only do I completely doubt that they just happened to give him an extra shake (strawberry, no less), but

Nick lives on the opposite side of town. Not exactly "in the neighborhood."

But then again, he does have a strawberry shake with him, so who am I to call him out on his blatant lies and send him away?

I reach out my hand for the ice cream goodness and wait until he passes me the cup. There's already a straw stuck in the lid, so I take a quick sip and savor the smooth velvety richness of the milkshake laced with chunks of strawberry heaven. Nick's eyebrow arches toward the sky as he waits. "It's amazing. Okay, you can come in."

"I don't have to come in. I just wanted to drop that off," he says, nodding toward the cup.

"But you have food, right? Might as well come eat it inside while it's still warm."

"You know how much I despise cold fries," he retorts with a grin. "Are you sure? It's getting late."

"Definitely. I'm not ready to go to sleep yet. You can keep me entertained for a while." I open the door and motion for him to enter.

Nick proceeds to step through the door, but there's no missing the way his eyes dart to my chest. When I glance down, I see exactly why. My boobs are practically on display, completely visible beneath the thin, gray material of the shirt. What's more embarrassing than showing my boss my girls is that my nipples choose that exact moment to stand at attention and salute.

Oh, goodie.

I take a step back and cross my arms over my chest. Nick's eyes fly up to meet mine, my cheeks burning with mortification.

However, Nick looks...hungry. And I don't think it's for the cheeseburger and fries he's about to consume. But that can't be right, can it? He has always treated me in a perfectly respectful, friendly manner.

The hunger in his eyes must be for his double cheeseburger.

"Umm, go ahead and make yourself comfy," I instruct, closing the door behind him and keeping all of my bits and pieces covered up. When I turn around, his eyes are focused on my ass.

My ass.

He's blatantly staring at my ass, which is completely covered, thankfully, but the way he's devouring my body makes me feel naked.

And surprisingly, not uncomfortable.

Why is that? I should be exposed, awkward, and incredibly embarrassed.

Instead, I feel...excited.

When the silence stretching between us continues, his eyes finally meet mine. That look that I saw only moments ago is quickly replaced by a sheepish, nervous look. He knows he was busted checking me out, and now neither of us knows what to do or say.

I know what I need to do.

Put on clothes.

I wave him toward the living room and make a beeline to my bedroom. When I'm finally safely behind the closed door, I finally take a deep breath. My reflection catches in the mirror above the dresser and I'm surprised at what I see. Even though my boobs are showing and my nipples clearly begging for attention, I look…cute. Pretty. Completely normal.

Alive.

Running my fingers along my lips, for the first time in a very long time, I wonder what it would be like to kiss someone again. Maybe even Nick. To feel wanted and desired…and alive. Yep, there's that word again.

But it might be the truest adjective to describe this crazy feeling that has pushed to the surface, past the armor of hurt and make believe I keep firmly in place to protect myself. I haven't felt this way in so very long that I thought this bitter sadness may have been all that was left. Like every ounce of happiness and life was buried in that six-foot grave, along with the man I loved.

As I rip off the shirt, grab a bra, and throw on a new (and slightly more form fitting) shirt, I can't help but wonder if there really is life after loss.

And more importantly, am I too terrified to find out?

Chapter Four

Nick

I should be ashamed of myself.

I should leave this house, never to return. I should bleach my eyes and hypnotize my mind so I can't remember the way her breasts pressed against the thin shirt, the way her nipples beaded hard, begging to be licked.

See? That right there.

Friends don't think about their friend's nipples.

Bosses don't picture what it would be like to taste his employee's soft skin.

That's why I'm going to Hell. I'm a terrible friend (and boss). The hard-on in my pants proves it.

Who's the worst friend in the history of all friendships?

Nick Adams, D.D.S.

I've never had this problem with any of my employees, but especially not Meghan. She was always happy, safely tucked away in friend-zone Meghan. Josh would bring her lunch or take her to the deli down the street from the office. He was a great guy. The best. She'd laugh and smile, giving all of her love and affection to one man. And that was fine. I was in a relationship and didn't find her attractive.

Okay, lie.

She has always been pretty (gorgeous, really), but completely off-limits.

I didn't want her.

And I definitely didn't pop hard-ons in her living room and imagine touching her nipples.

Fuck, this is messed up.

So bad.

My stomach growls, reminding me that I have yet to eat. The sad part is, there's only one thing I imagine putting in my mouth right now, and it isn't the double cheeseburger in the bag.

Ignoring the discomfort in my pants, I grab a paper plate from her kitchen and the bottle of mustard from the fridge. By the time I'm back in the living room, pulling my burger from the bag, Meghan returns. She's wearing a form-fitting t-shirt that hugs her body, and a bra. She's definitely wearing one now. She's also still wearing the cotton plaid boxer shorts that make her legs look incredibly tan and a mile long.

Dammit.

That won't help the hard-on.

"Sorry about that. I wasn't expecting anyone," she says sheepishly, grabbing her milkshake from where she left it on the table and sitting on the couch across from me.

"I should have called first. It's my fault for assuming you were up for company."

"No, it's fine. I actually don't mind the visit." She glances around the room, as if waiting for the ghosts to make their nightly appearance.

Meghan pulls her legs up to her chest and quietly drinks her shake. Her movements make those tiny little shorts appear that much smaller, all but disappearing in the V of her legs. Ignoring her attire, I dump the fries on the plate and squirt a blob of mustard. Taking the fries two at a time (because it's practically a law that they must be consumed in pairs), I drop them into my favorite yellow condiment and pop them in my mouth.

"Gross!" Meghan says, a look of horror on her face.

"What?" I ask, dropping two more fries into the mustard before eating them.

"Mustard? What's wrong with ketchup?"

"Nothing's wrong with ketchup," I tell her. "I put it on my burger."

"But you dip your fries in mustard?" Again, she looks horrified, her mouth hanging open as she watches me eat.

"I do," I answer with a shrug. Dipping two into the condiment, I hold them out and wait. Meghan shakes her head in answer, but keeps her eyes on the fries. "Come on, you know you wanna," I egg her on.

She gives me a skeptical look, but slowly drops her legs and leans forward. I expect her to take the fries from my hand, but am pleasantly surprised when she just takes a bite, from my fingers. Her lip grazes my thumb and I can feel her breath settle on my skin. She closes her eyes as she chews, slowly sitting back onto the couch.

My cock? Throbbing.

"Well?" I ask, popping what is left of the two fries in my fingers into my mouth, and trying not to think about the fact that they were just touching Meghan's lips.

"I stand by my original statement," she replies, taking a long pull of her milkshake.

"You don't know what's good for you." With that, I eat my dinner, while engaging in small talk with my dental hygienist.

Before we both know it, it's approaching midnight. "I can't believe it's so late," I state, jumping up and rounding up my trash.

"Me neither. I never stay up this late, unless it's sisters' night."

"Well, you still have a few weeks to go before your next late night."

"Yep. Next one is to celebrate AJ and Sawyer. We're having a bachelorette party at Lucky's, while the guys go to a baseball game that afternoon. They should return about the time the alcohol starts to kick in," she says right before yawning.

"I know," I tell her, making sure I've got my phone and keys. "I'm going."

Meghan stops and looks my way. "You are?"

I shrug. "Yeah, well, maybe he's in the market for a new dentist and this was their idea of vetting me before sitting in the chair?" She just smiles that warm grin that recently started to make my heart pound like a snare drum in my chest. "Plus, my brother-in-law is going, so maybe that has something to do with it?"

"Oh, sure. I forgot about Stuart. Natalie is on the invite list for the bachelorette party," Meghan confirms.

"And she's very excited. She mentioned last night at dinner that she's looking forward to the decorations," I laugh.

"I still can't believe that. That's the last time we put Grandma in charge of decorating," she adds, referring to the wall-to-wall dicks used as décor for Jaime and Ryan's co-party.

We stare at each other for a few seconds, both still smiling, until neither of us know what to do or say. Finally, Meghan speaks. "Thank you for the milkshake. You made my night."

"Mine too." She has no idea. "I'll see you tomorrow," I add as I make my way to her front door. Glancing down, I see a pair of old, worn tennis shoes by the closet door. A man's pair of shoes. Josh's shoes.

Her eyes follow mine, and her once bright eyes turn dark and stormy. I can practically see the sadness sweeping in, transforming her right before my eyes. When I open the door, I hesitate. Part of me doesn't want to leave her here, alone, when she's surrounded by so many memories and could-have-beens. But I also know that I'm not her keeper, and even though I consider myself her friend, if she's not asking for help, I'm in no position to force her.

"Good night, Meggy Pie," I say as I step onto her small porch.

She gives me a look that's part amusement and part annoyance, but I'd take that over the look of angst that was there just a few moments ago. "Good night, Nicholas Adams, D.D.S.," she sasses.

Throwing her a smile and a wave, I head down the steps and toward my car. I slip inside, noticing that Meghan's still on the porch, watching me. I wait a minute for her to go back inside, but realize she's waiting on me to leave first.

I slide my key into the ignition, put the car in reverse, and pull out of her driveway. Giving her another wave, I slowly drive away, those long legs still visible from the rearview mirror.

And even though I try not to think about those sexy legs and mouthwatering breasts – and those nipples, holy hell, those fucking nipples – I know they'll accompany me as I drift off to sleep to images of my beautiful dental hygienist.

Employee handbook, be damned.

* * *

A six a.m. text wakes me from an amazing dream (one that starred a certain brunette with intoxicating green eyes and perky nipples). When I glance at the clock and my phone, I groan.

After getting home well after midnight this morning, I had a hard time falling asleep. Mostly because I was hard as a rock and refused to do anything about it, at least while picturing a certain someone who shall remain nameless.

Rhenn's name greets me on the screen. I already know what his message will say before I even swipe my finger. If you're not ten minutes early, you're already late, according to my friend.

Rhenn: *Where ya at? The mats wait for no one.*

Me: *On my way.*

Throwing my legs over the bed, I ignore the swelling in my boxers and grab a clean pair of basketball shorts and tee. Workouts with Rhenn are always tough, but now he's going to be exceptionally brutal in light of my tardiness.

Rhenn is my oldest friend. We met in grade school when I was being bullied by two junior high boys over my size. I was always a tad on the short side and always ridiculed over it. Rhenn found the boys pushing me around behind the dumpster and intervened. Actually, I believe he kicked one in the balls and told the other he would rearrange his face if he caught him messing with me again.

That was the start of our friendship.

Rhenn was always a big guy, but used his size for good. He owns the dojo where I teach a Wednesday Little Dragons class and help with his bi-weekly Friday self-defense class for beginners. I'm a first degree black belt, while Rhenn is a third. He's an electrician by day and always seems to have no trouble finding a lady-friend to keep him company at night.

After brushing my teeth, I slip on a pair of shoes, grab my bag, and jump into my car to head toward the dojo. By the time I pull in, it's quarter after six, which will probably result in an extra fifteen minutes on the treadmill.

Using my key, I unlock the door and am greeted by the heavy beat of AC/DC. Rhenn must have had a good night last night if he's already hitting "Thunderstruck" for a warm-up. I ignore the man on the treadmill and slip into our private locker room to change. By Friday morning, this place always smells like a sweaty locker room, with towels thrown in the basket in the corner and empty water bottles loitering the benches.

It's why Rhenn pays someone handsomely to come in every weekend and make the place not smell so…smelly.

When I'm ready to go, I join my friend in the weight room attached to the main dojo. He's already pounding the road, or more adequately, the treadmill. Rhenn's the type of guy, even with his big bulky frame, who thinks running five miles is fun.

I see no fun in running.

After stretching out my legs, I climb onto the machine next to his and slowly work up to a jog.

"'Bout fucking time," he pants, sweat already falling from his brow.

"Sorry. Late night." My legs immediately start to feel the burn.

"What was it this time? Damsel with a flat tire? Grandpa broke his crown? You didn't leave here until nine, which tells me it couldn't have been anything too exciting. Like balls deep in a beautiful woman," Rhenn says, throwing me a cocky smirk.

I snort. "O ye of little faith, my friend."

Rhenn glances my way. "Really? Because if you were up all night screwing a woman then I'm willing to knock a few miles off today's run."

Without answering, I increase my speed.

"That's what I thought. So what was it? The damsel or the tooth emergency?"

For nearly a minute, the only sound is the pounding of our feet on the treadmills and slight exertion (mostly from me). But that's the thing about Rhenn; he hasn't dropped the conversation. He's just waiting me out, like always.

"Meghan." I had to give him something.

"I already knew that, man. What was wrong with the damsel this time?"

The way he says it heckles my nerves, but I know he doesn't mean any disrespect. Rhenn likes Meghan. Hell, he liked Josh.

Lacey Black

Everyone did. My friend just knows that I have a soft spot for my dental hygienist, and that I would do just about anything to help her. That's what friends are for, right?

"Nothing, actually. I grabbed food after I left here and dropped off a milkshake."

Rhenn looks my way, his eyebrows shooting skyward. "Is that code for something kinky?" He wiggles his eyebrows suggestively, which causes me to reach over and punch him in the arm.

"Fuck off. I'm not like you. I don't sleep with my friends," I retort, referring to an incident in college, which left Rhenn short one female friend after he slept with her and didn't return her calls.

"Low blow, brother. I was hammered."

"Too hammered to answer your phone? The entire week after?"

Rhenn turns away, a regretful look on his face. "Yeah, well, sometimes, it's for the best."

We're both quiet as we finish out our run together and hit the weights. It's a light day, considering we just ran three miles. (Well, I ran three miles. He ran six.)

"So, I'm going to let you off easy today, and we're gonna skip the mat," Rhenn says as he's spotting my bench press.

"You're up to something," I say as I push the bar up for the tenth time this rep.

"A date. Tomorrow night."

"Excuse me?" I ask, sitting on the bench and turning to face him.

52

"I have a date tomorrow."

"Shit, it's not a mom, is it? We have a rule against dating moms of our students. Don't you remember the Jackie incident?"

"Of course I remember the Jackie incident! It was my balls that kid kicked when he found me sneaking out of her room in the morning!" Shaking my head, I stand up so he can take the bench. "And that's not it. I'm not dating a mom. I'm dating a perfectly respectable young lady, who happens to be home for the summer."

"A college student? You're dating a fucking college girl?"

Rhenn lies back on the bench and grabs the bar. "She just graduated."

"High school?" I ask, knowing full well that if he answers yes to my question, I'm letting the bar, and all of its weight, drop on his chest.

"Fuck off, Dr. Adams. She's in grad school. Twenty-four, which is a perfectly respectable age."

"Fine," I reply, keeping my eyes on the bar as it rises and lowers to his chest. "What does this have to do with getting off easy today?"

"You're going with me," he grunts before pushing up one last time and setting the bar in the cradle.

"What? The hell I am."

"You said it yourself, you're ready to start dating. Your dick probably hasn't been played with since Collette, and it's time to get back out there, my friend. There are so many women out there willing to help you out with your little problem," he adds with a smirk.

"It's not a problem," I reply, finishing off my bottle of water.

"Dude, anytime you've gone more than a week without dick-action is a problem. And it's been, what, nine months since the bitch from Hell stole your shit and left?"

I don't confirm nor deny.

"So that's why you're going with me to meet Shelli and her friend Becca. You're going to have a few beers and get to know this woman. And if you're lucky, she'll help you out with the dick-play part."

"You're horrible," I reply, wiping my face with a clean hand towel.

"Actually, I'm fucking phenomenal. At least, that's what the ladies keep saying."

The shitty part is, the asshole is right. It's been a long time since I've enjoyed the company of a woman (dental hygienist excluded). There's no better time to get back on the horse than now, right? I don't even have to waste time trying to find a date, since my friend has pretty much already arranged one for me. That beats the hell out of Internet dating.

"Fine. I'm in."

"Of course you are," he says, tossing his used towel into the basket. "You and your dick will thank me later."

Ignoring his parting comment, I head to the shower, his laughter fading as I go. It's now or never. No, I don't expect the first woman I date to be "the one," but it'd be nice if she wasn't a cat-stealing, raging bitch on wheels.

Hell, I just need someone who likes to laugh, drink coffee by the Bay, and enjoys Mexican food as much as I do. Someone who kisses like a dream and maybe lets me hold her hand while we're watching a movie. And shower sex. Someone who doesn't mind getting wet and dirty, while you're supposed to be getting clean.

Is that too much to ask?

Chapter Five

Meghan

On Saturday morning, I find myself picking at the paper napkin in my hand, waiting for Cindy to arrive at the coffee shop. She's not late. I'm early. Like twenty minutes early.

When eleven finally rolls around, Cindy walks in wearing a bright yellow top with little pink flowers and Bermuda shorts, with sandals. Her smile is warm and genuine and her eyes light up when she approaches my table. "I'm going to grab a quick coffee. Do you need a refill?" she asks.

"No, I'm good." She doesn't need to know that I'm on my third cup of the morning already.

While I wait for Cindy to return, I glance at the small menu that's printed on an index card on the table. They don't offer too much, but what they do have is supposed to be out of this world.

"Sorry I'm a few minutes late," Cindy says as she slides into the booth across from me.

"No, you're not. I'm early." I pick at the napkin once more, dropping little pieces of paper on the small pile I created earlier.

"So…how have you been?" she asks, her warm blue eyes friendly and filled with a bit of concern.

"Fine, I guess." There's that word again. Fine. I'm always fine. Fine, fine, fine, fine, FINE! "Actually, no. That's not necessarily true."

"Okay, what's up?" she asks, sitting up a little taller in the booth.

"I mean, things really are...fine, but there's just something that I wanted to, maybe, talk to you about. But if it's none of my business, then I completely understand. You can tell me to get lost and I wouldn't hold it against you."

"Meghan," she says, reaching over and resting her hand on mine, "whatever you want to ask me is fine." Fine. See, even Cindy uses that word.

"Okay, well, what I was wondering...it's been a few years since, you know, your husband passed away." Deep breath. "Have you ever thought about, I don't know, dating?" Holy shit, I can't breathe.

Cindy smiles once more and just that slightest gesture on her part starts to put me at ease. "Actually, yes. Dale passed away almost four years ago this July. While it was difficult the first couple of years, lately, I've been spending a bit of time with someone."

"And what made you decide to...you know, do that?" I spin my coffee cup in my hands just to give them something to do.

"Well, I think it was when I realized how lonely I truly was. Dale and I had twenty-five wonderful years together and two great sons. They were both in college when he passed, living in their own place in Richmond. I was all alone at home. Even though I had friends and family who would stop by, it wasn't quite the same, right?"

I nod my head in agreement.

"Well, after I grieved for Dale and the love we had, I decided that it was time to start living again. I wasn't doing anything but sitting at home, or joining groups to keep myself occupied. I certainly wasn't living anymore. I was going through the motions.

"One day last year, my boys came home and they told me it was time. They encouraged me to go out and meet new people – men, actually – which was as awkward of a conversation as you could imagine."

I offer her a smile, trying to imagine how uncomfortable it would be for both mother and sons to openly talk about dating. Lord knows my grandparents don't seem to have that particular uncomfortable gene, but that doesn't mean I enjoy their little sex-laced powwows.

"Anyway, to be honest, I had been thinking about it for a bit, but didn't know how they would feel. He was their father, for heaven's sake. The last thing I would want is them to feel like I was trying to replace him."

I nod in understanding, though my emotions seem to have gathered in my throat and are making it difficult to speak.

"It was like they gave me that last bit of encouragement I needed to take that step. Now, don't get me wrong, they were baby steps at first. I had coffee with a couple of nice gentlemen in town, and a few dinners, but nothing serious, really. Until about six months ago. I met someone who makes me smile again."

And now I'm smiling in return. Her eyes light up when she speaks of this man, and I can tell she's completely smitten. "That's wonderful. How did you meet?"

"Actually, we met at the grocery store. He had his granddaughter with him, buying stuff for s'mores, when I dropped a can of peas. It rolled toward him, he bent to pick it up, and that was it. We talked for just a few moments, but it was nice. For the first time, it didn't feel forced or uncomfortable. When we ran into each other again a few weeks later, we decided to grab a cup of coffee. We've been enjoying casual dinners and outings ever since."

Reaching over, now I'm the one squeezing her hand. "I am truly happy for you. He would be a lucky man to spend time with you, Cindy." And I absolutely mean it. I've come to really enjoy our conversations, though always much more brief and not quite as personal before today.

"Thank you." Cindy glances at me before she continues. "You know, they say there is no timeline on grief, and I truly believe that, Meghan. You can't force these things; not when love was involved. You lost someone. Someone very dear to you, and there's no set time on when you should move forward. It's your schedule, your life. Take it day by day."

Nodding, I take another sip of my lukewarm coffee. "I, uh…I have a date tonight."

"Is this your first?"

I nod and blink back tears.

"How do you feel?"

"Scared. I mean, I'm not afraid of him – Adam, Adam Sullivan. We went to school together and ran into each other last weekend. He was always a nice kid. Anyway, he asked what I had been up to and wanted to catch up. At first, I almost said no. It felt wrong, like I was cheating on Josh, but then I remembered that Josh was gone. It was like that smack upside the head that leaves you a bit stunned and your head kinda foggy. Before I could talk myself out of it, I said yes."

"And now you're freaking out?" she asks with a smile.

"I'm totally and utterly in the freak-out mode."

"That's natural. Fear is logical when facing something like this. But you could either let fear run your life or overcome it. It takes a strong person to not let fear win, to stand above it, but when you do, the rewards are so much sweeter."

Again, I nod my head in understanding, as it seems I've done so much since we started talking. She's completely right, of course, but sometimes, something as powerful as fear, it's hard not to slink back in the corner and let it control your life. I've been doing that for more than two years now, and I'm not sure I'm really strong enough to overcome something that has controlled me.

"Tonight, try not to get lost in your head – or more accurately, your memories. Tonight, is a stepping-stone. Think of it like trying on a pair of shoes. Give them a whirl, walk around in them for a bit, and test the feel. It doesn't mean you have to buy the shoes."

Her analogy makes me giggle. "Shoes?"

"It was the first thing that popped into my head," she replies with a shrug and a smile. "But, Meghan," she continues, reaching for my hand, "most importantly, have fun. You deserve it. And whether you want to think about it or not, you know, in your heart, Josh would want you to."

The tears come unchecked, without care or worry that I'm in a public setting. Cindy squeezes my hand, but doesn't say a word, just lets me shed a few tears. Tears of fear and understanding, because at the end of the day, I know she's right. He would want me happy. That's what our nightly visits mean, right? When he arrives in my dreams and his words from that night – that night everything changed – play over and over again. Like a record that keeps repeating, I hear his words, but am too afraid to really listen.

We sit together for the next hour, enjoying lunch and talking. She tells me about her sons, her first grandson, and what keeps her busy. She talks a bit more about dating, though doesn't go into too many details. I want to ask her who this special man is that she keeps referring to with a smile on her face and light in her eyes, but I don't feel right. I don't want to overstep. It seems so personal.

So I sit quietly, and listen.

And enjoy our time together.

When it's time to say farewell, Cindy gives me a hug and wishes me good luck tonight. We exchange cell phone numbers, and I promise to text her tomorrow with how it went. The thought of having someone – someone who has been in my shoes – actually makes me smile. A real smile, not one of those fake ones that I've been wearing for so long.

As we part ways on the sidewalk, I think about the one other person I want to share my news with. He's the one man who has always been by my side, holding my hand while I cry. The other person who understands what I'm going through, maybe more so than anyone else I know.

My dad.

* * *

When I pull into the driveway, I see his car parked by the garage. He steps out of the garage, wiping something that looks like grease off his hand with a red shop towel. "Hey, baby girl, what brings you out here today?" he asks, a broad smile on his face.

"I wanted to see you," I answer, walking up to him and placing a kiss on his scruffy face. "What are you doing?"

"Changing the oil in the mower. I didn't get a chance to do it this spring, and since your grandparents were on their way to have a nap – which I'm pretty sure is code for something I don't want to think about – I thought now was as good of a time as any."

"Mind if I join you?" I ask, following him into the two-car detached garage.

"I'm always up for a visit," he says, walking over to where the push mower is positioned on the workbench.

I watch him work for a few minutes, wondering if he knows that something's on my mind and that's why he's not pushing me to talk. He seems to always be a bit more in-tune with me than with everyone else. Maybe that's because he understands more than anyone else.

"So, I have something to tell you," I start slowly, sitting down on one of the stools by his workbench.

"What's up?" he asks, turning and giving me his undivided attention.

"Well, I have a thing tonight. I guess you might call it a date, even though I'm not one hundred percent sure it's classified as one. One of my classmates from high school is home and asked me to dinner." I'm nervous, I can tell. My hands wring together on my lap as I play with the ring that still adorns my left finger.

Dad offers me a warm smile. "That's good, Meggy. Whether it's a date or not, it's good to go out and enjoy the company of friends."

"I know," I start, my eyes diverting to the floor. "It just seems weird, you know? Like I'm cheating or something."

Dad exhales and comes to sit on the stool beside me. "Now *that* I understand completely. And to be honest, you never really get over the guilty feeling. The longer you live without someone, the more you start to accept that new life that they are no longer a part of. Part of me will always feel guilty that I'm living and your mother isn't."

"You've never really dated." It wasn't a question.

He glances my way. "No, not much. For the longest time, I was busy raising six daughters and working. The last thing I had time for was dating."

"You should, you know. You're a very handsome man, father," I tell my dad with a smile. His hair is graying much quicker than it used to, but his green eyes still sparkle bright and his smile is warm and friendly.

Dad chuckles and glances my way. "Well, thank you, daughter."

We sit there silently for a few moments before I continue. "We would all be okay with it, you know. I mean, we don't all sit around and talk about it, but I think we all want the same thing: for you to be happy."

"I am happy, sweetheart. I have a beautiful family that seems to be growing in leaps and bounds lately. I do enjoy friends on occasion, and that does include lady friends."

"Wow, more than one? Dad, you're a playboy!"

That makes him laugh. "No, never more than one at a time. I don't think I could handle any more than that in my old age."

"You're not old, Dad."

"No, but I'm getting older."

"You know, I was talking to my friend Cindy from book club. We met for coffee and had a nice chat. She's a widow too and shared some of her thoughts with me. She's super sweet and would make a great dinner companion, you know, if you're ever looking," I add with a shrug.

"My own daughter trying to set me up? How did I get so lucky," he says, wrapping his arm around my shoulder and pulling me close.

"No, how did *we* get so lucky to have *you* for our dad?" I ask, giving him another kiss.

"Thank you, sweet girl. And for the record, I'm very happy that you're going to dinner with this young man tonight. I know it'll be difficult for you. I know it may feel a bit like cheating, but the thing to remember is that Josh would want you happy and to move forward. You know it, and I know it." He gives me that look that makes tears well up in my eyes. If anyone knows that for a fact, it would be my dad. After all, he was in that emergency room with me when I talked to Josh for the final time.

Nodding, I set my head on his shoulder and just enjoy the moment. Memories of my childhood come flooding back, as I used to do this exact same thing when I was younger. Especially after Mom died and I needed to feel comfort and be close to my remaining living parent. "I miss him so much, Daddy."

"I know, baby girl. I know." He lets me cry on his shoulder for a few minutes until the tears no longer come.

Before I can wipe away the remnants of the shed tears, a shadow falls over us. "Oh, look, Orvie! Our Meggy Pie is here!" Grandma bellows, clapping her hands victoriously.

"I see, Emmie. There's nothing wrong with my vision," Grandpa says, adjusting his glasses.

"What brings you home on this Saturday afternoon?" Grandma asks, walking over to Grandpa and goosing his behind on her way by.

"Behave, naughty girl," Grandpa coos, waggling his eyebrows suggestively. The entire display makes my stomach churn and bile catch in my throat.

"I thought I'd come see Dad."

"Oh, I enjoy that myself," Grandpa adds.

"Hanging out with Dad?" I ask, glancing toward the older man who slightly resembles my sisters and me.

"No. Coming." Grandma cracks up laughing at her husband's comment.

"Jesus, see what I have to deal with here?" Dad mumbles quietly beside me. "It's like living in a brothel."

I crack up as my dad rubs his temples.

"Have you seen Payters lately? I bought her a book and wanted to drop it off. Maybe I'll go to the shop Monday," Grandma says.

"Not in the last few days, but I'm sure she'd love a visit in the middle of her workday from her grandma." She'll hate it, actually, but serves her right for sending Grandma to my house a few weeks ago to talk about vibrators. Apparently, my sweet oldest sister told my dearest grandma that mine was broken. Grandma came racing right over with three new models to choose from.

And test.

She offered to let me test them out and report back on my findings.

"The book has many theories and predictions for conception. A few old wives' tales too. There's this one about butter and the flesh sword."

"It has pictures, too," Grandpa boosts.

"I'm sure she'll love and appreciate the gift."

"We went ahead and practiced the entire chapter twelve. We want to make sure *the sex* we're recommending is safe," Grandma adds.

Grandpa leans in closer. "Chapter twelve was my favorite. When paired with one of my love pills, my sword was able to attack the pink fortress for hours that night."

I choke on the very air I try to breathe. "You should tell her that, you know. Payton and Dean really appreciate the first-hand knowledge."

"Oh, there wasn't much *hand* involved. When my pill is in full effect, we can be paddling up Coochie Creek half the night, if you know what I mean."

"Yes, Grandpa, we all know what you mean."

"Well, we better get back inside. It's almost time for Family Feud and I promised Orvie a little late night puffin' on the doobie before beddy-by."

With that, Grandpa wraps his hand around Grandma's waist, resting his hand on her ass, and leads her back to the house. He whispers in her ear and makes her giggle in a way that makes my heart lurch in my chest.

"And you wonder why I don't date? You expect me to bring someone to my house and have to deal with that?" Dad asks, following my mom's parents with his eyes as they make their way up the front porch and disappear into the house.

"They're definitely not for everyone," I reply with a laugh. "But we were all able to find someone who can deal with their brand of quirkiness. You can too."

Dad snorts. "You may be right."

"I am right," I reply, walking over and giving him another kiss on the cheek. "Thanks for the talk."

"You're welcome. My door is always open for you, Meggy. Just remember to take it day by day. He would want you to live."

Swallowing over the tennis ball sized lump that has suddenly appeared in my throat, I nod my head. "I'll try."

"Start with tonight. Take it slow. You don't have to decide anything after one evening, Meg."

"I know. Thanks, Dad." I give him a hug and start to walk toward my car.

"Hey, Meg?" When I glance over my shoulder, I find him standing in the doorway of the garage. "The heart is an amazing thing. You don't have to replace someone who once filled your heart with joy. It turns out it'll make room for more, providing you with enough love for two people. It has taken me a long time, but I'm learning this."

Glancing down at the ring still adorning my left hand, I nod, blink away the tears, and slip into my car. It isn't until I'm halfway between Dad's house and my own that I really stop to think about his words.

Wait.

He's learning about enough love for two people?

Does that mean what I think it does? Is dad dating someone more seriously than he may have let on? Could he be falling in love with someone new, someone who isn't my mother? And how do I feel about this?

I'm happy, this I know right away.

Yet so confused on how this actually happens.

My heart aches for one man. It craves him like the desert needs water.

Could it really be possible to love another?

Chapter Six

Nick

The Mexican restaurant is packed.

Rhenn and I arrive a few minutes before six, but are unable to find a parking spot within a one-block radius of the place, which results in us walking in a few minutes after our scheduled plan. I can already tell Rhenn is irritated (tardiness, and all), but it seems to fade away quickly when we spot two women in a booth toward the back.

Following behind my friend, we maneuver through the busy restaurant until we're standing at the table. "Rhenny!" a bleached blonde woman (I'm assuming is Shelli) screeches as she stands up and throws her arms around my friend's neck. Her very large, very fake breasts are pressed firmly against his chest, which is probably what has really put that smile on his face.

"Ahh, the lovely Shelli," he says before kissing her neck and whispering something in her ear. When she giggles, I glance away, trying to not witness something that can't be unseen.

"I'm Becca," the woman opposite Shelli's bench says, holding her hand out to me and fluttering her eyelashes.

"Nick," I reply, her hand small and warm in my own.

"Nice to meet you, Nick. It looks like you're with me," she says sweetly as we glance over to see Shelli and Rhenn take their mini make-out session to the booth.

"Excellent." I mean, what else am I supposed to say? This is awkward as fuck, and the reason I hate blind dates.

"Shelli and I were just about ready to order drinks," Becca says, glancing down at her menu.

"Margaritas! Tequila makes my clothes fall off," Shelli whispers as if she were sharing some state secret. The thing is, I could have already told her that. I mean, she's on a date with my best friend, right? He prefers them easy and surgically enhanced.

"You don't say," I mumble, glancing at my own menu, even though I already know what I'm having. It's the same thing I get every time I come here.

After we place our orders, Becca and I make a few awkward attempts at small talk, while Rhenn and Shelli eye-fuck each other over their margaritas. The entire evening just feels strained and uncomfortable. Maybe that's my fault. Maybe I went into this with a closed mind, therefore I'm not giving this date a chance.

"Shelli is wrapping up grad school," Rhenn says, giving me that 'don't start your shit' look.

"Really? What for?" I dip a fresh, warm tortilla chip into the bowl of salsa in front of me.

"Hotel Management and Hospitality. I love everything about hotels," she coos, her bright red lips parting widely.

"You don't say," I reply, fretting interest.

"And what about you, Becca? What are your post-college plans?" Rhenn asks the woman who's apparently supposed to be my date for the evening.

"No grad school for me," she says, dipping a chip in the salsa. "I graduated two years ago with a degree in retail merchandising."

"Interesting. Isn't that interesting, Nick?" Rhenn asks, shooting me another one of his looks. This one says 'quit being a dick and acting bored.' And maybe even 'if you play your cards right, she'll be riding your dick by seven.' But honestly, that doesn't really get me excited. Becca seems nice and well put together (nothing like Shelli who's apparently two seconds away from offering a below the table BJ), but there just isn't any spark. Any connection.

Well, unless you consider her lips connecting with her margarita glass as a connection. There's plenty of that. In fact, she's already on her second peach drink before we even have our dinners.

"Very interesting," I say, just as I see movement across the room. When I glance that way, I find Meghan taking a seat across from some preppy-looking guy with gel in his hair. She's wearing a pretty lavender dress with a white sweater over the top. Her hair is down in long, wavy curls, just begging for a set of fingers. Of course, it'd be a hell of a lot better fantasy if they were *my* fingers sliding into those luscious strands and grabbing hold.

Meghan offers the man across from her a smile, but it's not one of her genuine ones. It's guarded and timid, and frankly, isn't real. Those smiles are rare, and reserved for special occasions.

What's she doing? She didn't mention having plans tonight, not that she needed to. But the way she's dressed and the way he's eyeing her like he wants to lick her from head to toe as if she were a fudge pop on a hot July day indicates this is more than just a chance meeting amongst friends. This teeters more into dating territory.

I watch a bit longer while she picks at the corners of her napkin, a nervous habit that she probably doesn't even realize she has. When the guy across from her laughs and leans forward, his hand resting on her arm, I almost come out of my seat. Meghan tenses at the touch, her back going ramrod straight. She doesn't appear scared, just uncomfortable. Nervous.

She slowly pulls her arm back without drawing attention to the fact she was removing it from his touch. She smiles tightly at him, nodding her head after whatever question he asked, and glances down at her menu.

"Earth to Nick," Rhenn says, drawing my attention back to my own table.

"What? I'm sorry," I reply, shaking thoughts of Meghan from my head.

Only it doesn't work.

Meghan is still very much present in my mind and in this restaurant.

"We were discussing *after* dinner," Rhenn says, giving me another look. I know what's coming. It's not my first ride as the infamous Rhenn Burleski's wingman. It's the reason we rode together so that when my friend and his date are ready to get to the more naked part of the night, they'd drive off into the sunset, leaving me behind to hitch a ride with the fourth wheel in this operation. And lest we forget, my friend is hoping I'll get my dick played with tonight, so he thinks he's doing me a great service by leaving me at the restaurant with no mode of transportation.

Good times.

"So what are the plans?" I ask, knowing that I'm not going to like them.

"Well, Shelli and I have…someplace to be." The insinuation is so evident that the deaf man down the block could pick up on it. "And since you rode with me, I figured Becca could take you home."

Called it.

"That's not necessary," I reply just as our food is delivered to the table. "I don't want to put Becca out."

"It would be no problem," she chimes in, offering me a friendly, half-drunk smile over her glass. One that says she'd be up for a round of bedroom aerobics if I'd offer. To confirm my suspicions, she reaches over and rests her hand on my thigh.

Tensing in my seat, I reach for my fork, ready to dive into the food. The faster I eat, the sooner we'll be finished with this double date from Hell and I'll be home with a beer and Sports Center. Becca removes her hand, grabs her own fork, and begins to eat her dinner.

Conversations are had around me, but I don't pay them any attention or actively participate anymore than the occasional grunt or head nod. My mind keeps wandering (and my eyes too) over to where Meghan sits with some guy. I can already tell I don't like him. He's too preppy, too pretty in his pressed blue jeans, for her.

I continue to watch her body language, not really liking what I see. She never really relaxes or seems to be enjoying herself, and a few times, I even catch her spinning the ring that she still wears on her left hand. Sure, the guy in front of her probably has no idea, what, with her fake smiles and bright green eyes, but I can tell.

She's not herself. I know this because she's my friend – my employee – and it's my job (as a friend) to know these kinda things.

Our dinner is cleared away as hers is delivered. She slowly picks at her food, moving it around on her plate as if she weren't hungry. This isn't Meghan. My Meghan loves Mexican food. It's why we order takeout at the office from this place at least once a week.

"Is that who I think it is?" Rhenn asks, drawing my attention to his face. But he's looking off to my left in the same direction as Meghan's table.

"Who's that?" Becca asks, peering around me to get a good look.

"Ex-girlfriend?" Shelli asks, glancing at her friend with wide eyes.

"No, she's my dental hygienist," I answer, looking around for the waitress so I can get the check.

"Oh, that's right, you're a doctor!" Shelli exclaims, leaning forward and setting her store-bought boobs on the table.

"A dentist, really," I reply, though not out of necessity. I'm honestly not sure Shelli knows the difference.

"Yes, a doctor," Becca replies, her hand sliding up my arm, her nails digging into my forearm. "That's so sexy," she adds, whispering in my ear.

Before I can reply, I see Meghan get up from the table, excuse herself, and make a mad dash toward the ladies' room like her ass were on fire. The guy she's with turns and watches her go, the gentle sway of said ass hypnotizing most of the men in the room.

I completely understand.

But I'm not focusing on her ass right now. I need to find out why Meghan is so upset, and what in the hell she's doing here tonight with the guy who looks like he could model sports coats and expensive watches for a living.

"Excuse me, please. I'm going to use the restroom," I say, dropping my napkin on the table and dislodging Becca's nails from my arm.

I make my way to the opposite side of the restaurant and slip down the short hallway that leads to both restrooms. Waiting outside the door like some crazy ex-boyfriend stalker, it only takes Meghan a few minutes before she reappears in the hall and almost walks into me.

"Sorry," she mumbles, taking a step back. That's when realization sets in. "Oh, hey. What are you doing here?"

"I'm here with friends," I tell her. "I saw you across the room and you looked, I don't know, upset, I guess. I just wanted to make sure everything was all right."

"Oh," she says, offering me a sad smile, her eyes filling with tears. "I..." she starts, but stops.

"Are you okay? Is it the sport coat model? Did he do or say something to upset you?" My protective big brother instincts flare to life, though this crazy attraction I feel for Meghan is anything but brotherly.

She gives me a look. "Do you mean Adam?"

"Adam. Joe. Richard. Does it matter? Do I need to go have a word with him?" A word that involves respect and ladies and why I'm about to throw my fist into his pretty face.

"No," she says, her eyes dropping to her shoes as if they were about to share the location of buried treasure. "He's nice, actually. We went to school together."

Watching her try to find the right words, it all starts to click into place. "You're on a date. With the suit coat model. And you're upset about it."

When she glances back up at me, the tears in her eyes almost bring me to my knees. Her tears are my undoing. I've never been affected by tears until they were hers. "He's a nice guy, but it just feels...wrong."

Nodding, without thinking, I pull her into a hug. We've hugged before, but with each one I feel myself slipping further and further into the deep end of the pool. Soon, my leg is going to be caught in the drain at the bottom and there'll be no way out.

"I'm proud of you for trying," I tell her, taking a subtle whiff of her hair and committing it to memory like a creeper. And I am proud of her. She's putting herself out there for the first time since Josh's death, and even though I'm not a fan of the douchey model wannabe at her table, I'm glad she has finally taken this step toward moving forward.

"Thank you," she mumbles, pulling back and noticing the wet mark on my shoulder from her tears. "I'm so sorry."

"Ehh, don't worry about it. No one wears tears like I do," I quip, making her smile. A real one. I love that smile.

"So, you're meeting friends?" she asks, turning those hypnotic green eyes my way.

"Yeah, Rhenn made plans with a woman, who ended up bringing a friend, which is why I'm hiding out in the bathroom hallway with you instead of enjoying the rest of our dinner."

"You're on a date, too. I'm sorry, you should get back," she says, brushing any remnants of tears off her pretty face.

"Did you hear what I said? I'm hiding out in the hallway with you."

"That's weird," she laughs. "What's wrong with her? Buckteeth? Lisp? Black olives in her teeth? Oh, wait. Is she picking her ear wax with her pinky and wiping it on her napkin?"

"Gross. What kinda women do you hang around with?" I gape with wide eyes and my mouth hanging open.

She laughs again. There. That smile right there.

"I was just trying to figure out what was wrong with her for you to be hiding out in a hallway with me instead of enjoying your date."

"Well, she's probably perfectly nice, but I'm just not feeling it."

Meghan glances around my shoulder toward the dining room. "We should probably get back out there. We both have dates waiting for us."

"I've been gone long enough now that the only way out of this mess is to fret digestive issues."

She laughs. "Oh God, me too! He's going to think I've died in the bathroom with stomach troubles, isn't he?"

I offer her a big smile in return. "Probably. At least you don't have to worry about the second date. Come on," I say, indicating the doorway that leads back to the dining room.

When we round the corner, I find our table empty, the busboy working to clear what was left of our dirty dishes. Glancing around the room, I don't find Rhenn or Shelli anywhere. What I do find is Becca sitting in the seat that was vacated by Meghan, the douchey sport coat model, who I know now as Adam, leaning over the table, eyes riveted on Becca's chest.

"Plot twist," Meghan whispers, her delicate little fingers gripping the back of my shirt.

"I suddenly feel like the third wheel. Again."

"Should we just slip out the back door or do I walk over there and pretend that woman isn't picking at the cheese left on my Taco Salad?"

"Slip out the back. We definitely sneak away," I tell her, just as Becca glances up and sees us standing there.

"Hey!" she exclaims, waving wildly and causing her boobs to bounce. Adam definitely notices.

"So the date crasher is your date? Seriously?"

"Agreed. Plot twist," I mumble as we start to walk over to the table.

"I thought you got lost," Becca coos, sending a flirty glance to the man across from her.

"Yeah, sorry. I ran into my friend Meghan. She had stomach issues." I can hear her gasp behind me and feel that soft, delicate hand grab a hold of tender flesh right at my waist. When she twists, it makes me jump.

"I thought you were the one with stomach issues. I found you practically doubled over in the hallway, groaning in pain," she replies, her green eyes lighting up with a wicked glimmer.

"You may be right. I think we both ate something that didn't agree with us," I reply, glancing down at the horrified woman who was considered my date for the evening.

"We should get home. Alone. Not together. We don't live together," Meghan says, sending Adam an apologetic look. "Sorry to cut our evening short, Adam. It was so great catching up with you. Next time you're in town, give me a call."

"But I don't have your number," he says as I pull her toward the back door.

"Thanks for dinner," Meghan replies, her hand tucked into mine, completely ignoring his statement about not having her number. We're so close we can practically smell the fresh air.

"It was nice meeting you, Nick. I know Rhenn left you without a car, but if it's okay, I might stay here with Adam and have a drink." Or sex. The way they're looking at each other, sex is definitely on the table tonight.

"Yep, sure, fine. Nice to meet you," I say, just before we make a break for it and hit the parking lot.

When we reach the outside, we both stop and break into fits of laughter. "Our dates are going to be bumping uglies very soon," Meghan says through her giggles.

"Definitely. I bet parking lot sex is on the menu tonight," I add, glancing at the smiling, happy woman next to me. "Hungry?"

"Starving. I didn't eat much of my dinner," she confesses, even though I already know.

"Hamburger from the drive-in or foot-long hotdog from the beach vendor?"

"Foot-long. I definitely need a foot-long." Suddenly, she realizes what she said and starts to blush a deep shade of fuchsia. "Hotdog. I mean, I need a foot-long hotdog."

"Not helping," I laugh, wrapping my arm around her waist and pulling her into my embrace.

"I can't believe I said that. So embarrassing," she mumbles, her face pressed firmly into my chest. I stand perfectly still, afraid to move or even breathe. Meghan is in my arms and I'm not sure it's the right move or not, but I don't want this moment to end, so I just hold her and revel in the way her breath penetrates my shirt and warms my chest.

Suddenly, she stills. When she pulls back, dropping her arms to her sides, she gives me a sheepish look laced with embarrassment. "Sorry about...the hugging...thing," I say, desperately looking to get back to our easy camaraderie from just a few minutes ago.

"Oh, no problem," she shrugs her shoulders and glances over to where her car is parked. "So...food?"

"Definitely."

Together, we make our way to her vehicle and head toward the best little food shack in Jupiter Bay. For foot-longs.

And I won't watch her eat it, allowing dirty thoughts to penetrate my brain.

Yeah.

Good luck with that one, buddy.

Chapter Seven

Meghan

"A How-To book on conceiving? Really, Meghan?" Payton seethes as soon as I step foot inside Blossoms and Blooms on Tuesday.

I glance around at the laughing faces of my sisters and immediately start to giggle myself. "There's pictures," I reason through my laughter.

"I know," she growls. "Grandpa showed me." That makes everyone in the room laugh that much more.

"Did he tell you they tried the entire twelfth chapter? I bet it was dog-eared and highlighted, wasn't it?" I sass, setting my purse down on the metal workstation that houses today's lunch.

"He told Dean. And apparently went into so much detail that my husband had a nightmare last night. He dreamed about butter, Meghan, and had to eat his toast dry this morning."

I can't help it. I laugh. Hard.

"Clearly, I don't need book help," Lexi says, reaching for the slice of pizza that is sitting on a paper plate, which is balanced on her enormous belly. It's not the first time I've wondered if my baby sister wasn't carrying twins. Again.

"You could have written the book," Jaime chimes in, rubbing her back and making her own basketball belly stick out that much more.

"The first chapter: My husband's a hot, horny bastard that I want to have all *the sex* with all *the time*," Lexi says between bites.

"He is pretty hot," I tell her, which results in her waggling her eyebrows suggestively at me.

"Speaking of hot, why is it four hundred degrees in here?" Jaime asks, fanning herself with a paper plate.

"It's a very comfortable seventy-two degrees, Jaime."

"Hot. I have the air on already and the thermostat set to sixty-five."

"Shut up, you do not," Payton says, grabbing a slice of pizza.

"Hell yes, I do. It's so hot. Ryan came to bed last night wearing socks, sweats, and a long-sleeved t-shirt."

"Pour guy," Abby says, sitting over by the cash register.

"Don't feel sorry for him. He got me into this mess; he can deal with a little frostbite on his balls. And besides, he wasn't complaining when I stripped him naked and climbed on top for a ride, which was wayyyyy longer than eight seconds," Jaime announces just as a male customer walks through the door. He stops and looks at all of us, clearly considering making a break for it out the very door he just entered.

"Hi, sorry about that. I was just on lunch with my sisters. How can I help you?" Payton asks the gentleman who slowly approaches the counter.

"I need to grab some flowers for my wife."

"Aww," we all reply in a lovesick chorus.

"Yeah," he replies as he looks around the counter. "It's our second anniversary."

"So sweet," Jaime coos, her wide eyes and giddy smile focused on the customer.

"Are you looking to take something with you from the case or would you like a custom arrangement?" Payton asks.

"I'll just grab something from the case. We're meeting for lunch down the street in a few minutes."

"Seriously, that's the sweetest thing ever! See, some guys know chivalry isn't dead!" Abby exclaims, her hands folded over her heart.

"Oh, knock it off. Levi dotes on your every breath. Besides, this guy knows that the quickest way to *the sex* is with flowers," AJ replies, making the poor customer's face turn beet red. "He shows up with flowers and they'll be banging in the hallway before the front door is even closed."

"Speaking from experience, again?" I tease AJ, all of us knowing full well that AJ and Sawyer get it on in random places throughout their house.

"Anyway, I'll just take those dozen red roses over there," he says, pulling his credit card from his wallet.

"Red roses? I mean, they're all fine and dandy, but don't you think it's more fitting to go with something a bit more unique? You know, like your wife?" Lexi chimes in. She always hated it when her ex-husband would send her red roses.

"Excuse me?" he says, panic filling his brown eyes.

"Look at those beautiful calla lilies over there. I'd get up and show you, but I'm a big fat pregnant woman, and I might have to pee for the eighteenth time this hour the second I stand up." The poor guy actually pulls at the neck of his shirt as if it were choking him.

"You can pick whatever you like," Payton says, trying to reel this sale back in. "The calla lilies are gorgeous and very unique, but the roses are timeless and classic."

"Umm," he starts, glancing around from woman to woman. "Maybe...I'll take the calla lilies?" It comes out a nervous question.

"Good choice, champ! She'll be putty in your hands and you'll be sexing it up in no time," Lexi adds right before shoving more pizza into her mouth.

Payton grabs the vase from the case, rings up the sale, and sends the customer on his merry way. Before he leaves, he gives us all one more long, uncomfortable look and practically runs out the door. "I think that went well," Payton grumbles.

"I'm sure he'll be back soon." This from Abby.

"He wouldn't survive five minutes with Grandma and Grandpa," Lexi adds, making us all laugh.

"No shit," Payton says.

"I only have ten more minutes before I have to get back to the school," AJ replies, and together we all gather around the pizza and dive in.

* * *

Tuesday afternoon proves to be much busier than normal. Two dental emergencies showed up at the office, and when that happens, Dr. Adams does everything he can to accommodate the added patients. A hectic afternoon transformed into an even busier evening. Tuesdays are our late night, as we schedule patients through seven o'clock. Tonight, we're just doing everything we can to get all of our patients taken care of.

When the clock strikes eight, Patty is ready to take off, only a few minutes after flipping the closed sign and shutting down the front office. Erika, the part-time dental assistant who helps Nick with procedures, leaves with her a few minutes after that. And as soon as I finish tidying up my room, sterilizing my instruments, and get everything set for tomorrow's round of patients, I'm out of here too.

At eight thirty, I've finally completed my tasks. My feet are starting to ache, even though I get to wear comfortable tennis shoes all day, and I'm pretty sure there's a bottle of wine in my near future.

Tuesdays are always the hardest for me. Sure, every day can be labeled as difficult, but this particular day of the week is downright excruciating.

Every Tuesday, Josh would get home from work, start a load of whatever had the biggest pile in the laundry room, and cook dinner. After we were done seeing patients, I would go home to my warm, cozy house, where my fiancé had dinner ready. He would ask me about my day, share with me a few tidbits of his, and we'd enjoy dinner and a movie together.

Every Tuesday.

And now those days are filled with emptiness and a Lean Cuisine microwave dinner. The television is on, but I don't pay attention. I need it for the noise. The distraction. The familiarity. The entire house is hollow, just like my soul. It died the day my best friend and lover was taken from me.

Blinking back tears, I make my way to Nick's office. He's been fighting with the computer software company since the final patient left, and it looks like he's not done yet.

I knock on his door and wave when I see the phone plastered to the side of his face. He looks beat. Even though he smiles as soon as I step into his office, the smile doesn't quite light up his hazel eyes the way it normally does. His dark hair is standing up, as if he just ran his fingers through it. It does nothing to change the fact that he's a very handsome man.

My heart actually does this weird tap dance in my chest.

I push it away.

"Hey, are you done?" he asks, moving the receiver away from his mouth.

"Yeah, I'm heading out."

"I'll walk you," he says, standing up. This is something Nick has always done on the late nights, especially when it's winter and dark by now. He won't let any of us leave alone.

"No, you're on the phone," I tell him, adjusting my purse over my shoulder.

"I'm on hold. I suppose Patty and Erika already left?"

"Yeah, they left together a little after eight," I reply, offering him a small smile as he runs his big hand down his tired face.

"Shit. Okay, I can set the phone down for a few minutes and walk you out," he replies, starting to set the receiver on his desk.

"No, that's silly. You've been on hold forever waiting to talk to a representative. You know as well as I do that the moment we set the phone down and walk outside, they'll pick up and then hang up because you're not there."

He gives me a look, one that says he totally agrees with my statement, but doesn't like it. Nick is a great guy and always escorts his employees out at night. This isn't sitting well with him, that I can tell.

"I'll be fine. My car is literally right outside the back door. What could happen?" I ask, giving him a carefree, worry-free smile.

"Text me when you're home safe," he concedes, dropping back down into his chair.

"Will do, Bossman," I salute.

Just as I go to wish him a goodnight, he starts talking to whoever finally picked up on the other end of the phone. I throw him another wave and head toward the back door, flipping off a few of the lights as I go.

When I slip out the door, car keys in hand, I notice how dark and quiet it is. The days are getting longer as summer approaches, but for some reason tonight, it just appears darker than normal. Maybe it's the storm blowing in that has my hair swirling around my head and shadows dancing on the concrete. The rest of the businesses in the area are closed up, which leaves only Nick's car and mine in the small lot.

As I approach my car, parking in the back row, the hairs on the back of my neck stand up and a weird feeling sweeps through my body, making my blood run cold. I double click the key fob to unlock my door and pick up the pace. Just as my hand grabs the handle, movement catches out of the corner of my eye. When I turn, a strong arm wraps around my body, while the second wraps around my neck.

Gasping, I drop my keys and purse and reach for the arm that's restricting my airway.

"Shhhh, don't do anything that'll get ya hurt, 'kay?" the man breathes against my ear, making bile rise in my throat.

"What do you want?" I gasp, my nails digging into his forearm.

"Just some cash, sweet thing. You got anything good in that big bag of yours?"

Again, I wiggle in his grasp, trying to steal a full breath of fresh air. "Cash. I have a few…bucks."

"Let's bend down and get it, shall we?" he says, bending us both over and reaching for my purse. He sets it on my hood, and with one arm still wrapped around my neck, starts to riffle through my belongings.

As he holds me against his body, I can smell the alcohol on his breath and the gasoline on his clothes. His voice doesn't sound familiar, but we have enough tourists who travel through Jupiter Bay that there's no way of knowing everyone in town.

The stranger pulls my wallet from my bag and slips it into his shirt, tossing the rest of my belongings over my car and into the bushes. "You sure are a pretty little thing, aren't you? You feeling lonely tonight?" he asks, sliding his nose down my jaw.

I'm going to throw up. My vision starts to blur, a combination of being short of oxygen and fear. I start to twist, ready to fight my way out of this situation, when I'm pressed hard against my car. My head slams into the unforgiving metal, which sends pain ricocheting through my body. Just as he starts to loosen his hold on my neck and spin me around, I'm falling. Falling to the ground, slamming my knees and hands onto the gravelly, cold asphalt.

I gasp for air, ignoring the ache in my knees and the burn of the exposed flesh of my hands. The sound of a grunt, followed by something hard hitting bone grabs my attention. When I glance up, I see the man who grabbed me on the ground, his legs and arms protectively, and slightly awkwardly, extended in front of him.

And there's Nick.

Standing over the man, his fists balled up at his sides and breathing fire.

"Nick?" I whisper in a voice that doesn't sound like mine.

As soon as he glances down at me, his eyes soften and his shoulders relax. That's also when the man on the ground jumps up and tries to make a break for it. Nick reaches for him with reflexes so quick, I almost miss the movement. He spins him around and kicks out one leg, sweeping the man off his feet and sending him hurtling to the ground.

The man moans in pain. "You broke my wrist!"

"Your wrist should be the least of your worries," Nick replies, his voice husky and threatening.

I watch as he holds the perpetrator down by applying pressure to the groaning man's chest with his foot. Nick is still wearing his work attire, his tie loosened around his neck and the two top buttons popped open. He glances my way once more, his eyes full of concern and sorrow.

"Meg, are you okay?" he asks, the man twisting in agony beneath the pressure of his foot. I hear him say the words, but I can't seem to open my mouth to reply. My heart pounds in my chest like a snare drum and my vision is a little fuzzy. I can't seem to get enough oxygen in my lungs. It's like I'm here, but not really. I'm floating around the scene, not in my own body. "I'm going to call 911 and as soon as the police get here, we're going to get you checked out, okay, honey? Stay with me, Meghan."

His voice is soothing and soft. It sounds nothing like the voice that spoke just a few moments ago when he was knocking the man to the ground and threatening to do more damage than a broken wrist.

My stomach lurches and I scramble for the bushes. Ignoring the pain in my knees and palms, I crawl past my car and lose whatever contents were left from my lunch with my sisters. My eyes burn from the tears, my throat raw from emotions. I can hear Nick talking, but don't understand what he's saying. I try to focus on the words, on his voice. After a few moments, my body starts to relax.

It could be five seconds or five hours later, the sound of an approaching ambulance fills the empty night. A car pulls into the lot, lights blinding and carrying a speed a bit too fast for a parking lot. But I don't care. I don't have the energy to move.

A minute later, he's there.

By my side.

His eyes check me over from head to toe, surely taking in my horrible appearance and the pile of vomit just over my shoulder. "Hey," he whispers softly, kneeling beside me and taking my arm.

"Hey," I finally say, my voice dry and fatigued. Suddenly, I can't keep my eyes open. Sleep is pulling me under, my body willingly following.

"No, no, no, Meg, you have to stay awake. I saw the blow to your head when you hit the car. You have to stay awake for a bit, okay, honey?" He cradles me in his arms, positioning me between his legs. Comfort wraps around me like a worn, familiar blanket from my past. It's nice.

"I just want to take a quick nap," I reason, my eyes already falling closed once more.

"Meg!" I hear moments before Levi drops to his knees in front of me, surveying the damage from tonight's ordeal. "Jesus, Meggy. What the hell happened?" he asks, grabbing a little flashlight and shining it in my eyes.

"Stop that," I grumble.

"We need to get you to the ambulance and checked out."

"I need to go to sleep," I retort, slipping back into the warm little cocoon I've created in Nick's arms.

"No can do, sweetheart. You need to get checked out. You could have a concussion. The only place you're going is to the hospital," Levi says, taking my hands and making me wince. "And you need to get these cleaned up," he adds when glancing down and seeing the damage to my hands.

"Come on, Meg. Let's get you looked at," Nick says, sweeping me into his arms and somehow standing up without needing assistance. Before I can even think about protesting, he's walking me toward the waiting ambulance.

Levi's friend Tucker is standing there, as we climb inside the waiting rig. Nick gently sets me down on the gurney, my body becoming stiff, sore, and protesting all movements. Levi grabs the blood pressure cuff and wraps it around my arm, while Nick hovers at my head. With the doors open, we have a front row view of the police as they place the cuffs on the man who attacked me, read him his rights, and slowly walk him toward the awaiting cruiser.

Lacey Black

"How's the head?" Tucker asks, writing stats down on a form on a clipboard.

"Sore. I think I'll have a lump," I answer, reaching up to gingerly touch the side of my head, wincing as my fingers connect with the swollen, sore skin.

"Definitely a nice little goose egg," he replies with a smile.

I answer Levi's questions as he gauges my injuries and helps get them cleaned up. "I think we need to go to the hospital. You have a slight concussion and should be seen by a doc. Plus, we want to rule out a brain bleed," he says, reaching down and setting his hand on my knee in a comforting manner. When he does, I wince. "Sorry," he adds, giving me a sheepish grin that I'm sure makes Abby's knees buckle.

"Is it really necessary? To go to the hospital? I mean, I feel like I just need to sleep it off and I'll be fine tomorrow."

"Absolutely. I'd insist if it were any other patient, but because it's you, I'm more than insisting. And I like my balls. One of your sisters would rip them off and toss them in the Bay if I didn't make sure you were taken care of," he replies with a wink.

I try to smile back, but it just hurts. "Fine."

"I'll go finish locking up and meet you there," Nick says, slowly brushing hair off my forehead with his finger. When he does, it leaves a trail of fire against my skin.

"You don't have to. I'm sure Levi has already called Abby," I respond without moving. For some reason, I kinda like the way his finger feels. I kinda like it a lot. Way more than I should, that's for sure.

"Texted her. She'll meet us there," Levi says, not even embarrassed that he probably broke some sort of confidentiality law or something.

"I'm going." He's firm and direct as he crosses his arms over his chest, daring me to argue further. But all I notice is the way his dress shirt molds to his arms, his muscles ripe and taut beneath the material.

Stop it, Meghan! He's your friend. You don't ogle friends!

Even if they do have arms that make your mouth water...

"You really don't have to," I reply, somewhat lamely. The truth is: I kinda want a friend with me right now.

He doesn't reply with words, just gives me a look. It says, 'Forget about it, Meghan. I'm going and that's that.'

So instead of replying with my own words (because frankly, words hurt), I nod my head gently and relax on the gurney. Levi follows Nick out of the ambulance where they exchange a few words. I can't tell what they're saying, but when they both glance up at me, I know who they're talking about.

Just as I'm about to ask what's going on, Levi slaps Nick on the back of the shoulder and hops back into the ambulance. Nick hurries off in the direction of the office, and Tucker jumps in the front seat. "We'll be there in a few minutes," Levi says, taking a seat next to me.

"Did you really text her?"

"I had to. If she found out I didn't, she'd have my balls. I did tell her just to come by herself until we know more. Hopefully, that'll save us all at the hospital from being taken over by your bossy family."

I snort a laugh. "Doubtful."

"A guy could hope," he replies with a shrug.

As the ambulance starts to move, I close my eyes, replaying everything that happened tonight. I was scared that he was going to hurt me. The thought of what could have happened if Nick hadn't happened upon it outside makes my blood run cold.

It definitely could have been a lot worse than a few scrapes and bumps.

But there was something more I saw in Nick's eyes tonight.

Guilt.

It's that look that will haunt me later as I try to drift off to sleep.

* * *

"You're all set, Miss Summer," the blonde nurse says, while stealing a few appreciative glances at the man who's quietly hovering in the corner of the room.

"Any other instructions?" Abby asks the nurse before I have a chance. Though, if I'm being honest, I'm very thankful someone is here to ask questions and hopefully remember all of the details and instructions they're sending me home with. I've talked to the police, though I have to stop by the station tomorrow, give my formal, written statement, and collect my belongings.

All I want to do is go to bed.

"No, she should be set. Just make sure to take it easy for the next twenty-four to forty-eight hours and acetaminophen for any pain."

"Thank you," I say, already swinging my legs over the hospital bed, thankful that the blow to my head didn't result in anything more than a slight concussion.

"She'll take plenty of time off. She's taking the rest of the week."

I glance over at my boss with my mouth gaping open. He appears all casual, leaning against the wall with his arms and ankles crossed, but appearances can be deceiving. Anyone who really knows him can see the storm clouds brewing, which makes his hazel eyes appear much darker, giving off a shadowy, brooding vibe.

"What? I can't take the rest of the week off. That's three days!" I argue.

"You will. It's not negotiable."

"Who made you the boss of me?" I ask with venom, my green eyes turning to little laser beams, focused directly on their target.

"Actually, I am the boss."

"Only while I'm in the office. Outside of the office, I'm the boss. Me."

Nick takes a step forward, and another. He keeps moving until he's standing directly in front of me, his hands now firmly on his hips. "You're my friend, Meghan. First and foremost, before my employee, you're my fucking friend. And tonight was my fault, so you're taking the next three days off with pay, all right?"

I gape up at him. "You're fault? How was this your fault? You didn't arrange for that lunatic to jump me for the twenty-three dollars I had in my purse, did you?"

"Hell no, I didn't. But if I had waited until you all left before making my phone call, you wouldn't have been hurt. What do I always say? Safety in numbers, Meghan. It could have been Patty, or even Erika who was hurt..." His eyes transform right before my very own. They change from dark and stormy to a lighter shade of green. I can see all of his pain reflecting in them. "But it was you." His words are almost inaudible.

Reaching out, I touch his jaw with my hand. I'm not sure what made me do it, but it seemed right. He's upset and blaming himself for something that wasn't his fault, and the only thing I want to do is wrap my arms around him and take away that pain and blame. If he's shocked by my touch, he doesn't show it. Instead, I swear I feel him tilt his head ever so slightly and lean into it.

"This was not your fault, Nick. Nothing about tonight was your doing."

He opens his mouth to argue, but I cut him off. "No. You don't get to take the blame away from where it should be placed. It belongs on the man who came out of nowhere and tried to steal my money. The man who pushed me against the car and probably would have done something far worse if not for my friend, *Nick*, who arrived at the right time and pulled some of his karate chopping kung fu shit out and took the jerk down."

His eyebrow rises and he gives me a smirk. "Karate chopping shit? Haven't I taught you anything?"

"This is so hot. I wish I had popcorn. Lexi is going to be so upset she missed it." Glancing toward the voice, I find Abby completely entranced in our conversation, eavesdropping like the meddling pain in the ass she is. Grandma would be proud.

Dropping my hand like I was burned, I take a step back, putting much needed space between my boss and myself. The man I suddenly feel like hugging. And maybe rubbing my hands over those little bulges on his shoulders. It's like his shoulders have shoulders. Hard, muscular, lickable shoulders.

Anyway…

"You outta here?" Levi says, stepping into the small exam room and instantly heading toward my sister.

"I am." Walking over to the chair that houses a bag containing my clothes, I grab my personal belongings and step toward the restroom.

"I'm going home with her," I hear Abby say as I close the door, rolling my eyes.

It takes me a few minutes to get dressed, but when I'm comfortably back in my scrubs, I finally take a gander at my reflection in the mirror. Jesus, Mary, and Joseph. I look like I took a two by four to the side of the head. The goose egg is a hideous shade of purple and protrudes from my head like someone stuck a ping-pong ball on my melon. My eye makeup is smeared, reminding me of an all-night bender from back in college.

"Nice," I grumble, reaching for a paper towel to try to wipe away some of the black.

When I do the best I can (or more accurately, when I become too tired to worry about it anymore), I rejoin the party in my little ER room. "Well, what did you all decide on my behalf?" I ask, dropping down into the chair where my bag was sitting.

"I'm going home with you to make sure you follow instructions and don't drop in the shower. Levi is going to have

Tuck drop him off at the office to grab your car and take it home. Nick is going to his house to pace the floor and be pissed that he's not at your place, taking care of you," Abby says with a smile.

"I just said I'd be more than happy to stay with her since this was my…since I don't mind helping," Nick returns with a huff, glancing at me out of the corner of his eye. "I mean, I'd stay on your couch, of course."

"And while everyone would appreciate his offer, I don't have anything going on and you're my sister. Plus, Levi is coming over when he gets off work to check on you."

Glancing Nick's way, I find his attention locked on the floor. I get up and walk his way. "Thank you for caring enough to want to help. Abby won't leave it alone until she's completely basking in the Mother Hen role," I reply, shooting for a bit of humor.

"I do not Mother Hen," she huffs behind me, making both Nick and I smile.

"Well, if you're going to be okay at home, then I'm good with that," he whispers, his eyes dropping to my lips. Reflexively, my tongue darts out and wets them, his eyes dilate and darken.

"I'm going to be okay," I confirm, and before I can stop myself, I step into his personal space, wrap my arms around his neck, and hug him, my cheek pressed against his shoulder. His arms meet at my back as he pulls me tightly against him, his head coming down to rest on my head.

It's oddly comfortable.

And probably a little inappropriate, considering the work thing.

But neither of us seem to care.

As he said before: first and foremost, we're friends.

"Thank you. For everything." Emotions clog my throat and I have to blink back the tears. I'm not sure why I feel like crying, only that I do. Relief, maybe? The stress of the night finally catching up to me? A sense of gratefulness that I had someone who helped me, and family to help take care of me?

That right there is a big one.

I don't have to be alone.

Abby goes to get her car, while Levi and Tuck take off to retrieve my vehicle back at the office, which leaves Nick and I standing just outside the Emergency Room entrance. He's holding my tattered purse, in a completely masculine way, mind you. The image makes me smile. And remember.

Josh used to carry my purse.

Before I can rip off that particular scab of pain and start to bleed all over the concrete, Abby pulls up and grants me a mental reprieve. As soon as the car is in park, Nick walks to the passenger door and opens it. When his eyes connect with mine, they're both weary and alive.

"Your chariot," he says, giving me a little grin.

"Thank you," I reply, stepping to the door. Before I climb inside, I throw my arms around him one more time and hug him. He doesn't hesitate to comply.

"You're welcome, Meghan. I'm glad you're okay."

"Thanks to you," I whisper, pulling back slightly. And because I have no control over my mouth, I lean upward on my tiptoes and place a gentle kiss on his cheek. It's slightly scruffy from his five o'clock shadow, but I find the feeling a bit intoxicating and exhilarating. My lips start to tingle.

Without saying another word, or waiting for his reply, I slip into the passenger seat of Abby's car. Nick hands me my purse and shuts the door. He steps away from the vehicle and watches as we slowly pull out of the circular drive and onto the street.

My eyes instantly close and the weight of the day starts to settle in. It's almost midnight and my body is starting to shut down. It only takes a few minutes to arrive home, and with Abby's help, I settle into my bed, ready to let this entire day just melt away.

Chapter Eight

Nick

I've been tossing and turning, and have watched the clock go from one to two to three. I have yet to fall asleep. Every time I close my eyes, I see the way that man pinned Meghan to her car and then practically threw her against it. I can still see the fear in her eyes, even through the darkened night, as she gazed up at me from the cold, dirty concrete.

My gut churns with anxiety and my body hums with a powerful urge to put my fist through a wall. It's been a long damn time since I've felt this reckless, this irritable.

Tossing my blanket off my legs, I run my hand down my weary face and throw my legs over my bed. The hardwood floors are cool as I head to the kitchen for some water. The night is still black, the neighborhood silent. No dogs bark, no horns honk, and no kids play outside. It's almost peaceful.

If only my mind were in the same state.

Instead, my brain is like the ball in the Pinball game. Roll...bounce off the side...clang into the bumper...roll...get smacked in the face by the flipper. That's me. The ball slammed into objects by the damn flipper. For fun.

I'm tired, but I can't sleep. I need to let off a little steam, and there's only one thing to do. Heading to my bedroom to change into workout clothes, my attention is pulled to my vibrating cell phone. Glancing down and expecting to see the emergency service I use for immediate dental situations, I still when I see her name.

Meghan.

Swiping my finger, I pull up her message.

Meghan: *I'm sure you're asleep, but I wanted to tell you that I'm starting to feel better.*

Me: *Really?*

The bubbles appear right away.

Meghan: *No, not really. Actually, I can't sleep. My head is pounding and every time I close my eyes, I see his face.*

Me: *I'm the same way. I still feel horrible this happened to you.*

Meghan: *Please don't start that "it's my fault" crap again.* *insert winky face*

Me: *Fine. I won't say it.*

Meghan: *Or think it.*

Me: *Anyway, you should try to get some sleep.*

Meghan: *Pot, meet kettle.*

Me: *I caught a catnap.*

Liar.

Meghan: *I don't believe you. What are you doing?*

Drinking the last of my water, I take my phone into the living room and have a seat on the couch.

Me: *Thinking about going to the gym.*

Meghan: *That sounds horrible.*

Me: *It's not so bad.*

Meghan: *I'd rather have my ducking fingernails pulled off with tweezers.* *insert getting sick emoji*

Me: *What's ducking fingernails? You have some sort of fungus that I need to know about?*

Meghan: *Autocorrect hates me. No one says ducking. No one. It's fucking, autocorrect. F.U.C.K.I.N.G.* *insert angry emoji*

Suddenly, I'm sweating.

And horny.

And not sure how to respond, because all I can think about is fucking, and not in the adjective sense as she just used. I'm imagining the dirty, sweaty, naked kind, and I'm ashamed to acknowledge who has the starring role in the fantasy. I'm a horrible person.

Meghan: *Anyway, I'm going to take more Tylenol and try to rest. I tried to read, but it hurt too much to focus on the words. Maybe if I find one of those boring war history shows you like to watch, maybe I'll fall asleep.* *winky emoji*

Me: *I think you were autocorrected again. Those shows are amazing and educational.*

Meghan: *Nope, no autocorrect.* *sticking out tongue emoji*

Me: *You'll be able to tell the difference between an eighteenth century bayonet and a Civil War Bowie knife in no time.*

Meghan: *I'll be asleep in no time.*

Me: *Then I guess my work here is done.*

Meghan: *I actually do feel a little sleepy. Thank you for the talk.*

Yawning, I sag into my couch, realizing just how exhausted I really am.

Me: *Me too.*

Meghan: *Good. G'nigh Nicholas. Balk at you toon.*

Me: *smiling emoji* *Autocorrect and exhaustion don't mix. G'night, Meggy Pie.*

Meghan: *sleepy emoji*

My eyes start to cross as I set my alarm for six thirty and place my phone on the coffee table. I grab the blanket on the back of the couch and use it for a pillow, as I lie on my side and get comfortable. It doesn't take much, since my body is just done. My limbs feel like they're numb and my eyelids are weighted. The magnitude of the last eight hours has finally caught up to me.

I don't think about the asshole who hurt Meghan. I don't think about the pleasure I felt when I punched him in the face and knocked him down. I don't think about the fear in her eyes or the dark purple bruise that developed on her head.

Oh, I think about her, but not the bad. I think about her smile when she greeted me yesterday morning and the way she intentionally kicked my chair when I came in for the final exam on one of the patients she just finished.

It's that smile and those sparkling green eyes that lull me into a deep sleep.

* * *

"And you didn't beat the shit out of him?" Rhenn asks, moving from his fighting stance and dropping his gloved hands to his side.

"It took everything I had not to. I wanted to," I tell him, letting go of the bag he was just pummeling. "I almost did, but then I looked over at her on the ground and knew killing him wasn't the answer."

"You should have called me. I would have taken care of that asshole," Rhenn says right before slamming his fist into the bag once more, sending it flying into my face since I'm not holding it steady.

"Nice, asshole." His chuckle follows me over to the water cooler as I grab another drink of cold water.

We've been working hard as we approach the end of the season. Rhenn always finishes classes by the end of May. It's too hard to compete with all of the other summer activities and vacations, so we'll finish out this year at the end of the month and pick it back up again in September.

"I think you've been a little pissy since your last date dumped you for another guy," he says, dropping his gloves on the bench and grabbing a cup of water.

"That's all you got out of that, isn't it?" I huff.

"She was a sure thing. If she was anything like her friend, she would have been blowing your mind all fucking night," he smirks.

"You're something, man."

"I know," he boasts with a big smile as if that were a compliment.

"Anyway, next Wednesday, I'm bringing Meghan by after class to show her a few things. I hope that's okay."

Rhenn actually turns serious. "Of course it's okay. Do you want my help?"

"No, I think I can handle it."

Again, he smirks. "I'm sure you will, but be careful. You've been friend-zoned so long, you'll probably have to forward all of your mail there."

I shake my head and refuse to comment. I decided last night when I was teaching my Wednesday night Little Dragons class that Meghan needed to learn a few basic self-defense maneuvers. If it goes well, I'm going to suggest she attend next Friday's class for women. My thought process is she can learn a few things next Wednesday night, and then hopefully I can convince her to come the following Friday when Rhenn and the rest of the students will be there. It'll be good practice for her.

"You should bring her Friday," he says.

"The thought crossed my mind," I reply casually. "I'm not sure if she has anything going on already. Maybe one of her sisters' gatherings," I add with a shrug.

"Sisters! I forgot about them. Bring them too," he says, waggling his eyebrows suggestively.

"Take a cold shower, dude. They're all either married or in committed relationships. Besides, they'd all have too much class for a loser like you." I'm able to smile moments before the gloves come flying at me and nail me in the face.

"Take that back," he says.

"Never. You're a whore, and you know it."

"I am," he grins mischievously.

"One of these days, someone is going to knock you off that self-imposed throne you have yourself perched on. She'll have you eating out of the palm of her hand and your balls stuffed so far in her purse that you won't know what to do with yourself."

He advances quickly, but I know his games. We've been friends for too damn long and fought together on the mat for me not to learn a thing or two about Rhenn. He throws his arms around my neck, but I spin and sweep my leg at his. He counters quickly, throwing his right leg at my left, ultimately knocking us both down to the hard floor.

"Damn," I laugh. "Couldn't you have done that on a mat?" I ask, rolling over to my stomach.

"Me? You kicked me first, asshole," he grunts as he lifts himself up onto his elbows. "I'm going to make you pay for that Saturday morning on the treadmill."

I snort and look over at my friend. I really can't wait for some woman to knock him down a few branches and make him a one-woman man. It's happened before. In college. He was completely into Suzanne Jaskula, throwing around the I-love-you's and making plans for the future, until he caught her in bed with one of our frat brothers. You know, that asshole guy that *no one* in the fraternity likes, but was old enough to buy beer and had the money none of us working college kids had to keep our fridge stocked? After that, my best friend turned into a manwhore, completely closed off from any sort of relationship outside of the physical. Surprisingly, there are plenty of women out there looking for a little no-strings fun, and Rhenn always has a way of finding them.

Me? I've never been into one-night stands. I'm more of a committed relationship kinda guy, and it has always been one of the constant sources of ribbings from my friend. But I don't care. It's just not my shot of vodka. Doesn't mean it hasn't happened; just that it doesn't happen often.

"Monday I'm taking the boat out. Be at the dock at ten," he says, referring to his thirty-eight foot sailboat docked at the Marina. It has way more speed than Rhenn needs, but he has always been about barreling full-steam ahead as often as possible.

"Fine. I'll bring the food this time," I reply. Last time we took the boat out, he remembered about every type of alcohol imaginable, yet forgot to bring substance for our stomachs. It made for a long, miserable day at sea.

"Drinks tomorrow night after class?" he asks, getting up off the floor.

"Sure. I'll drive myself since you have a habit of ditching me for blondes in short skirts," I answer, getting up off the floor myself.

"Why you gotta be like that?" he asks, fretting hurt. "It's not just blondes, dude. I like brunettes, too. And redheads. I fucking love redheads. They're wild as hell." He barks out a laugh that leaves me shaking my head.

Oh yeah, I'm going to enjoy watching him fall hard.

Hopefully, sooner. You know, before he comes down with an STD.

Chapter Nine

Meghan

"Are you okay?" Cindy asks as soon as we break apart from the group to enjoy appetizers and drinks at Thursday night book club. Of course, I'm not quite up to drinking yet. My head hasn't hurt much today, but still carries an ugly shade of purple.

I've decided it's not a good color for me.

Plus, it's my first time driving since Tuesday night's incident.

"I'm fine, thank you. I'm feeling much better today. Yesterday, I kinda slept the day away, but I was feeling up to moving around a little more today. My grandma came over and sat on the back porch with me for a few hours this afternoon."

"That's nice," Cindy says with a smile. "I've been worried about you. I wasn't sure if you'd be here tonight or not."

"Honestly, I wasn't sure I was coming until about five. Then I decided I needed out of the house for a bit." The walls were starting to close in on me, as they often do when I'm there alone for long periods of time, but I leave out that part.

"Well, I'm glad to see you, and so happy you're okay," she adds, reaching over and rubbing my upper arm.

"Thank you. How did you hear? I mean, I know it's a small town, so I'm sure it's grocery store fodder."

She seems to blush a bit and hesitates before answering. "Oh, uhhh… I ran into your dad. At the grocery store." Cindy seems to blush even more.

Interesting.

"Oh." I knew Dad and Cindy knew each other, but didn't realize they were friends enough to share personal details like that.

"Anyway, I wanted to stop over last night, but figured you wouldn't be up to visitors quite yet."

"You're welcome anytime," I tell her honestly. I really do like Cindy and find value in our friendly chats.

"Can I get you anything? Wine?"

"I'm good, thank you. I'm not quite up to drinking yet, but my appetite is returning tenfold. I've been eyeing those stuffed mushrooms and crab dip like I haven't eaten in days." And maybe I haven't. Grandma forced me to eat some soup today, but I was so tired yesterday that I don't think I ate much of anything all day. Even with Lexi babysitting me.

"I'll go grab you some," she replies with another smile. It's a nice smile. Friendly. Easy. Pretty.

A few other ladies come over and ask about my head, and I find myself sharing the story several times throughout the rest of the evening. Some had heard the story, but many hadn't. Since I showed up right when book club was starting, no one had the chance to ask about my lovely purple bruise accessory I was sporting when I arrived. But now, everyone wants to know what happened.

By the time we dismiss, I'm starting to get very sleepy. It's definitely time for me to head home. Saying goodnight to everyone, including receiving an extra hug from Cindy before I leave, I make my way outside in the late May night and toward my car. The air holds just the slightest chill to it, which may be of benefit to me as I make my way home. Rolling down the windows, I check my phone before I leave and find a message from Nick.

Nick: *Just checking in. How are you feeling?*

Me: *I'm feeling better. Decided to go to book club tonight.*

Nick: *That's good. I'm happy to hear.*

Me: *I could probably work tomorrow, you know.*

Nick: *No. You'll be back Monday, unless you need more time.*

Me: *You're so bossy. I don't need more time. I'm fine to work now.*

Nick: *Sorry, you're breaking up. I can't hear you.*

Me: *Very funny, Mr. Miyagi. When did you develop a sense of humor?*

Nick: *Ouch. You wound me.*

Me: *You know I'm joking. Anyway, I'm heading home now.*

Nick: *I'll let you go. Night.*

Me: *Good night, Nicholas James Adams, D.D.S.*

Nick: *inserts man shaking head GIF*

I set my phone down in my cup holder, laughing. He hates it when I pull out his full name for some reason, which is why I use it. Much like him calling me Meggy Pie. One time Grandma used it in his presence and he hasn't let it go since.

It's a short drive home, the cool air tussling my hair and chilling my cheeks. I'm expecting to come home to a still house and the kitchen light on above the sink. What I'm not expecting is to see Nick's car in the street. Pulling into my driveway, he gets out and meets me at my car, his right hand holding a familiar cup.

"What are you doing here?" I ask with a smile, even though I can already see the answer in his hand.

"The kids at the burger joint made an extra strawberry milkshake. I thought I could find someone to drink it. You know, so it didn't go to waste." His smile does something weird to my heart and makes my breathing hitch in my throat.

"Again? They're going to have to do something about that employee. That can't be good for business if he keeps making extra milkshakes," I tease as I climb out of my car.

"Yeah, you're probably right," he replies, rubbing the back of his neck.

Nick follows me up my stairs and watches as I unlock the door, but he doesn't follow me in as I cross the threshold. For several seconds, we just stand there, staring at each other. The desire to invite him in, to come in (and not as my friend, Nick) and stay for a while, is strong. The words are on the tip of my tongue, but for some reason, I don't say them.

"Here," he says, extending his hand with the milkshake.

"Do you want to come in?" The words are small, my heart hammering in my chest. I can't stop the yawn, and immediately bring the hand with the shake to my mouth to cover it.

He shakes his head. "Not tonight. You've had a long few days and you're tired."

Nodding, we continue to watch each other. I can tell he wants to say something else, but he doesn't.

"Well, thank you for this," I finally say, bringing the straw to my lips and taking my first drink.

"You're very welcome, Meghan. I'll talk to you soon. Sleep tight." He stuffs his hands into his pockets and heads down the stairs.

I watch as he climbs into his car and starts it. He doesn't pull away, though. His eyes are locked on mine in a way that's both familiar and scary. There's a different look to him tonight, and if I'm being completely honest, I've noticed it before tonight. He's still my friend Nick, but there's more there. Longing, maybe? That thought leaves me both excited and fearful. Not because I'm afraid of him, but more of the fact I'm afraid of the feelings.

Because I've done everything to avoid feeling anything for more than two years.

Feelings lead to pain.

Excruciating, miserable, all-consuming pain.

As I close and lock the door to the sound of Nick's car driving away, I'm instantly surrounded in the silence, the pain. It's familiar. Much more familiar than any other pesky feeling that I may or may not be having toward Nick, or anyone else.

Taking a hearty pull from the straw, I can't help but smile as the creamy strawberry shake hits my tongue. He thought of me enough to bring me my favorite treat. Again. He really is a sweet and caring man. Someday, someone (not Collette) will be lucky enough to win his heart and love.

Climbing into bed, I settle in for the familiar uneasy sleep. The tossing and turning. The dream that's sure to come.

* * *

"Did you hear Clayton and Christine are engaged? I did that! I set them up!" Lexi hollers across the table with a wide smile on her face.

"Really? Good for them. I really like them together. She's so much better for him than his ex," Abby says from her seat. We're at the café having Sunday brunch. Our family is big enough now that the biggest table doesn't fit our crew. We have to add another table to accommodate our group.

"Aren't they the ones you practically forced to go to lunch together after their hair appointments?" AJ asks next to Sawyer.

"Well, duh. I knew she was into him. Had been in school, too. So I just arranged his hair appointment at the same time as hers. The rest, as they say, is history," our baby sister boasts proudly, clapping her hands together victoriously before setting them on top of her big belly.

Jaime sits at the end of the table beside Dad looking as miserable as ever. She's getting closer to her due date with only three and a half weeks to go. "How ya feeling, Jaime?" I ask, watching as she continues to squirm in her chair.

"Fine," she says with a fake smile. Ryan gives her a sympathetic look and then kisses her on the cheek. "I'm just ready. Our little one doesn't like me to be comfortable for more than thirty seconds." She rubs her very round belly and gives me a small smile.

"She's not sleeping," Ryan adds, pulling her into his arms and letting her rest her head on his shoulder.

"I can't get comfortable," she adds with a shoulder shrug.

"I hear ya. But the good thing is I don't sleep anyway. Not when these two seem to think sleepy-time is when the crib party starts," Lexi chimes in, a tired but adoring smile on her face as she stares down at Hemi in the highchair beside her.

"I didn't party nearly this much in my early twenties as I do now between one and three a.m.," Linkin adds, picking up a dropped toy that Hudson keeps throwing over the tray of his chair. I'm pretty sure it's just a game to the little guy now.

"It gets better," Dean chimes in, his daughter, Brielle, sitting next to him and coloring with Payton.

"I hope so," Lexi whispers.

"I have an idea, why don't you bring the boys over to my house on Friday night," Dad says from his end of the table. "You guys can go have dinner and enjoy your evening."

"Or just have *the sex*," Grandma says way too loudly from the opposite end of the table.

"Grandma," Abby chastises, her cheeks instantly turning pink.

"What? It's a part of life, Abbers. Everyone has *the sex*."

"Yes, but we don't necessarily need to discuss it over eggs and bacon," AJ says.

Grandma waves her hand dismissively. "Pfff. Orvie will have to help you for a bit. I'm signed up to take the women's self-defense class uptown. In fact, I'll go ahead and call that sexy karate instructor and tell him I'm bringing my granddaughters."

Wait. Sexy karate instructor? Is she talking about Nick?

"Jaime isn't doing a karate class," Ryan says firmly.

"Neither is Lexi," Linkin adds.

"Fine, not those two since they drank the Preggers Kool-Aid. They'll both be busy with *the sex* that night anyway. But Abbers, Payters, Alison Jane, and Meggy Pie will all be there." It's like she's already decided for all of us.

"Why do I have to take it?" Abby asks.

"Because any one of us could get jumped. It would be good for all of us to learn some basic self-defense," Grandma says decisively with a firm look my way. I start to blush when everyone else glances at me.

"I'm in," I tell her before I can second-guess my decision.

"Great! Now the rest of you will join us," Grandma says before glancing down at her menu. "I think I'll get the biscuits and gravy today. I love a good, firm biscuit."

"Me too, my love," Grandpa whispers loudly beside her. He reaches over and takes her hand, bringing it to his mouth for a kiss.

TMI alert.

"You ready to go back to work Tuesday, Meghan?" Dean asks from across the table.

"Wait. Tuesday? I'm going back tomorrow."

"Tomorrow is Memorial Day," Levi says.

"Oh. I forgot," I mumble, surprised that something as big as a paid holiday off completely slipped my mind, and apparently, Nick's too, since he keeps talking about coming back Monday. Although, it's not like I've been at work, staring at my calendar as a reminder. "Anyway, I guess I go back Tuesday and I'm so ready. I hate sitting at home doing nothing."

"You haven't been sitting at home," Payton says, giving me a look. It says 'I'm about to bust you out and tell everyone you came up to the flower shop and worked until I sent you home to rest yesterday.'

Sisters are horrible. Don't have them.

"I'm *fine*," I insist, anxious to order food and get on with my day so I don't feel like I'm being watched under a magnifying glass.

"You are fine, Meg, but it never hurts anyone to take it easy for a few days. We just care about you and want to make sure you're on your way to being one hundred percent soon," Dad says with a smile.

One hundred percent? I'm not sure when the last time I felt that was.

Actually, I do.

But I'm not going there right now.

"We're heading up to the shop for a bit after brunch," Lexi says to me. "Abby's roots make me want to cry."

"This is why I hate dyeing my hair. It's too much maintenance," Abby groans.

"They're highlights and lowlights, sister dear. Plus, I have a new shade of purple I want to try," Lexi says as she gives the boys little pieces of baby cereal. They absorb water (or drool) super fast, which is why they have remnants of the food already smeared all over their adorable little faces.

"I'm not putting purple in my hair," Abby disputes.

"I want purple!" our niece, Brielle, exclaims.

"Maybe a strip," Payton replies to her adopted daughter, to which Dean gives her a look. "It'll wash out," she assures her husband. "Plus, it'll be fun to have Bri come along while I get my hair done."

"Whatever you think, love," Dean croons at his wife, leaning over and kissing the tip of her nose.

"Stop it. I'm trying to eat," AJ grumbles. Sawyer laughs, pulls her into his arms, and kisses her senseless. "I mean, do whatever you want," AJ adds, her eyes dazed with lust.

"You should come up and hang with us," Lexi says, pulling my attention away from the mini-make-out sessions happening around me.

"Oh, umm…I have plans afterward. Maybe I'll stop by later," I reply with a shrug. Lexi's face transforms into one of sympathy as realization sets in. She knows where I'm going, but doesn't call me out on it. I go every Sunday.

The rest of brunch is pleasant, with very little talk about sex, which I chalk up on the plus category. Dad pays the bill, and before I know it, we're all heading outside. It's a beautiful Sunday, the sun shining high in the sky and the smell of salt wafting from the Bay. We all say our goodbyes, and hugs are passed around like candy at Halloween.

"Want me to join you?" my dad asks quietly as he gives me a hug.

"No, I think I'm good today. Thanks for the offer," I reply, fighting the tears that threaten to spill.

"The offer stands if you change your mind," he adds before placing a kiss in the middle of my forehead. "Love you, Meggy."

"Love you too, Dad."

I make my way to my car, keeping my head down. I tell myself it's to keep the sun out of my eyes, but let's be real: it's to keep the others from seeing the tears swimming in my eyes. As soon as I'm inside my car, I grab my sunglasses and slide them onto my face. Automatically, I place my keys into the ignition and pull away. A few of my family members are still gathered on the sidewalk as I drive past, probably talking about me.

They're always talking about me.

Pushing all thoughts of the sadness they poorly hide in their eyes, I make my way to the one place I feel both joy and ultimate sorrow. The narrow roadway winds through the land as I head toward the single plot. I park on the lane, my car as familiar to this place as the markers surrounding it.

The breeze has picked up slightly out here. Trees are everywhere, extending as far as the eye can see. It's another two miles before you get to houses, to happy families and the lives they lead.

My life is here.

The cemetery.

I get out of the car and make my way to his final resting place. Even now, after more than two years, the sight of his name on that piece of granite steals my breath. It makes it real. I crouch down on the grass, reaching out and tracing my fingers along his name.

Joshua David Harrison.

Beloved Son, Brother, Fiancé

"Hi, Josh, it's me." He knows who I am, yet I always feel the need to start my conversation off with an introduction. Old habits die hard, I guess. "I'm sure you've heard what happened this past week. I'm fine, though I was a bit shaken up at the time. It could have been a lot worse," I state, sitting and crisscrossing my legs, while reaching for a blade of grass. I pick a piece from the ground and start tearing it into little pieces. "Nick was there at the right time. He came out of work and found that man hurting me. I'm okay, though, really I am.

"I know what you're thinking: I should have never went out by myself. It was stupid of me. Well, Nick usually walks me out, but he had something else to handle. I feel horrible because the poor guy blames himself, even though it's not his fault. He's a good friend to me, Josh. Besides my family, he's one of my only friends," I confess.

I sit there and stare at his name, the two dates below jumping out at me like a beacon in the night. The name starts to blur as the tears start to come. Lying down beside his headstone, I cry for everything I've lost, everything I'll never have. Every dream we shared that was crushed alongside his body. The breeze picks up, the air wrapping around me like a warm hug. "I miss you so much," I cry, giving in to the gut-wrenching sobs that steal my breath. "I wish you were here. I don't want to do this alone."

"You're not alone, Meggy," my dad whispers behind me, crawling to the ground and pulling me into his arms. I cry in his arms until there seems to be no more tears. I have no idea how long we sit there, but he never moves. He just holds me and lets me grieve for the man I loved more than life itself. "You're never alone."

When the tears finally subside and I'm able to breathe somewhat normal, I sit up beside the man who has held me more in the last two years than he probably did in the twenty-six years before this happened. I wipe my eyes and glance back at the stone, my dad keeping his arm around my shoulder.

"He's proud of you, Meghan. I know it doesn't seem like it, but you've been taking baby steps toward healing and moving forward."

"It feels wrong," I confess, my words barely a whisper. "I feel guilty for moving on with my life when he lost his."

"I understand," Dad says, his eyes cast downward. "When your mother was sick, I would stay awake at night, watching her sleep and praying that God gave me her cancer. I would have taken that pain away in a heartbeat if I could, for all of us. After we lost her, I even begged God to take me too. I wasn't sure how to live without her."

His confession is like a bullet to the chest. It's painful and raw...and familiar. I understand exactly what he's saying, because I felt the exact same way. It would have been so much easier if God would have just taken me right along with him.

"But that's not how it works," Dad continues. "I was still alive, and more importantly, I still had you girls to look after. The thought of you all losing us both, well that pretty much gutted me. So, I got up and did what I had to do.

"It's okay to miss him, sweetheart. You'll miss him for the rest of your life, but the important thing to remember is that *you* still have a life. And if you go through the motions, if you just merely exist, you're not only shorting yourself, but Josh too. He wanted you to live, Meggy. He wanted you to love because your heart is made for that. You are an incredibly smart, generous, and caring woman who deserves to share her life with someone who sees what Josh saw."

Tears stream down my face as I listen to his words – really listen to them.

"It's not easy, honey. I'm the first to admit, but the older I get, the more I realize that life is worth living, and loving is the greatest joy in life."

"Are you saying," I start, leaving my statement open.

"Yes, that's what I'm saying. No, I'm not in love, but as I mentioned, I met someone who makes me feel alive again. For the first time in forever, I smile. Not that you girls don't make me smile, because between you and your sisters, and now the slew of grandbabies being added to the family, I have plenty of reasons to smile. But this is a different smile."

I nod, understanding what he means. The love you share with your soul mate is different than that of your family. And that's okay. Love comes in many forms and ways. I don't know, maybe there is room for more than one great love, more than one soul mate. The thought gives me both hope and hives.

"Can we meet her?" I ask, glancing down at Josh's stone.

"I invited her to the wedding," Dad says, offering me a smile.

I smile back at him, truly happy that he is taking this step. I'm sure it's not easy, but the thought of Dad spending time with someone who puts a smile back on his face makes me a bit giddy. "I can't wait."

Dad nods. "And when the time is right, when the right person comes along, you'll find your reason to smile again, Meghan. Just don't give up on the idea, okay? There is so much love and joy around us that I'd hate for you to miss out on the beauty that surrounds us." He pauses and holds my eyes. "Josh wants nothing more than your happiness, sweet girl. He wants you to live."

Just then, the breeze picks up again.

It's as if Josh is speaking to me too.

Nodding my understanding, I rest my head on his shoulder and finish my visit with the man I was going to marry. I tell him about the babies coming and AJ's wedding. Dad doesn't speak as I talk, just continues to hold me close.

When I'm finally finished with my visit, I turn to my dad. "Can we go say hello?"

"I'd be sad if we didn't," he replies with a gloomy smile.

Hopping up, he extends his hand down to me. Before we walk away, I turn toward Josh's headstone. As I do every Sunday, I kiss my fingers and place my hand on his name. "I love you. Always."

Turning to Dad, he offers me a hand and leads me toward the tree line a few rows back. There, under a blooming Eastern Redbud tree, is the large double heart stone with the names of my parents. One has a death date and the other doesn't.

I try to hold back, giving Dad time to visit with his wife, but he won't have it. He guides us both to the stone and takes a seat on the grass beside it. I'm quiet, lost in my own memories of the woman who never got to see her six daughters grow up. The reflections are fuzzier now than they have been in the past, and I wonder if that's just part of life. The details start to fade.

"I've told her all about the woman I've been seeing. I think Trish would have liked her." Dad smiles fondly at the stone that bears his wife's name, along with his own.

"Mom liked everyone."

"She did. She was an amazing person who could find the good in anyone. I see a lot of her in you. Probably more than any of the girls."

The accolade warms my heart, because honestly, being compared to my mother is one of the greatest compliments in life. She really was a caring, joyful, amazing woman.

"We're going to be okay, Meghan. I know it." Dad wraps his arm around me and pulls me close. Together, we sit there and talk to Mom.

By the time we both walk to our cars, I feel like I've cleansed my soul. Do I think our talk today magically healed the hurt and pain in my heart? Absolutely not. But maybe, just maybe it's a step in the right direction.

After another hug and a forehead kiss from my dad, my phone lights up with a text message. An instant smile spreading across my face as I swipe the screen to read his message.

Nick: *Going sailing tomorrow with Rhenn. Please say you'll come. I'm bringing food so no one starves. We're meeting at the marina at 10.*

I look up from my phone, the smile still extending across my face, and gaze out at the many stones until I spot one specific one. The breeze picks up, rustling my hair, and the sun chooses that moment to shine brightly on the screen. I gaze up, the heat warming my face, close my eyes, and smile. It feels good to…feel.

Turning toward the car parked behind me, I notice Dad standing with his door open. He gives me a warm grin and nods his head, solace spreading through my body. Before climbing into my car, I fire off a reply.

Me: *I'll be there.*

Nick: *I'll pick you up.*

Chapter Ten

Nick

I'm trying not to stare.

I'm failing.

Meghan is seated beside me in the passenger seat, a pair of short khaki shorts and boat shoes framing her long, thin legs. And let's not get me started on the tank top that hugs her upper body like it was tailor-made just for her. Her hair is up in a high ponytail, and she's sporting a visor on her head to shield her eyes from the sun.

I can also see strings around her neck.

She's wearing what is probably a bikini.

I most likely won't survive the day.

As I pull into the parking lot of the marina, I quickly notice the lack of available parking. Instead of searching for a spot, I pull up to the walkway that leads to the dock where Rhenn's boat is located, and stop.

"We can unload here, and then I'll go hunt for parking."

Popping the trunk, I remove the cooler with food and a bag with condiments and extras. Meghan joins me with her own bag, a towel sticking out of the top. The thought of Meghan sunbathing on the deck of the boat has me already half-hard.

"Wait here. I'll go park and be right back."

I'm saved from having to park in the back lot when a car vacates their spot only a few rows back from the marina. When the vehicle is locked and I make sure my keys and wallet are in my pocket, I join Meghan back on the walkway. "Ready?" I ask, throwing the bag over my shoulder and reaching for the cooler.

"Here, let me," she says, coming over to grab the bag. Her hand brushes against my shoulder, and I'll be honest, the casual touch doesn't suck. In fact, it is pretty much the exact opposite of suck.

When she has both bags, I grab the cooler and head toward where Rhenn moors his boat, year-round. "Watch your step," I instruct, setting the cooler on the ground when we approach the sailboat.

"Thanks," she says, taking my hand and stepping onto the decking.

She quickly sets the bags down and tries to help with the cooler. "I got it." I offer her a smile as I step around her and set the cooler down.

"You brought a friend? I didn't know we were bringing friends," Rhenn says, stepping up from the cabins below deck and retrieving his cell phone.

"Don't you dare," I tell him.

"Give me five minutes. I could have some friends here in thirty."

"Not happening. It's a perfect day for a sail, and I'm going to spend it with my two favorite people."

"But…one of your favorite persons is a dude…who likes the company of women."

"You'll have to use this five-hour dry spell to sit and reflect on your life," I tease.

"That's bullshit," he mumbles. Honestly, I'm surprised he doesn't already have a cabin full of half-naked women on board. "At least I get to spend the day with this gorgeous lady," Rhenn croons, turning all of his charms on Meghan. He reaches out and takes her hand, bringing it to his mouth for a kiss. "Meghan Summer, always a pleasure spending time with you."

"Knock it off, Burleski. Your charms don't work on me," Meghan fires back, making me bark out a laugh.

"Ouch. You wound me, Meghan."

"I'm sure you'll survive. You have enough ego to pad your fall," she sasses. You couldn't wipe the smile off my face with a putty knife.

Rhenn joins me and helps carry the cooler down to the galley below. "Dude, I think I'm in love with her. She's the perfect combination of sweet and sassy. If you don't claim her, I'm going to. Make your move and now is the perfect time. Ladies dig boats. If you play your cards right, I might even let you play Captain for a bit."

Rolling my eyes, I look over at my friend. "You're such an idiot. You can't just claim women like a table at Starbucks. Besides, Meghan has way too much class for a loser like you."

"Don't I know it," he replies, unloading the food and placing it in the small refrigerator. "It was worth a shot, though."

"You weren't even playing the same game," I snort before climbing up the stairs and joining her on deck. "Hey."

"Hi. So…"

"So…" I mimic.

"So, if you guys are going to talk about me, you should probably make sure to do it behind closed doors, or where the sound doesn't travel upward to where I'm standing."

Believe it or not, I blush. I've never blushed in my life. Okay, that's a lie. I'm pretty sure I blushed in high school, freshman year, when the senior head cheerleader walked into Science class and gave me a little smile. You don't want to know what sort of embarrassing things happened in my pants that day.

"Oh, sorry. Rhenn doesn't think sometimes. Actually, all of the time. He sort of just speaks without thinking. You don't have to worry about him, though. He won't bother you," I assure her.

She shrugs her shoulders. "I'm not worried about him." Then she walks over to her bag and pulls out sunscreen. I watch, helplessly, as she lathers up her arms and legs, making sure the thoughts filtering through my mind are completely inappropriate.

"Ready to hit the water, Romeo?" Rhenn comes up behind me and slaps me on the back. Hard.

I don't flinch as I turn toward my friend. "Let's do this."

Together, we get his boat ready to sail, and fifteen minutes later, we're slowly making our way through the harbor and out to the Bay. It really is a beautiful day. The sun is shining brightly, with not a cloud in the sky. Plus, there's a beautiful woman sitting port side across from me. Her hair is pulled up high on her head, a pair of big, dark sunglasses don her face, and she keeps looking up at the sky and smiling, as if she enjoys feeling the wind and sun on her face.

Realization sets in, hard and fast. Meghan Summer may very well be the most remarkable woman I've ever met, and what I'm starting to feel for her goes so much deeper than the friend's category. She's breathtakingly beautiful, whether in scrubs or dressed up. She's sweet and loyal. Her smile could brighten even the darkest nights.

And she's in love with a ghost.

We sail for approximately an hour and a half, and no one so much as utters a word. Rhenn, though slightly reckless with his personal life, is great behind the helm. He maintains a great speed, but never goes too fast. His boat is built for speed, but he doesn't quite stretch her legs in the open waters. For that, I'm grateful. He doesn't need to scare the shit out of Meghan like he has women before.

Honestly, I think he only does it in hopes of blowing their bikini tops off.

Rhenn finally slows down and comes to a stop. "This okay?" he asks me, which earns a nod in return.

"Looks good."

I jump up as he releases the anchor and prepares for our afternoon. We're a few miles out from land, but toward the southern edge of Virginia. We've sailed down here several times before. It's a gorgeous and common area for boats to gather, with minimal waves. There are already about a dozen boats in around us, though no one gets close enough to bother any other boaters.

Meghan hops up and stretches, the hem of her tank top riding up a bit on her stomach, exposing smooth, creamy flesh that makes my mouth water.

"I'm heading down to grab the food," I announce, taking the stairs below to put a bit of distance between me and the only woman on board.

"I'll help," she replies, quickly following me down below.

Great.

So much for trying to give myself a few minutes to calm down. You know, think shit out. Nothing calms a half-mast dick like thinking about your ancient English teacher with her black knee-high socks and floral calf-length skirts.

Together, we pull the containers of chicken salad, coleslaw, and potato salad from the fridge. I grab the bag with chips and buns and set a few bottles of water in the bottom before turning back to the stairway. "I'll grab utensils," Meghan adds, her arms loaded with food.

Back on deck, we work seamlessly to set lunch out on the table. "You didn't bring beer? What's this water shit?" Rhenn asks, making a face at the bottles of water.

"You can have beer after you drink some water," I tell him.

"Thanks, Mommy." He pops the top off the first bottle and chugs away. When it's empty, he heads below, only to return a few moments later with a bottle of Coors Light. "Ahhh, this is better."

I pull out a chair and start to make a sandwich. Meghan joins me, reaching for a bun, and that's when I notice something is missing.

Her tank top.

She took off her fucking top, her blue and yellow bikini top on full display. I almost groan. Almost. My eyes are riveted to her chest like some perv getting his rocks off. I'm such an asshole.

"So tell me about the boat. Did you pick the name?" Meghan asks Rhenn when he joins us at the table.

"It's a two-thousand fifteen Catalina that I got for a steal when the original owners went through a divorce. He wanted the boat more than he wanted anything else, and since it was in her name – she bought it as a gift for his fortieth birthday – she decided to sell it cheap just out of spite."

"Wow, that's…vengeful," she replies between bites.

"It was originally named Stephanie, which turned out to *not only* be the wife's name, but also his secretary's name – total coincidence, so he says – and when I took possession, I knew I had to rename it."

"You can just rename a boat?" she asks, totally enthralled with his story.

"Oh, sweet Meghan," he starts, reaching over and taking her hand. The movement makes my blood start to boil. He notices right away, of course, and offers me a quick 'fuck you' wink. "The renaming of a boat isn't to be taken lightly. The legend goes that the captain must consult Poseidon, as to not invoke his wrath. There's a fancy and totally necessary ceremony that must commence in order to purge the old name from Poseidon's memory before the new name can be made official."

"That's so cool," she says, hanging on his every word.

"He had to chant some weird saying and fling champagne. I'm pretty sure it was just an excuse to drink," I add.

"And drinking we did. I was able to unveil the new name as soon as the ceremony was complete."

"That's pretty radical. Why Runaround Sue?" she asks.

"Because it's a reminder that not all women are the staying-type," he replies with a smile, though I can see the painful memories brewing in his eyes. "Plus, it was the first song I heard once I signed the papers for my new boat. Let's go swimming!" he adds with a blinding smile.

We spend the next three hours basking in the sun and enjoying the day. It feels completely natural to spend it with my best friend and my…other friend. Meghan appears relaxed and seems to enjoy her time on the boat. In fact, I've seen her smile more in the last few hours than I have in the last few months. I've even caught her checking out my bare chest a few times while we sunbathe.

"His ex was named Suzanne," I confess quietly as we both sit on the deck. Meghan is reading a book, tanning her incredible body. "She cheated on him and broke his heart."

She glances over at me, and even though I can't see her eyes beneath her glasses, I can tell they're full of sympathy. "Makes sense."

"What does?" I ask, turning toward her and giving her my full attention. Rhenn is down below showering off the sea.

"Why he sleeps around so much. He's protecting himself."

I grin. "You're very smart, Miss Meghan Summer."

"Don't I know it," she sasses, setting her book on the table. I use the opportunity to talk with her a bit more about Wednesday.

"So, I have an idea."

"What's that?" she asks, leaning forward and giving me her full attention. My eyes drop down to her bikini. Thank fuck for sunglasses.

"I was hoping you'd swing by the dojo on Wednesday. I have a class that night, but wanted to show you a few things. Like self-defense things."

She sits up tall in her seat. It's the first time I really notice the markings on the side of her head from last Tuesday's assault. The bump has gone down and the bruising is fading, but the memory of what happened is still fresh in my mind. "Well, I'm already taking a class Friday night with some of my sisters."

"You are? Good. I'll be there with Rhenn. I always help with his beginners' self-defense class."

"Do you think I should still come Wednesday?"

Yes. Not because you need more work, but because I want to spend time with you. Of course, I don't say that aloud. Instead, I go with, "Wouldn't hurt. I can show you a few things before Friday's class. Then you'll be ahead of the curve," I reply lightly.

"Okay." She doesn't even hesitate. "But you'll be gentle, right? I've never done this before."

Okay, let's hold up a moment. I know she means it lightly, and more importantly, is referring to the moves I'll be teaching her, but my male brain runs right past all logic and lands firmly on inappropriate. My cock twitches in my swim trunks at the thought of showing her *moves*. And I'd definitely be gentle. Unless she didn't want me to be.

Clearing my throat, I reply, "Absolutely. Just a few moves to help a woman protect herself if needed."

"Then, yes. I'll do it. What time?"

"My class is from six fifteen to seven fifteen. Anytime after that."

"I'll be there."

Chapter Eleven

Meghan

I'm early.

After work, Nick took off to the dojo thingy to get ready for his class, while I ran home to change. I debated on what to wear for at least twenty minutes, finally opting for a pair of capri yoga pants and workout tank top.

Now, here I stand, out on the sidewalk, trying to build up the courage to actually walk in. I'm not sure why I'm so nervous, but I am. Maybe it's the thought of having to learn hand-to-hand combat and knowing that I might actually have to use it someday. Or it could be that it's because *Nick* is the one who'll be teaching me.

We'll be close.

Touching.

Finally, curiosity gets the best of me, and I enter the building. There's a small sitting area where a few women are chatting, and when I walk in, a couple of them sitting in the corner turn my way. They really seem to take in my appearance with a very critical eye. It makes me feel self-conscious, like they find me lacking.

"Meghan," Rhenn croons like a verse in a love song, approaching from the small hallway that leads to the back.

"Hey, Rhenn," I reply, offering him a smile. "I'm a little early."

"You're fine," he says with his own killer smile. He really is a good-looking guy. "Come with me, darlin'." Rhenn places his hand on my lower back and guides me to the hall. Glancing over my shoulder, I find a few sets of eyes glaring daggers into the back of my head. "Ignore them," he whispers. "They're jealous because I don't sleep with the moms. Learned that lesson the hard way when I first started this place," he adds with a wink.

"So they think I'm with you?"

"Of course, they do. Do you see how gorgeous of a couple we make?" he asks with a laugh, ensuring the rest of my tension ebbs from my shoulders.

At the end of the hall is a large, open room. It's well lit and has a large red and blue mat on the floor. There are mirrors at the front of the room, with some stuff in the back that looks like workout equipment. The entire room is clean, accessible, and doesn't smell like a locker room.

"Five punches, let's see it," Nick bellows with authority, drawing my eyes back up to the front of the room. He's standing there, wearing his white...outfit (or whatever it's called) with a black belt cinched around his waist. His feet are bare, and I'll be honest, it's kinda hot.

"One," he instructs, followed by eight little preschoolers wearing white, all punching with their right fist, yelling, "Huhhh!"

"Two." They punch with their left fist and yell once more.

They continue until Nick says five, eight little fists flying with force and determination. "Good job," he says, offering the kids a smile that does something to my stomach. It flutters like ten thousand butterflies, and when he glances my way and notices me standing next to Rhenn? That thousand-watt smile is completely disarming, making my panties practically useless.

"The kids love him. He has way more patience than anyone I've ever met. That's why he's perfect to lead this class," Rhenn whispers as we stand there and watch Nick work with his little students. Even when the kids bounce around and "practice" their moves, he remains completely patient and always encouraging.

"Let's see high kicks," Nick instructs, walking into the group and placing his hands out. "One," and the kids kick. In fact, one little girl with brown pigtails and a toothless grin, kicks so high, she knocks Nick's hand up.

"Two." Again, they kick, as Nick moves through the group and allows different kids to kick at his hands.

"Greyson, your kicks are looking great, bud. And Emma, I think you hurt my hand," he boasts at the sweet little girl in the back row. She gives him a shy little grin, but I can tell she appreciates the compliment.

"Great job tonight, everyone," he says, walking into the middle of the group for a bow and a round of high fives. Each student jumps up and slaps his hand, some earn a pained face from Nick as well as a shaking of his hand, like their slaps hurt. "Tonight was our last class for the spring. Is everyone coming back this fall?" he asks.

"Yes!" the entire group of students hollers at the same time.

"I'll be right back," Nick says as he approaches. "I'm running up front to make sure all of the students meet up with their parents."

And with that, I'm left alone in the back...with Rhenn.

"Feel free to set your stuff down over on one of the benches," he says, pointing to the side of the room.

Within five minutes, Nick rejoins us, and Rhenn makes his excuses to leave. "I'll be in the office if you need me."

Suddenly, being alone with Nick in the dojo has me nervous. I'm shifting my weight from foot to foot and not completely sure what to do with my hands. "Hey," he finally says, offering me a small smile.

"Hi."

"You ready?"

"As I'll ever be," I grumble, not really sure if I can do this.

Or if I should.

No, I definitely should. After what happened last week, a woman should know a few basic self-defense moves.

Nick heads over to the bench and unties his belt, dropping it on the bench beside my bag. Then, he strips off his white jacket.

My jaw hits the floor.

Unlike our time on the boat Monday, where he wasn't wearing a shirt, this time he's wearing a white tank top underneath, and if it's possible, I think it makes him hotter. It hugs his very hard, very muscular upper body in a way that I've only read about in books. (Or saw one time when Linkin stripped for my sister, Lexi.) His shoulders...my word, his shoulders. The definition and muscles are like a work of art. Nick turns back to face me. "Is this okay? It's hot."

Yep. Definitely hot.

"Umm, sure. Whatever. Fine." I know I try to sound casual, but really, it just comes out like a bumbling, blubbering teenager.

"Good. Now come here," he instructs, and the tone goes straight to the apex of my legs (which are practically shaking, by the way). Why does it sound dirty?

"I'm going to show you just a few moves to help you escape an assailant. The first is an open hand strike. You're going to use the heel of your hand to strike some of your assailant's most sensitive areas," he teaches, demonstrating the move. "Aim for the eyes, nose, mouth, or neck." He stands in front of me and holds my hand, positioning it and showing me the correct ways to execute. "Here," he adds, moving my hand to his face.

I can feel his breath on the palm of my hand as I slowly shadow his movements, practicing without actually striking him.

"Good. Now, if he comes at you from behind, your elbow is a valuable weapon. It's hard, and when thrust into his face, neck, or stomach, you could definitely buy some precious time to get away." He moves behind me and I immediately thrust upward with my elbow. He easily dodges the blow, as mortification tinges my cheeks.

"Oh my God, I'm sorry. I didn't mean to try to hit you, it just…was a reflex," I insist.

"You're fine," he chuckles. "It's good for you to actually practice the moves. Well, except this next one. No need to practice the knee to the groin. Just know it's one of the most effective ways to disarm an assailant. If done right, your perp will be lying on the ground, crying for his mommy while you run away," Nick teases, holding his hand over his…area.

Of course, my eyes drop down.

Why wouldn't they?

He was just referring to someone's…package.

"Yeah, no need to practice that," I quickly reply, again a blush burning my neck and cheeks.

Is it hot in here?

"Let's go over a few ways to block a punch or slap," he says, showing me a few techniques using my arms and hands, before finally demonstrating what to do if the assailant gets me down on the ground.

Yep, I've officially lost my mind. I'm practically rolling around on the mat with Nick, who is trying to teach me moves that might one day save my life. And all I can think about is the way his arms feel when they wrap around me or the way his *package* brushes up against my thigh, not once, but five times.

Five.

Yes, I counted.

"Okay, that's the basics. I want to do a few of them in a real-life situation. Stand over there, and I'll come at you. I want you to take me down."

"Wait, what? I can't take you down. You're…big."

And, cue the blush…

Nick chuckles. "I'll be okay, honey. Promise." Then he winks at me, and my entire body seems to catch fire. "Ready?"

No. I'm definitely not ready for this.

But before I can give the idea of Nick attacking me another thought, he moves and is on me. He tries to pin my arms, but I block his hold and thrust the heel of my hand into his stomach. It's hard and unforgiving, and doesn't have the effect I thought it would.

That kinda pisses me off.

"Good," he says, allowing me a moment to catch my breath. He doesn't wait too long, though, and I hear him say, "Again."

This time, he comes at me from behind, wrapping his big, strong arms around me in a bear hug. He pulls me along, showing me how easy it would be for a man of his size to overcome me and practically cart me off to wherever. I can't breathe.

"Come on, Meg. Fight. Don't let me win."

Fear starts to spread through my entire body, and I start to wiggle. I try to twist and free my arms, but he just holds me that much tighter. My fear turns to anger. I'm suddenly very pissed off. I'm angry at Nick for showing me just how easy it is to overcome me, at the man who tried to hurt me last week and almost got away with it. I'm angry at everyone who has treated me as if I were broken and talked to me in that sad, pitiful voice. I'm angry at the world for showing me its ugly, dark side.

And I'm angry at…Josh.

I'm so fucking angry at the one man who vowed to always love and protect me. I'm livid that he broke that promise, that he left before we were truly able to live our life. I'm furious at the hand life has dealt me, at the pain and the sorrow. I'm outraged that I'm alone.

Suddenly, I'm crying. Big, fat angry tears slide down my face, but I can't stop. I fight off my assailant, turning every ounce of anger that has been bubbling beneath the surface for so long onto the innocent man in front of me. I kick, I punch, and I fight.

Lacey Black

And I scream.

"Why!" I bellow, swinging my arms wildly, feeling the strike of flesh beneath each blow. "Why did you leave? Everything was perfect, and then you just left! You took everything. You lied. You broke your promise. You died and I couldn't do anything to stop it! You swore to always love me and you lied!" his words from that night – those final, heart-wrenching words – the ones that are repeated every night in my dreams – come back to me.

"You were wrong! It wasn't supposed to be the end, and it was. You were wrong, Josh. Wrong."

The tears pour from me like a faucet and all of my energy just seems to vanish. I'm tired, exhausted really, and that's when I finally know the truth, something I've hidden from, fought, and ignored for the last two years.

Josh is never coming back.

Gazing down, realization slams into me like a semi. "Oh my God!" I bawl, noticing for the first time the blood. I'm straddling Nick on the mat, a steady stream of blood oozing from his nose and lip. His eyes are locked on mine, but it's not fear or anger that I see.

It's relief.

The same relief I feel sweep through my weary body.

He moves quickly, just as the humiliation starts to set in, and wraps his arms around me. I don't even realize I'm crying again until I hear him. "Shhhh," he coos, his hand gently on the side of my face in a comforting manner. "I've got you."

And I know he does.

I cry against his shoulder, gripping his top as if it were a lifeline, as everything washes over me. It's like losing Josh all over again, but I guess if I'm being honest, it's more accurately like I'm finally accepting that he's gone. I've carried it around with me, like a security blanket, but now I'm facing it – really staring it down, face-to-face. He's not coming back.

Ever.

"I'm going to get up, okay?" he whispers gently, his hand still stroking my face. Unable to speak words, I just nod.

Nick stands up, me in his arms. I hear him holler for Rhenn, who helps gather up my bag, as well as Nick's stuff, and follows us out the back. Nick sets me in his passenger seat, his nose no longer bleeding. He wipes the remaining blood off with the back of his hand and closes my door. He speaks to Rhenn for a moment before coming around and climbing into the driver's seat.

Without saying a word, he takes me home.

I try to get out on my own accord, but Nick won't have it. He meets me at the passenger door and instantly pulls me into his arms. He carries me up the steps and to the door, where he digs in my bag and retrieves my keys. I'm so grateful because I'm not sure I have the strength for the simplest of tasks right now.

Inside, he secures the front door before carrying me back to my bedroom. I feel the soft mattress beneath me and Nick's arms disappear. Reflexively, I reach for him. "I'll be right back," he whispers before placing a kiss on my forehead. It's unexpected, but a welcome comfort.

Nick returns just a few minutes later and sets a glass of water on the nightstand. He moves around to the opposite side of bed and climbs in, wrapping his arm around me. "You okay?" he asks softly, stroking my hair where it's tucked behind my ear.

"I'm so sorry."

"Please don't be sorry. I'm proud of you, actually."

"Proud? How can you be proud of me? I beat the crap out of you and made you bleed," I argue, though my words hold no bite.

"Because you just released two years worth of feelings that you've kept bottled up inside you."

"I do feel better," I confess, tears threatening to spill once more. "I don't know what came over me. It was like everything that has gone wrong in my life, all just sort of exploded like a volcano. And once it started to erupt, I couldn't stop it."

I take a deep breath before continuing. "I know he's gone, but it was like, tonight, I finally let go. Everyone kept saying anger was part of the grieving process, but I didn't believe it. I guess I proved them all right, huh? And only two years late."

"There is no timeline for grief," he says softly.

"I guess," I shrug, feeling small and tired. "It's time, isn't it." It's not a question. "It's time to stop living in the past and...let go." Just saying the words feels like someone sliced my chest open with a box cutter. "I don't know if I can do it, though. I'm letting go of everything I've ever envisioned for myself. Our life together."

"You don't have to let him go completely, you know. There's room for him and whatever your future has in store for you, Meg. Josh will always have a place in your heart."

Blinking the tears, I nod my head. "I know. I was always so afraid to acknowledge that, but I guess tonight, it happened all on its own."

"Not a bad thing. Now, you can live. I knew Josh well enough to know he would want that for you."

Again, I nod and sniffle. "I know. You're completely right, and everyone keeps reminding me of that. It's just so…hard, you know? Everything we had planned, every wish we had ever made was together. It's just gone, and I don't know how to deal with that."

"Well, you start with baby steps. Dreams come in all shapes and sizes, right? So let's start small and work our way up," he suggests.

"We?" I ask with a smile.

"We. We're a team."

The way he says that makes me smile. It's a small one, but it's there nonetheless. The idea of being a part of a team once more, of having a friend or someone close to you to share the burden is awfully appealing.

Plus, there's Nick, and he's quite appealing himself.

We lie in silence for a while, the occasional noise of a passing vehicle mixed with our breathing are the only sounds. I think about Josh and everything we shared, and then I try to look to the future. It's scary and dark. A mystery. But if I think about what Nick said, about taking small steps toward whatever the future may hold for me, then it doesn't look so daunting.

It almost feels manageable.

"You know, there's never been another man in this bed."

"I can go," Nick says, starting to get up.

"No," I reply immediately, reaching for his arm. "Stay. I want you to stay." And I'm surprised to realize how much truth is in that statement. "Please."

His hazel eyes look dark in the moonlight, and they follow my every move. They appear so relaxed, so familiar, and yet hold so many secrets. His cheekbones are high and his jaw covered in two days' worth of stubble. Nick hasn't shaved daily since Collette moved out of his life and took his cat.

I glance at his nose, which is usually fairly straight, but tonight is a bit tweaked and puffy. You know, from where I punched him?

And then my eyes fall to his lips. His perfectly kissable, soft lips. I probably shouldn't be thinking about them that way, but I can't seem to stop myself. "Your lip is swollen," I whisper, lightly touching the smarted flesh of his bottom lip.

"Pssh, you should see the other guy," he teases, trying to give me a grin, but realizing it pulls against the broken flesh.

"I'm sorry."

"I'm not. I've never been beat up by a gorgeous woman before. Not that I'll be telling all my buddies, but it wasn't so bad."

"You think I'm gorgeous?" The words are out of my mouth before I can stop them. Dammit!

"I think you're incredibly beautiful. And smart. And funny. And when you smile, I think the sun shines even brighter."

My heart gallops in my chest and I almost forget how to breathe. I have no idea what to say, or if I'm supposed to say anything in return. What do I say, "Thanks, you're pretty damn hot yourself?"

Instead of saying words, I place my arm across his side, resting it on his back. The movement brings our bodies much closer than they've ever really been – especially on this more intimate level. Nick brings his arm up and sets it on my side. He moves so slowly, as if testing the waters.

I don't stop him.

When our arms are crossed, essentially holding each other, I lean my head forward against his jaw. I exhale deeply, then breathe in his woodsy scent. Sure, there's a weird mixture of sweat and blood, but it's oddly familiar. He just smells like...Nick. Leaning in even more, my cheek comes to rest on his chest. His very firm, muscular chest. I can hear the steady beat of his heart beneath his tank top, a solid reminder that he's alive. That *I'm* alive.

I close my eyes and relax into our new (and really nice) position, entwined together on top of my bed. The events of the night, the day, the week, and hell, probably the last couple of years, finally catch up to me and start to drag me under. My eyelids can no longer stay open and my mind just wants to shut down. For the first time in...forever, I don't dwell on the past, like I normally do at bedtime. I don't think about what I lost or the one who was stolen from me. I don't picture our future and what could have been.

For the first time in so very long, I'm not alone.

Chapter Twelve

Nick

I wake to sunlight in my eyes and a warm hand against my chest. It's almost a startling revelation, but then memories of last night flood my mind quickly, reminding me of where I am and why I'm here.

Meghan.

I try not to move. I'm afraid that if I move, so will her hand, which is under my shirt and splayed on my chest, and in the respect of full disclosure, I really, *really* like her touching me. I like it so much, in fact, that the proof is in my pants. And they're not exactly the best pants to camouflage such evidence. The loose, white material pretty much looks just like the six-man tent I used to camp with in my youth. *That's* something I need to change – and quickly. The last thing I need is for Meghan to wake and see my dick saluting her.

Grandma, Grandma, Grandma, Grandma. Nothing kills a hard-on like the memories of your grandma making you a Spiderman birthday cake when you're ten years old, right?

Right.

Just when my pesky cock starts to act appropriately in the presence of a friend, I get a good look at the beautiful woman in my arms. God, she's breathtaking. She looks completely relaxed, vulnerable even, as she sleeps on my arm. Even when she's drooling on me, she's still a vision.

Her brown hair is sorta wild, splayed out against the soft blue and brown comforter. We're both still curled up on our sides, the way we fell asleep together last night – even if she fell asleep much sooner than I did. For almost two hours, I watched her sleep like a creeper, memorizing everything I could possibly commit to memory of the woman who was sleeping against my chest.

Last night. That was something. My nose feels fine, but my lip is a bit tender this morning. But I don't give a shit. She could beat the shit out of me again if it meant letting out all of that anger she'd been hanging on to for so long. I've never seen her like that – upset to the point of violence, but I'm glad it happened. It was almost like a cleansing, a washing of her soul and the demons that plague her.

Is she healed? Ready to move on with her life? Hell no. But maybe now she'll actually start trying, instead of merely existing. That's what I want for her – to try. To see her easy smiles every day, to hear those little bubbles of laughter. I've heard anger is an important part of the grieving process, and maybe now that she's unleashed two years worth of fury, she'll finally face what troubles her.

And I wasn't kidding. I feel like we're in this together. She needs a friend, more than anything. Even if it means I'm permanently benched in the friend zone, I'd do it just so she gains that little spark of life back in her beautiful emerald eyes.

Which is why I should probably get up. I should remove myself from this comfortable little bubble I'm in, and leave. She can wake up on her own and go about getting ready for her day, without anything like regret setting in. I think that's my biggest fear: that she'll regret asking me to stay. Even though nothing happened, I don't want her to feel uncomfortable that I'm here – in her bed.

Though, it's a pretty fucking fantastic place to be.

Before I can slip from the place where she sleeps, a pair of green eyes open and meet mine. I feel her tense, but then immediately relax. Instead of the panic I expect her to feel, she offers me a small smile. That fucking smile is my undoing.

"Good morning," I whisper, still terrified to move.

"Hi." Her eyes seem to smile as she looks at me, her head still firmly resting on my forearm. She stretches her body out straight, the movements pushing her chest upward, toward my face. My cock notices. My eyes do too. Meghan also seems to notice where her hand is. I feel her fingers flex against my peck, but they don't move. Instead, they almost seem to explore. I'm pretty sure no one is breathing at the moment as her fingers dance on my skin. "What time is it?" she finally asks, a small yawn slipping from her lips.

Glancing over her shoulder, I spot her alarm clock. "Six fifteen."

"Wow, really? I never sleep this late or hard without waking up at least once," she says, almost absently to herself.

"You were rather exhausted when you fell asleep." She doesn't answer with words, but merely nods her head.

"Your lip is all swollen and bruised," she says after a few long seconds of silence. I also notice she still hasn't moved her hand from my chest.

"I'll be okay."

"It's probably going to hurt to eat for a while," she says softly, her eyes full of concern and guilt.

"I'll be fine, Meghan. I won't starve."

"I'm sorry."

"Please stop saying that. I'm not sorry at all."

"I still feel bad that I hurt you."

"I'll live." My stomach chooses that moment to growl. She's not the only one who slept soundly last night. I'm usually up by now and at the gym with Rhenn. He hasn't blown up my phone, which I'm grateful for. I think even he knows that last night was kind of a big moment for her and is letting us be. "I'll tell ya what. You can make it up to me with breakfast."

Her eyes light up. "I'm buying."

"I didn't say that."

"Well, I am, so get over it."

"Fine, but only if I can buy lunch." The words are out of my mouth before I can stop them.

"Perfect." She moves, as if to get up, and glances down at where her hand disappears beneath my shirt. Instead of ripping it away like I expect her to, she slowly drags her hand down my chest, grazing my abs. Yep, there goes my cock again. He's thinking about one thing, and one thing only, and it's not about the friend line that's clearly drawn in the sand. My entire body tightens as her soft fingers practically caress my abdomen before slowly pulling from my shirt.

I miss her touch immediately.

But then she does something I'm completely not expecting.

Meghan Summer winks at me and gives me a saucy little smile before turning and climbing from the bed. "I'm going to jump in the shower," she says over her shoulder before strutting into the adjoining bathroom. Yes, strutting. It's not the walk of someone who's embarrassed or shy. It's the walk of someone who rather enjoyed copping a feel.

I like this side of Meghan.

I like it a lot.

When the shower starts up, I make my way to the kitchen. I know how much she enjoys coffee in the morning, so I fire up the coffee maker. While it's percolating, I take a few minutes to check out her domain. Yeah, I've been here before, but I've never really gotten a good look at the place – well, except for the pair of men's shoes still by the door. It's a comfortable space with soft colors and lighting, and accents of a feminine touch. Not too many, but a few things here and there, like a purple throw pillow that says Home and a pink candle that's been used a few times.

The scent of coffee fills the air, so I return to the kitchen to pour two cups. I grab the two mugs sitting in the cabinet above the sink and fill them both about three-quarters of the way. I know Meghan needs to add creamer to hers, while I'm more of a plain sugar man.

A few minutes later, I hear soft footfalls in the hall and am greeted by a freshly showered Meghan. A trace of her shampoo fills the air, mixing with the coffee, which could forever be my new favorite scent. She's wearing green scrubs with toothbrushes on them, her long hair in a standard ponytail, and minimal makeup. Yet, she still looks as beautiful as ever.

"I made coffee," I tell her, nodding to the two mugs sitting on the counter.

She smiles but then stops when her eyes meet the cups. A look takes over her face. It's part sadness, part confusion. Shit, what the hell did I do? "Is something wrong?" I ask, wanting to take a step toward her, yet not wanting to upset her any more than I clearly have.

"No," she says, shaking her head. When her eyes connect with mine, she gives me a sad smile. "I'm sorry, I'm being silly." She seems to be looking for the right words, so I wait. "It's just that…that cup. It was Josh's."

Oh.

Shit.

I'm drinking out of her dead fiancé's coffee cup.

Swell job, Nicholas.

"Shit, I'm sorry," I reply instantly, grabbing the cup, intending to pour it out.

"No!" she says, quickly coming at me. "Please don't." Meghan holds my hand, which is holding the cup, and our eyes connect. "I want you to use it."

"I don't have to." Why do my words feel like they're choking me?

"I need you to. Please."

She lets go of my hand and watches as I bring the cup to my lips and take a sip. The hot liquid against my smarted lip doesn't feel so great, but I ignore the discomfort and focus on the fact that something bigger is happening here. She's acknowledging that it's okay to let go of something from her past – something as small as a coffee cup.

To me, it's a huge step.

153

When she seems satisfied that I'm drinking from the mug, she reaches for her own and adds the creamer I placed on the counter. "So," she starts.

"So," I mimic, both of us leaning a hip against the counter. "I realized something while you were in the shower. I don't have any clothes here and you don't have a car." Her eyes immediately drop to my outfit – the white tank top I was wearing under my karate gi.

"Shit, you're right," she mumbles, a pink tint sliding up her neck.

"I was thinking that we still have time for this breakfast thing. Since you're ready for work, I'll drive to my place, hop in the shower, and get ready. I at least need shoes."

"You don't have shoes?" She seems mortified.

"I was a little preoccupied last night to put them on," I tell her casually with a shrug. "Anyway, we can stop at the café for a bite to eat, and then, I can either take us to work or drop you off at the dojo to get your car, depending on the time."

"That sounds like a solid plan. I can't believe you left without shoes."

"I was fine. My feet where the last thing I was worried about," I answer honestly.

"I'm sure. You were more concerned about the blood gushing from your nose and lip," she says sheepishly.

"No, I was more concerned about Meghan, who was in desperate need of a friend at that moment."

Her eyes soften and lips curl upward. "Meghan did need a friend, and she's very grateful to Nick for being there for her."

"There is no place that Nick would have rather been."

"I'm not sure about that," she replies with a laugh. "I didn't know crying, emotional women were Nick's thing."

And again, before I can stop myself, I reply, "I think Meghan is Nick's thing."

She looks up at me with wonder, excitement, and maybe even uncertainty in her eyes, but she smiles nonetheless. She doesn't run screaming from the room, nor gently remind me that I'm her friend and *only* her friend. I'll chalk that one up in the win category.

No, I'm not entirely sure where this is going, or what the future may hold for her and I, but the door to finding out feels cracked open. I just have to be careful to enter slowly, and not kick the door and bust in the way I want to.

Slow and steady is the key.

* * *

After a quick stop at my house, in which I run through the shower in record time and throw on the first pair of Dockers and dress shirt I can find, we're off to the café for breakfast. Having Meghan sitting in the passenger seat seems almost too natural. Like she was meant to be there. I try not to let my mind go there, but it does.

And now I can't unthink it.

The café is fairly busy with both families and individuals heading into work. We're able to find an open booth, but before we can sit down, our attention is drawn to the opposite side of the room. "Youuwhooooo, Meggy Pie!"

"Crap," Meghan mumbles as we both turn to the couple waving their hands. "We should go say hello."

"We should," I reply, following behind as Meghan makes her way toward her grandparents.

"Well, look at this! What a wonderful surprise," Emma says, her entire face lighting up with excitement. "Join us," she adds, motioning with her hand to the booth opposite of where Orval and she sit together.

"Oh, we don't have much time. We just stopped in for a bite before heading to work," Meghan replies.

"You'll get food as quickly here as you would on the other side of the room," Orval contradicts. It's the first time I notice that his hand is holding hers on top of the table.

"Unless, you know, you two would like to be *alone* for a bit. Then, by all means, please go sit over in that quiet, private little booth in the corner," Emma adds, an ornery glint in her sparkling eyes.

"No, no. No privacy needed. We can sit," Meghan quickly replies, sliding into the empty booth.

I follow suit, the outside of my thigh gently touching hers beneath the table. She doesn't move over farther, so neither do I.

"So, what brings you two out? Together." Oh, that mischievous ol' woman is definitely up to something. She's like a dog with a new bone.

"We just ran into each other and decided to have a quick bite before heading into the office." I notice Meghan doesn't mention anything about the sleepover, not that I blame her.

"Sure, sure. Everyone's gotta eat, right?" she says, that look still in her eyes. "Besides, I'm sure it was easy running into each other." Emma shrugs casually before taking a sip of her black coffee.

I can feel Meghan tense in the seat next to me. "Why do you say that?"

"Well, since his car was at your house all night, I imagine you probably ran into each other a few times. You know, in the hallway, the kitchen…the bedroom." Emma's smile turns victorious as she gazes at her granddaughter from across the table.

Meghan gasps next to me. "You were spying on me?"

"Of course not, dear. I sent Orvie out for ice cream, and he happened to mention seeing Nick's car."

"I'm not on the route to the ice cream parlor, Grandpa," Meghan glares across at the old man.

He shrugs at her comment. "I always drive past your place, Meggy Pie. I check up on all of my granddaughters." There's no remorse, only compassion as he makes his confession.

"You do?" Meghan asks.

"Always. How do you think we knew about Jaime and Ryan's long history of having *the sex* in their driveway?"

"Oh my God," Meghan mumbles. "They live in the country," she reminds them.

"And we still check on all of you. You won't make me feel bad for that," Orval says.

"I'm not trying to make you feel bad, Grandpa. I just…didn't realize you did that."

"Do you really think your grandma needs ice cream three to four nights a week?" he asks, humor dancing in his eyes.

"I do love ice cream," Emma chimes in. "But usually, I prefer to be licking it off your…"

"Stop!" Meghan interrupts, and for once, I'm so thankful she did. I'm pretty sure I was about to hear something that can't be unheard. You know, like when you're a kid and hear your parents having sex? A nightmare like that sticks with a kid.

"Anyway, Grandpa drove by and noticed your car gone and that Nick's was there. He was afraid something was wrong, but I figured you were finally having *the sex.*"

"Would you stop saying that before breakfast?"

"So? Which was it? Something wrong or *the sex?*" Emma asks, patiently waiting out her granddaughter's reply.

I sit silently, not knowing how much of last night Meghan is going to give up, if anything. She values her personal space, and even though her grandparents are a bit like bulls in a china shop, I know they love her and respect her need for it.

"Actually, it was the former," Meghan starts softly. "Nick taught me a few things last night at the dojo, and I ended up getting upset. Not at him, but I just…well, I sort of got angry and emotional and freaked out a bit. He brought me home in his car and stayed to make sure I was okay."

"And were you? Okay?" Emma asks gently, reaching her wrinkled hand across the table and setting it atop Meghan's.

"Yeah. I think last night helped. I actually feel much better this morning," Meghan replies, turning those green eyes my way for a few seconds.

"Good. I'm proud of you, Meggy. You've come a long way," Orval adds.

"Thanks. But right now, my stomach could use some pancakes and bacon," she replies, trying to lighten the mood.

I look over the menu, even though I already know what I'm going to have, as Emma says, "I always crave a big hearty breakfast after *the sex* too."

Meghan glances across the table. "No, we didn't...I mean, there was no...that."

"Well, maybe not for you," Grandma says coyly just as the waitress delivers a huge plate of eggs, bacon, sausage, and hash browns, and sets it in front of Meghan's grandma.

"That's gross," Meghan mumbles just loud enough for me to hear.

"Oh, there was nothing gross about it, Meggy Pie. In fact, your Grandpa is a magician in the bedroom. He does this thing –"

"NO! For the love of God, please stop talking," Meghan pleads, and I do everything I can to keep the bubble of laughter from spilling out.

"Fine, but one day, you'll be into sharing details with all of us again."

"I've never been into sharing the details. In fact, I don't think any of us have been into sharing. You guys just take it upon yourselves to over-share."

"Good sex will do that to you," Emma retorts with a grin before turning and kissing her husband square on the mouth.

And I'm pretty sure there was tongue.

This family is…well, interesting. They obviously love each other, and that love overflows down through the generations.

I like it.

I like it a lot.

Chapter Thirteen

Meghan

We make our way to the office, a box sitting on my lap containing a couple of éclairs for the other ladies. There's no time to stop at the karate place to get my car, so I'm stuck being driven around by Nick. Not that it's a bad thing.

Not at all.

In fact, I kinda like spending all this time with him, outside of the office.

The morning flies by as patients come and go from my chair. When Nick comes into my little room, he's charismatic and engaging with the patients as always. I also catch him stealing sly glances at me and offering these cute little smiles, like he knows some big secret. It makes me feel all schoolgirl giddy, a feeling that I haven't felt in so very long.

When lunch rolls around, Patty takes off to walk at the park, as she usually does over the lunch hour, and Erika leaves for the day, only working part time on Thursdays. "Ready?" Nick asks when he enters my little room.

"Yep," I respond, grabbing my purse from the cabinet.

As we make our way to the rear of the office, Nick places his hand low on my back. Warmth floods my bloodstream and I couldn't stop the smile from spreading across my face if you paid me a million kajillion dollars. It's a pleasant feeling, one that not only makes me smile but makes me feel alive. Wanted.

Together, we walk to the end of the block to the deli with amazing panini sandwiches. There are only a few tables open as we make our way to the front of the room to place our order. "Do you know what you're having?" Nick asks as we wait behind another couple for our turn.

"Absolutely! Is there any other sandwich than the turkey?"

"Not if you like spicy mustard," he says, glancing at the menu.

"Are you telling me you don't like the turkey panini? That's it. We can't be friends," I tease.

"It's all right, but I have issues with the onions."

"You have issues with grilled red onions? And here I thought you were a good guy."

"Why do you like grilled red onions? Don't they make your breath smell like...grilled red onions?"

I can't help it. I giggle. "I'm going to eat grilled red onions now for lunch right before you clean my teeth."

That makes him laugh. "Thank God I'm not kissing you after that," he says with a wide smile. Then his face falls, as if registering exactly what he just said. "I didn't mean..."

"It's okay," I say with a shrug. "I guess I'll just have to make sure to brush my teeth after I eat grilled red onions...and before you kiss me."

Why does my heart feel so light and free in this moment? It feels amazing to smile and joke, even if the pun is about kissing another man. Nick. Specifically, kissing Nick.

"Can I take your order?" the young high school girl asks from behind the counter.

"Yes, we'd like a turkey panini special with a Sprite and a ham and Swiss panini special with water, please." He orders for both of us, but that doesn't bother me. The fact that he knows exactly what I want is actually a little comforting.

Nick pays, even though I had told him earlier that I was buying lunch today. While we wait for our number to be called, I find a small table over by the window. He pulls my seat out for me, which isn't really surprising, since Nick has always been a complete gentleman. But that begs the question: I wonder what he's like when he's *not* a gentleman? No, I have no right wondering such a thing, especially about my boss...my friend, but now that the seed is planted, it's growing deep roots and sprouting leaves.

I kinda need to know what Nick would be like when he loses control.

"Are you all right? Your cheeks just turned red. Do we need to sit closer to the air conditioner?" he asks, concern written all over his very handsome face. In fact, he's gorgeous. In his work attire, his trunks on the boat, or his white outfit thingy at the dojo, he's simply a stunning specimen of man.

"I'm fine," I reply, waving my hand dismissingly. Nick takes the seat across from me, his eyes seeming to know exactly where my mind had wandered.

Our number is called quickly, and he makes his way up to the counter to grab our tray. When he returns to the table, my mouth waters at the sight of one of my favorite sandwiches.

"Thank you," I say as he sets my food in front of me.

Lacey Black

"You're welcome."

We both dive in, knowing that our time away from the office is limited. My station is all ready to go for our first afternoon patient, but we're still expected to return before everyone starts to arrive.

"So, I was thinking," Nick says, wiping his mouth gently on his napkin. A perfectly, kissable mouth, if you ask me.

Not that I'm thinking about kissing Nick.

Okay, yes I am. I'm completely thinking about kissing him. Especially now that my attention has been drawn to those full, impeccable lips, even though they're still healing from my violent attack on them just last night.

"What do you think?" he asks, pulling my thoughts away from his mouth.

Another blush sweeps in as I realize I just missed whatever he suggested. "I'm sorry, what?"

"You don't have to if you don't want to," he says quickly, seeming to retreat away.

"No, I'm..." I close my eyes and prepare for the embarrassment. "I missed what you said. I'm sorry, I was distracted."

"Oh. Umm, I just asked if you had plans tomorrow night. After the self-defense class. I thought maybe we could go get something to eat."

"Like a date?" I ask, a bubble of hope growing in my chest. Going on the date last week was terrifying. The prospect of going on a date with Nick is exciting.

Nick looks at me from across the table, as if weighing his words carefully. Finally, he replies, "Yeah. Like a date."

My heart pounds in my chest and a smile threatens to spread widely across my face. "You want to take me on a date when we're all sweaty and gross?" I tease.

He seems to think about that for just a second. "Well, I guess it doesn't have to be a date," he starts to backtrack.

Finally, I start to laugh. "I'll make you a deal. You can take me out on a date Friday *and* Saturday. This way, I still get the full-date experience with Nicholas Adams, D.D.S."

A smile that surely matches mine spreads over his lips. "Friday and Saturday night, huh? You drive a hard bargain, Meggy Pie."

Smiling like a loon, I finish off my sandwich and chips, slurping the final drops of my Sprite from my cup. I didn't realize it was possible to eat and drink with a grin, but it is. And if I was ever wanting proof, all I would need to do is look across the table to Nick, who is throwing subtle grins my way between bites as well.

* * *

"Do you see the ass on that man?" Grandma mumbles beside me as we watch Rhenn and Nick demonstrate the first of several moves we'll learn tonight in the beginners' self-defense class.

"Which one?" AJ asks, her eyes clearly checking out both Nick and Rhenn's rear ends.

"Either. Both. Does it matter? They're both tight enough to bounce a quarter off of. I wouldn't mind getting my hands on one.

Or both." Grandma fans herself, as if the thought of grabbing one of their asses has her hot and bothered.

It's disturbing, really.

"Knock it off, will you? You're disrupting class," I chastise the old woman next to me.

"I get dibs on Nicholas. I have a feeling his ass is a work of art. Every time he comes in to check my teeth, I imagine biting it. Like a dog with a bone." And then to prove her point, she growls. And pretends to attack a bone.

Kill. Me. Now.

"Everything all right over here?" Nick asks, joining our group.

"Fine, fine," I say too loudly and much too quickly.

"Meggy was just asking us whose ass was nicer," Grandma says to Nick with a smile.

I gasp. "I was n–"

"Oh, don't be shy, Meggy Pie. I'm sure all of the women in this class are here for one reason only, and it's not to learn self-defense. They're hoping they'll be picked as your victim for the night. A few demonstrations now, a few later in bed – naked. It's every woman's fantasy, really. Chapter six, right Payton?" Grandma asks our oldest sister, who's just staring at her. Mute. Payton is actually mute. Who would have thought?

"Anyway, Meg wants to be your guinea pig. She can't wait for you to throw her down on the mat and work her over," my completely psychotic and absolutely crazy grandma says to Nick with a smile.

"Well, that's perfect, actually. I was about to have Meghan come up front and help demonstrate," Nick replies, giving my grandma a wink. He extends his hand toward me, and while I'd much rather the floor open up and swallow me whole, I grudgingly make my way to where Rhenn stands.

"Make sure you grab his ass, Meggy!" I hear hollered from behind, followed by giggles from the room.

"I'd totally be okay if you grabbed my ass," Nick whispers before dropping my hand and turning to face the room.

For the next forty-five minutes, Nick and I help demonstrate the moves as Rhenn explains them to the group. A few times, a small cluster of young, perky-boobed women in tight tank tops ask for help to make sure they have the moves down. Rhenn usually is the first one to run over and offer his assistance (and probably his phone number), but a couple of times when he was busy, Nick had to help the giggly boob-shakers.

At the end of class, everyone seems to linger a bit. The giggly gaggle of wanna-be porn stars all flock to Rhenn, practically offering themselves up on some sort of orgy promising platter. That man is going to come down with something itchy on his balls if he's not careful.

Nick says goodbye to a few of the ladies before heading to where I hang back with my family. They don't know about our after-class plans, and I'd prefer to keep it that way. The last thing I need is for Grandma to start pulling on that particular thread and unraveling too much information. The Summer family phone tree would blow up, for sure!

"Ladies, how was class?" he asks when he joins us.

"I feel like I could kick someone's ass right now," AJ replies.

"You need to go home and put all of that energy into *the sex* with the sexy ball player. I know exactly how you feel right now, AJ. Your grandpa is launching the meat missile the moment I get home," she says, her face absolutely glowing with excitement.

And I think I'm going to throw up…

"Grandma," Abby chastises, her face a weird shade of green.

"Anyway, Nicholas, it was lovely to see you again. Thank you for a very informative, entertaining class," the little devil says as she steps forward, wrapping her frail little arms around Nick's midsection.

It's when he jumps and his wide eyes land on me that I know what happened. What she did.

"Oh, yes, a very fine ass indeed," she says sweetly before whistling and making her way toward the door.

"I'm so sorry," I mutter, not really sure what I'm supposed to say or do. I mean, what is the protocol for your grandma goosing the man you're not really dating, but kinda sorta seeing a bit – unofficially – who is also your boss. Is there some sort of rule for this situation?

"She totally had a handful of ass, didn't she? I'll never forget the first time she did that to Dean," Payton says with a smile.

"The first time?" Nick asks with wide, yet laughing eyes.

"Oh, yeah. She totally cops a feel as often as possible," Abby adds. "She came over and brought banana bread earlier in the week. Had her little hands full of Levi's butt before I could even slice the first piece."

"Truth. She's quite fond of Sawyer's sexy ass too, but actually it's Linkin's that she can't keep her hands off," AJ contributes.

"That's…" Nick starts, but stops when he can't seem to find the right word.

"Wrong?" I offer.

"Disgusting?" Abby says.

"Disturbing?" Payton adds.

"She says she's making sure we have great asses to go home to, but I think she's just a perverted ol' woman who enjoys feeling up young butts." This from AJ, who shrugs.

"We should head home. Levi has to work in a few hours and I promised I would be home to give him a goodbye kiss," Abby says, grabbing her bag and purse.

"She'll be playing the skin flute within the hour," AJ mumbles to Payton, loud enough that we can all hear her.

"Launching the meat missile," Payton says with a big giggle.

"Riding the bologna pony," I add before bursting into my own fit of laughter.

"You hang around Grandma too much," Abby grumbles, pointing her finger at AJ and Payton. "And you? I expected more from you, Meggy Pie."

"What can I say? We're all cut from the same cloth."

"On that note, we're out of here. Payton is our ride," Abby says, coming over to give me a hug, followed by my other sisters. "Do you need a ride?"

"No, I have my car," I reply, still not giving away a single detail about tonight.

"All right. We'll talk to you soon," Payton says, offering a wave before the three of them head out the door.

"You have a very interesting family, Meggy Pie."

"I can't argue that, Nicholas Adams, D.D.S. and karate chopping kung fu master."

That makes him laugh. "Let me change my clothes and we can head out."

"No way, you don't get to change. If I have to go in sweaty gym clothes, so do you."

"No worries, Meggy. I have a locker full of gross, stinky gym clothes that'll fit the bill just fine," he says with a wink before disappearing into the locker room. I'm left behind with a smile on my face and a happy skippy-beat in my heart.

Chapter Fourteen

Nick

I change quickly, and even though I don't put on nasty, wrinkled gym clothes from my locker, I still opt for a very casual appearance. I throw on a pair of black basketball shorts and clean gray t-shirt, dropping my karate top and pants into my bag to be cleaned.

"Where you running off to?" Rhenn asks when he enters the locker room.

"Nowhere," I answer, tying my tennis shoes.

"I call bullshit. You have this stupid grin on your face that tells me you're up to something. Plus, there's a hot brunette waiting by the back door for you. At least, I think it's for you. I guess Meghan could be waiting for me though, right?"

"Doubt it," I holler over my shoulder as I make my way to the doorway.

"Have a good night, kids. Make sure to wear condoms." His laughter is the last thing I hear before exiting the locker room, flipping him the bird as I go, and heading to the back door where Meghan waits.

"Ready?" I ask, taking her hand in my own.

"Yep." A blush creeps up her neck, and I'm not sure if it's from the hand holding or the fact that we're going on a date – even though this isn't exactly top five date night activities.

The parking lot is well lit as we make our way to my car. We both set our bags in the back seat before climbing in and heading toward the street. I ask about class, what she learned, but never ask what she's in the mood to eat. That's a surprise.

"You and Rhenn work well together. I can see why your classes are well attended."

"Thank you. Rhenn really is a great teacher. I just follow his lead."

"Well, you guys make a good team. Tonight's class was very informative. I think even the boob-sisters all came away with something, other than Rhenn's phone number."

"I'm pretty sure they already have that," I say, heading up the road to the Bay. "They've all taken the beginners' class about five times."

"Five times? Why not just ask him for a date?" she asks.

"Oh, they have. He doesn't date students or moms of students. I don't think they're smart enough to realize that. Plus, he's an attention whore just as much as a regular whore, so he eats up their fawning like he hasn't eaten in a week."

"Do you think he'll ever settle down?" she asks as we pull into one of the beach parking lots.

"Oh, I definitely think he will. When the right woman comes along and knocks him on his ass, he'll give up his bed-hopping ways. Underneath the playboy is a good man who will make a great husband and father. He just won't know it until it slaps him upside the head."

Parking in the pretty vacant lot, I jump out and meet her at the passenger door. She's all smiles as she gets out, her hair high on her head in a messy bun and the strap of her navy blue tank top falling off her shoulder. My eyes follow the material until I'm sure she realizes I'm checking her out.

"Hungry?" I ask, placing my hand on the small of her back and leading her in the direction of my favorite food vendor.

"Starving. I'm surprised by how much of an appetite I worked up by kicking and punching you for a half hour."

Her comment makes me smile. She kicked and punched at me maybe for five minutes, but who am I to argue? Rhenn used us as props for the class, demonstrating the moves he was talking about. It was really just an excuse to have my arms around her or her hands on me – even if they were used in more of an aggressive manner. But hey, I'm not picky. I'll take what I can get.

We walk down the road until I find the vendor with fair food. "Seriously? How did I not know this was here?" she asks, completely shocked when she reads the menu.

"You have to be in the secret fair food society."

"I want in!" she proclaims with a laugh.

"Well, there's only one way to get in the club, Meghan. First, you have to order one of everything on the menu."

"Done!"

"Then, you have to eat as much grease and fattening food as you can consume in the next thirty minutes."

"I'm on it."

"Finally, you have to wash it down with a lemon shake-up and proclaim 'Nick is a date God!'" I tell her seriously.

She giggles, her cute little button nose wrinkling up in a way I never thought would be sexy. But it is. Totally sexy. "So, taking me to a food truck and ordering a bunch of greasy, overpriced food makes this a great date, huh?"

"You forgot the God part."

Again, she laughs. "You're right, I'm sorry. Well, Date God, let's get some food so I can continue to rain compliments and accolades down on you for the next thirty minutes."

"Deal."

Chapter Fifteen

Meghan

A knock sounds at the door. He's early. Thirty minutes early. Holy crap, I'm not ready! I slip on my pink and white dress and run to the front door. I have yet to do my makeup, but that won't take me very long.

When I reach the door and glance through the peephole, I'm surprised to see the person on the other side of the door. "Hey," I say as I open the door and let my sister AJ in.

"Hey, sorry to just drop by. I was going to text, but I was already in the car driving." She seems to take in my dress. "Oh, are you going out?"

I swallow over the lump in my throat. "Umm, yeah. Actually, I am. I have…a date."

"You do?" she asks, smiling widely and practically vibrating with excitement.

"Yeah. Is that weird?" I ask, glancing down at my dress. Is it too much? Do people even wear dresses anymore on dates?

"Weird? Hell no! It's great, actually. I'm so excited for you. Who's the lucky guy?"

"Promise you won't get all weird on me?"

"I make no such promises," she teases.

"Fine. It's Nick."

AJ blinks once. Twice. "Nick? Your sexy boss who showed you how to take down an assailant with a few thrusted hand moves?"

"Yes, but…wait. Did you say sexy?"

"Hell yes, I did. Nick is totally gorgeous, Meg. He's also sweet and kind, and I'm not really surprised you're going out with him."

"You're not?" I ask my older-by-one-year sister. We've always been the closest of all of my sisters, and I always associated that to our close age. We were only a year apart in school. We were in the same clubs and sports in school, and even had some of the same friends.

"No way," she says gently. "You should have seen the way he was looking at you last night. He totally had googly eyes. I'm surprised Grandma didn't pick up on it."

"She was too busy staring at his ass," I mumble, recalling the embarrassing conversation last night.

"True," AJ laughs. "But back to my original point, I'm very excited for you. You deserve a bit of happiness in your life. Maybe Nick is that happiness and maybe not. I'm just glad you're putting yourself out there again."

"Thanks," I say, quietly, the word hard to find over the golf ball that I swallowed and stuck in my throat.

"Before you start to overthink this, it's important for you to know that we all support you one hundred percent. I think it's great that you're going on a date with Nick. You guys will have a good time."

"We, uh, kinda went out last night after class."

AJ whoops and pulls me into a hug. "I'm proud of you, really. Just go and enjoy. Smile again, but if there's one thing all of us miss it's a real Meghan smile." The look she gives me is warm and gentle, and lets me know that she supports me.

"Thank you." I choke on the words.

She waves her hand, blinking back tears. "So, this is what you're wearing? It's super cute. Why didn't I know about this dress?"

I laugh and know full well that if AJ had seen this dress in my closet, she would have taken it at some point. Like always. "I just bought it a couple weeks ago. At the time, I didn't really have a reason, but now I'm glad I did."

"Super cute. But your makeup isn't done. What time is he going to be here?"

Glancing at my watch, I'm surprised to find that I've been visiting with my sister longer than I thought. "Shit, in ten minutes."

"Hurry! I'll go so you can finish getting ready," AJ says, pulling me into a big hug. "I really am happy for you."

"Thanks," I say when she pulls away and opens the front door. "Oh, and AJ? Could you keep this to yourself? I'm not quite ready to tell everyone else about the date."

She gives me a knowing glance and nods. "Sure."

"Love you," I holler as she heads down my steps and toward her car.

"Love you too," she calls back.

"Wait!" I holler, stopping her before she can slip inside her vehicle. "You didn't say why you stopped by."

My sister just gives me a smile. "Doesn't matter. Enjoy your night," she replies with a big smile before getting in and driving away.

When the door closes behind me, I take a deep breath. I have eight minutes before Nick gets here. I better hurry.

* * *

Nick arrives just a few minutes after I step into the bathroom. Fortunately, most of my makeup is on, but I don't have a chance to slip on my sandals or spritz myself with perfume before the doorbell rings.

"Hey," I say, an immediate smile on my face when I take in the man standing at my door. He's wearing a pair of khaki shorts with a blue and gray polo. He's wearing brown leather sandals and a big smile. He also smells amazing. Like I want to climb up his body, stuff my nose in his neck, and just inhale for the next three hours.

He's also carrying flowers.

I smile, glancing down at the gorgeous yellow and pink bouquet in his hands. It's been a long time since I've received flowers. More than two years, to be exact. Josh was a big one for surprise flower deliveries to the office, but now isn't the time to think about that. Now is the time to focus on the man in front of me, who just so happens to be holding a pretty bouquet for our date.

"These are for you," he says when I step aside and let him in. "Wow, you look amazing," he adds, giving me an appreciative once-over that warms my entire body. The way he looks at me makes things tingle that haven't tingled in quite a while.

"Thank you," I reply, reaching for the bouquet. "For the flowers and the compliment. Come in. I'll put these in water real quick and then finish up. I'll only be another minute," I tell him, glancing over my shoulder. When I do, I find his eyes firmly locked on my backside.

Again, things are tingly and I start to get concerned about the state of my panties by the end of the evening.

"No rush. Take your time," he says as his eyes meet mine. If he notices that I busted him watching my ass, he doesn't show it. Instead, he offers me a smile that makes my heart skip a beat and dance around in my chest.

When the flowers are sitting in a crystal vase that was my mom's, I slip out of the room to finish getting ready. It only takes me a couple of minutes to finish up my makeup, slip on a pair of nude wedge sandals, and spritz my neck with my favorite perfume. After I set the bottle down, a thought crosses my mind. Josh bought me this perfume because it was his favorite. He said it drove him wild.

As I look at my reflection in the mirror, I can't help but wonder if the same will hold true for Nick. Will he like the scent or will I need to switch it up? Maybe try something new. It's definitely not something that has to be decided now, but it makes me pause, even for just a moment.

God, I miss him.

The woman staring back at me is so much different than the one she used to be. Little lines are appearing around her eyes that weren't there before. She looks tired, and maybe even a little scared, but that's to be expected, right? She's pretty, but not a supermodel. She's confident, but nervous.

Actually, she's petrified.

But, she's also determined.

A woman who is ready to live her life, not merely to exist.

I nod my head and dig deep for that determination I know is there, and then turn to meet my date. Nick. If it were anyone else, I'm not so sure I'd feel as resolute, but there's something about him that helps return the confidence I once had. Maybe it's the fact that I consider him my friend, too. Friendship and lovers seemed to work well for Abby and Levi, correct? Not that I'm thinking about the lovers aspect with Nick, but...

You never know.

I'm not ruling it out just yet, but it's also not in the plan for tonight.

Or is it?

It's been a long time since I've dated, even casually. Maybe it's expected? My heart starts to pound and I start to feel a little sweaty in the pits. Nick wouldn't expect sex tonight, would he? Not that it would be a bad thing, but I'm just not sure I'm *there* yet.

As I round the corner and see him standing there by the door, I answer my own question. No. Nick wouldn't expect any more than I'm ready to give. He's a true gentleman like that.

"Hi," I say lamely as I approach my date.

"Hi." He offers me another great smile, with perfectly straight, white teeth. He truly has an amazing mouth. Completely kissable.

Warmth creeps up my neck and settles in my cheeks as thoughts of kissing Nick pepper my mind repeatedly. He reaches down and takes my hand. "Come on," he says huskily, giving me a wink as he leads me out the door. I'm pretty sure he knows I was just thinking about his mouth and all of the things I wouldn't mind doing to it.

Or him doing to me. With that mouth.

"So where are we going?" I ask after making sure the door was secured and pushing all thoughts of Nick's lips and the possibility of kisses out of my mind.

"We're headed to Cooper, but I'm not telling you where we're going when we get there," he says as he holds open the passenger door for me. Cooper is a small coastal town, thirty minutes south of Jupiter Bay. It boasts small, quaint shops and cute bed and breakfasts, and is just as popular of a summer tourist trap as our town.

Small talk is easy when Nick is sitting beside me, and even though we start off talking about work, it turns to more personal conversations. Before I know it, we're reaching the city limits of Cooper, those thirty minutes eaten up quickly. He drives us to the center of town and turns off at the grocery store. As soon as we make the turn, I know where we're going.

"Roller skating?" I ask, suddenly really excited.

"I hope that's okay," he says warily.

"Okay? I haven't been since I was like eleven. I used to love coming here with my sisters." Memories of family outings with my mom, dad, and sisters flash through my mind. Some of them are painful, but mostly they bring happy recollections of a time where the eight of us would take a Sunday drive and skate the day away. "I can't believe it's still open."

Nick parks in the first available spot, which is closer to the back. I'm pleasantly surprised by the amount of cars in the lot.

"Well, it closed down for a few years, but not long ago, a young couple bought it and brought it back to life. They're only open on Friday and Saturday nights and Sunday afternoons now, but it's still a popular hangout."

With way too much enthusiasm, I give my seat belt a little toss and climb out of the car. My eyes light up when I see the neon marquee that reads "The Rink." A sign in the window promises the best pizza in Virginia, and to be honest, I really hope we get to test that proclamation.

"Is this okay? I wasn't even thinking about you wearing a dress," Nick admits, glancing down at my knee-length dress.

"It's perfect. Actually, I was the best skater in the family, so me being in a dress shouldn't matter at all."

His laughter fills the evening and makes me smile. "Well, that's good. Maybe your expertise will rub off on me. I'm only a so-so skater, and haven't been in a few years."

"I'm sure you'll be fine. Come on," I say, grabbing his hand and practically pulling him toward the entrance.

Best. Date. Ever.

Chapter Sixteen

Nick

She's all smiles as we enter the skating rink. At the counter, I pay for our admittance and give the teenager our shoe sizes. Two pairs of skates are placed on the counter, and for the third – or maybe tenth time today – I question my decision for tonight's date. Nothing about roller skates says romantic night out, but when I look over at Meghan's bright, happy face, I decide any amount of embarrassment I'm about to endure tonight will very well be worth it.

"Can we order pizza too?" she asks when we find an open bench to change from our shoes into the skates.

"Definitely. What kinda date do you think this is?"

"Well, I didn't want to assume," she replies, again that wide smile on her lips, as she grabs her skates. "Crap. I don't have socks."

"Shit. Me either. Oh, wait. They have disposable socks at the counter," I say, mentally slapping myself upside the head for forgetting to think of that part. I run up to the counter and grab two pairs of the cheap unisex, thin socks for a dollar, and bring them back to our bench. "They aren't the best, but they should keep us from getting blisters."

We both don our sexy brown and blue roller skates and head toward the rink. "This was easier when I was younger," she says, laughing as we both gingerly try to walk.

"Right? I'm starting to think this was a horrible idea. My injury recoup time is much greater now than it was back in the day,"

I reply as we grab the ledge of the rink and step through the doorway.

"Here goes nothing," she says, pushing off and slowly moving out into where traffic is. "You coming?"

Is that a loaded question? I'm not, but I would like to be. But that's probably not the right answer to her question when we're thirty minutes into our first official date. "Yep." I push off the side and glide to where she's standing.

"We got this," she says, offering me another award-winning grin, as she reaches for my hand. My entire body fires to life as my bigger one wraps around hers. Together, we push off with one foot and join the crowd of skaters, though at a slightly slower pace.

It all starts to come back to me as we both begin to feel more comfortable on our skates. We both pick up speed, yet we never let go of our hands. We start to keep pace with the faster skaters, though neither of us attempts any of the fancy footwork or moves of the experienced ones.

"I used to be able to do that," she says, pointing to a girl who lifts one leg in the air and weaves through the crowd on one leg.

"Maybe after pizza?"

"Definitely. All of my best moves come out after dinner," she says, making my cock twitch in my shorts. Nope, he definitely wouldn't mind seeing her *moves*.

We skate to about a half-dozen songs, both of us red-cheeked from exertion and a bit on the sweaty side. "Ready for food?" I ask, not ready to admit aloud that my feet are screaming in the skates.

"Starving. I forgot how much of an appetite you work up," she says as we make our way to the doorway. From there, we head into the adjoining room where you order food and sit and rest.

"Anything special on your pizza?"

"Don't tell me you've forgotten," she teases. No, I haven't forgotten. Not one bit. I actually remember quite a bit of random details about Miss Meghan Summer, but I try not to flaunt it. There's a fine line between observant and stalker.

"Sausage and mushroom," I state when we reach the counter. She nods with a grin, which makes me feel a bit like Superman. I could conquer anything if she just keeps smiling like that. It's a hell of a lot better than the tears I've witnessed over the last few years.

"Can I help you?"

"Large sausage and mushroom pizza with two Sprites, please," I order, pulling my wallet from my shorts. After she hands me my change and our order number, Meghan and I take our drinks and head toward an open table.

"My feet are going to be sore tomorrow," she says, dropping into the chair across from me. "I forgot how strenuous this is."

"Me too. Maybe this wasn't my best idea," I reply, reaching over and grabbing her hands.

"No, it was a perfect idea. I haven't been in decades, and I'm happy that I got the chance to skate again. I'm having a great time."

"You are?" I ask, not able to stop my own smile.

"The best," she replies, squeezing my hands with her own. "Maybe even the best first date I've ever been on," she adds casually with a shrug, but then realization seems to set in.

"It's okay, if it's not the best," I assure her, caressing her knuckles with my thumbs. My finger grazes over the ring on her finger, a subtle reminder of the pain she still carries.

Her eyes still sparkle, but you can see as she gets lost in a memory. "No, it really is the best first date. I know what you're thinking, and I appreciate it, but the first time Josh took me out was just your average, typical date."

"Where did you go?" I find myself asking, really wanting to know the answer.

"We went to the movies and saw some rom-com film that I don't even remember the name of. Then, we went for ice cream at the parlor uptown. It was nice."

"Sounds nice."

"But it was also awkward," she confesses. "We were both pretty shy, so it took us a while to get comfortable in our relationship."

"You're not shy or awkward now," I add.

"No, Grandma and Grandpa pretty much cured me and my sisters of any bit of bashfulness we may have had."

I laugh as our number is called at the counter. Retrieving our dinner, I join Meghan at the table and dive in. We consume most of the large pizza and keep talking like we've known each other forever. It amazes me how comfortable I feel around Meghan. I dated Collette for a few years – hell, I even moved her into my house and bought a ring (that I thankfully didn't give her) – and never felt this light and easiness that I feel with this particular woman.

More than an hour after we finish our pizza, Starship's "Nothing's Gonna Stop Us Now" begins to play over the sound system. "I love this song! Come on, one last spin around the rink before we head home," she says, standing up and reaching for my hand. I take it instantly, and even though my feet aren't excited for the last skate, I follow her back into the main area.

We keep our fingers entwined as we glide around the rink, singing along with the music. Every time she glances my way, I'm rewarded with a blinding smile. When I build up the confidence, I swing her out and watch as she does a little spin move. I snatch up her hand again as I cruise by, pulling her along until we're skating side-by-side again.

We are laughing, carrying on, and enjoying the moment, when suddenly, someone stops in front of us. I visualize the crash moments before I feel it. In an attempt to save Meghan from going down with me, I try to spin her out, only to get the front wheels of our skates tangled up.

The result is painful. We go down hard, a tangled mess of arms and legs, not to mention the fact that the weight of the skates makes it difficult to determine where exactly your foot is going to end up. For me, it ends up at an awkward angle that includes a pull, followed by a bit of a burn.

I gaze down at the woman lying next to me on the hard floor, ready to pull every apology I can out of my ass. Before I can open my mouth, she bursts into fits of laughter. In fact, she's laughing so hard, I'm pretty sure there are tears in her eyes.

"Christ, are you okay?" I ask, trying to keep from panicking at the thought of hurting Meghan.

Lacey Black

"That wasn't supposed to happen," she giggles, her green eyes sparkling like brilliant emeralds beneath the spinning disco balls.

"Fuck no, it wasn't. Are you all right?" I ask, glancing down to make sure no bones are protruding from her body.

"I'm fine," she says, a bit breathless from our spill.

When I finish my perusal for injuries, I discover where my hand landed and so much more. My eyes are riveted to her thighs, where her pink dress is pulled up to her waist. Her smooth, creamy skin is on full display, and my very male brain zeros in on the sliver of pink lace between her legs. My mouth goes dry and my cock rigid. Suddenly, it's hotter than Hell inside this place and I can't breathe. Quickly, I pull the hem of her dress down enough to cover what was exposed by the spill. I go to pull on the neck of my shirt, but my hand won't move. It won't move because it's plastered on her outer thigh, my fingers grazing the globe of her ass.

Sweet mother of God, I'm touching Meghan's thigh.

And saw her panties.

I'll jack off to this exact image for the rest of my life.

"Nick?" My name on her lips is both a question and a plea. My eyes zero in on her lips. Those full, lush, completely kissable lips. Suddenly, tasting those lips is the *only* thing I can think about, the only thing I want.

With our eyes locked, my head dips down, her lips drawing closer and closer with each passing second. I can feel her breath fan across my face until I'm right there – my lips are a whisper away from hers. It would take very minimal movement and I would be kissing Meghan.

188

I don't want to question it, but I do hesitate. I need to give her time to realize what's happening. When her sexy little tongue slips out and licks her lips, I know what her answer is. Her eyes close a moment later, and I get ready to make my move. I didn't even realize how much I wanted this kiss until this exact moment, and now, I want it more than I want air. No, I *need* it.

"Spill on aisle four!" a skater hollers as he whizzes by, pulling us out of the moment.

Meghan's eyes fly open and crash into mine, the almost-kiss moment shattering like a glass vase on the ground, and realization settles in. We're sprawled out on the floor, in the middle of the rink, and I was about to kiss Meghan. Publicly. Our first kiss was almost witnessed by half the town of Cooper, and two dozen teenagers with smart phones.

Superb job, Nicholas. Smooth. Real smooth.

Chapter Seventeen

Meghan

He almost kissed me.

I almost kissed him.

But more importantly, I'm completely overwhelmed with disappointment that the moment was broken. I didn't realize how badly I wanted him to kiss me until that teenager skated by and smarted off.

Now, the moment is broken, and I'm not too sure about the state of my ankle. It twisted in a funny direction the moment we went down, and the weight of the roller skates isn't helping. But surprisingly, there's no pain. In fact, I feel completely the opposite of pain when my body is entwined with his, even if we're lying on the floor like a couple of rag dolls.

"I was trying to avoid this," he mumbles, moving just a bit and getting his bearings.

"Avoid kissing me?" I tease, knowing full well that he was meaning the fall.

"What? No," he insists, his eyes wide as he starts to stand up. "I meant I tried to spin you out so you didn't crash into that guy."

"I know," I reply with a smile. Nick extends his hand down to me, ready to help me stand. My hand feels warm and tingly as I place it inside his, and all I really can think about is finishing that kiss – or starting the kiss.

"On that note, maybe we should leave the skating to the kids," he says with a smile, watching as people whiz by us at a higher rate of speed.

"Probably. Though, I still stand by my comment that this was the best first date ever. I mean, skating, pizza…"

"Twisted ankles," he contributes with a laugh.

Without hesitating, I move forward and wrap my arms around his waist. Resting my head against his shoulder, I can hear the beating of his heart vibrate through his body and smell the clean scent of his cologne. He smells so yummy. "Thank you," I whisper, breathing him in.

Nick wraps his arms around my shoulders, our bodies pressed tightly together. In doing so, I can now feel something very hard and very large sandwiched between us. He's either carrying a hammer in his pants or he's a bit worked up. (Probably from when he was basically gripping my ass a few minutes ago.) The thought exhilarates me in a way I wasn't prepared for. It's that reminder that yes, I am a woman. One that is still desirable, if Nick's reaction is any indication. "I can't believe you're thanking me," he whispers. I can feel his breath on my head.

"Why wouldn't I?" I ask, gazing up at him. "This was a great night."

He smiles down at me, his hazel eyes turning a deeper shade of brown. "You're right. It was a great night."

Together, we skate off the floor to the bench where we have our shoes stashed. There's a young couple, probably in their late teens, making out on one end. We sit down, careful not to disrupt the young lovebirds, and go about removing the skates. Every time I glance over at Nick, he's looking at me, smiling as if he has a secret. I slip my wedge sandals onto my feet and dispose of the thin socks.

"Next time, we need to bring better socks," I state, noticing a slight pink ring above my ankle where the skate rubbed against bare skin.

"Next time?" he asks, standing up in front of me after tossing his own disposable socks in the trash.

"Definitely. There should definitely be a next time."

Nick wraps his arms around me in another hug. "Then there will definitely be a next time." He places a kiss on my forehead and pulls me toward the door. "Come on," he says, reaching down and taking my hand in his.

We walk out to his car, the gentle rustle of the breeze cooling my overly heated body. Yes, it was hot inside the rink, but that's not the sole reason for my flushed state. I'm pretty sure my hot boss and what I felt pressed against my stomach a few minutes ago has a lot to do with my current condition.

He holds the passenger door open for me as I slide inside his vehicle. We're both silent as he starts the car, but there's no mistaking the third party riding alongside us: sexual tension. It's been a long time since I felt this inundated, raw need rush my body, leaving me yearning for more.

It's Nick. He makes me feel this way.

The ride back to Jupiter Bay passes just as quickly as the one to Cooper just a few short hours before. We talk about everything from favorite songs to movie remakes that we wished wouldn't have been touched. It's easy. Carefree. Comfortable.

But the moment his car pulls into my driveway, a weird sensation sweeps through me. Realization that our night is over settles in, leaving me a bit sad. I unbuckle my seat belt, but before I can open my door, he's there, opening it for me. He rests his hand low on my back, and all I can think about is a sudden hope that he spins me around, pins me against the side of my house, and kisses me.

And I mean, *kisses* me. The kind that steals your breath and your sanity. That single amazing kiss that becomes branded in your brain. The one that you remember for the rest of your life.

Yes, I'll never forget my first kiss with Josh. It was sweet and perfect.

But what I feel bubbling up inside of me is something completely different now. It's the need to be taken, to be dominated. To let him take complete control over the kiss (and whatever may happen next). Am I ready for *next*? No. I already know that answer, but I'm getting there.

"Thank you for an amazing evening," I say, turning and facing him when we reach the door.

"I'm glad you enjoyed yourself," he says, his eyes looking so much darker than ever before.

Nick steps forward, one hand snaking around my waist and resting on my lower back. His other hand comes up to cup my cheek. My breathing halts completely as I wait to see what happens next.

Kiss me, I beg.

Our eyes remain locked for what feels like forever. We have an entire conversation without saying a word. I can see everything swirling around from his own desire to his hesitation. We're treading in muddy water right now, trapped somewhere between friends and coworkers. An undercurrent is pulling us straight toward the tide that could either bring us together or rip us apart.

It's where friendship and coworkers still remains, but so does something more.

Lovers.

"I want to kiss you so badly," he whispers, my blood swooshing in my ears and drowning out everything around me.

"I really, really want you to kiss me," I say, and I do. I really, really do.

He moves slowly, much like he did when we were sprawled out on the floor at the skating rink, and I know he's giving me the chance to change my mind. But what he doesn't realize is that I won't. I *need* this kiss as much as I need oxygen.

So he moves the rest of the way, until his lips touch mine. Neither one of us moves for a heartbeat as we savor the feel of the other. His lips are soft, just as I imagined, and little shockwaves of lust zip through my body.

Then, he starts to deepen the kiss and doesn't disappoint. His hands grasp the sides of my face as he takes complete control of the moment. His tongue slides along the seam of my mouth, begging for entrance. The moment I open my mouth, I'm almost overwhelmed with sensations. I can *feel* him, *taste* him, *smell* him. I've never wanted someone, wanted something *more* than I do right now.

My arms wrap around his shoulders as I press my body against his. His shoulders are ridiculous, and the feel of those hard muscles beneath my fingers only seems to add fuel to an already burning desire. It takes everything I have not to climb him like a tree, wrapping my legs around his body, and swallowing him whole.

This is a kiss.

Before I have a chance to test out my tree-climbing skills, his lips start to slow. His open mouth outlines my lips as if he's memorizing the way I feel. I want to invite him in, and I almost do, but something has me holding back just a little.

I'm almost there.

Nick places one last kiss on my swollen lips before pulling back. My eyes are still closed and I'm afraid to move. If I move, I may break the spell or wake up from this dream.

When I finally do open my eyes, he's smiling at me, a look that conveys his excitement (and I'm not just talking about what was happening in his shorts. There was definitely something going on down there). He rubs the apple of my cheek with his thumb and whispers, "Best kiss ever."

Definitely.

One hundred percent.

Best. Kiss. Ever.

I can't even speak. He's rendered me completely speechless. So I just smile up at him, letting him know that I agree wholeheartedly, and wouldn't mind another round of tonsil hockey.

But Nick doesn't catch my subliminal request for more kissing, which is slightly disappointing. Instead, he takes another step back, putting great distance between us. "Can I call you tomorrow?" he asks with a bit of hopefulness.

"Yes."

I'm rewarded with a boyish grin as he turns to head down the steps. I should probably unlock my door, but I don't want to move. I want to stay right here, watching him. When he reaches his car door, he turns back my way. "I'm not leaving until you're safely inside."

"Well, then you might want to get comfortable," I sass.

"Meghan," he grumbles, my name a curse on his tongue. "Get inside."

"Fine. Good night," I reply with a smile, turning and unlocking my front door. Before I step over the threshold, I glance back his way one more time. He hasn't moved, letting me know he's not going anywhere until I'm safely tucked away behind locked doors.

I give him a wave and step inside, slowly closing the door behind me. As soon as the lock is engaged, I run over to the window, moving the blinds just enough to see his car through the cracks. He's still standing there beside his car, smiling at the door I just closed. He looks happy, which in turn makes me feel elated.

I step away from the blinds and set my purse on the table. A pair of running shoes by the door catches my attention, but for the first time, instead of feeling that all-consuming sadness sweep over me, I smile. I grin at the shoes and at the memory of the kiss I just shared with Nick.

Am I healed?

Hell no.

But am I looking ahead, instead of over my shoulder?

Yes.

Nick did that. He's making me feel again. And yes, that's both exciting and completely terrifying, but I know that as long as he's by my side, helping me, I feel almost invincible. Like I can do anything again.

Like I can live.

Chapter Eighteen

Nick

"What the hell are you swinging at, Bronson? That wasn't even close to the strike zone, you fucking bum," Sawyer hollers through the glass wall before bringing his beer bottle up to his lips.

The view from our Sky Suite at the ballpark is something. So is the language from the groom-to-be as he watches his former teammates on the Rangers get their asses handed to them by the Nationals. Of course, it doesn't help that the current batter is the one he caught his ex-wife in bed with not too long after his career-ending shoulder injury.

"Tough game," Stuart whispers beside me as we watch the Rangers continue their downward spiral in the fifth inning.

"No shit," I mumble, taking a pull from my own beer.

This place is pretty sweet. I've attended a couple of pro baseball games over the years, but never in a suite. The chairs are luxurious and leather, and there's a wall of food and drinks. The guys spared no expense when it came to today's bachelor party, and until the Rangers started to fall behind in the third inning, it was proving to be a good day. Now? Now everyone is screaming obscenities at the glass and drinking a little faster.

"You guys get enough to eat?" Linkin asks as he comes over to where Stuart and I are seated.

"We have. Thanks for inviting us," I say to the big guy married to one of Meghan's sisters.

"I'm afraid if the Rangers don't pull their heads out of their asses, Sawyer is going to come unhinged," Linkin replies with a laugh.

"You think?" Stuart teases as we watch the former ball player rant in front of us.

"Come on, Joel! We need a hit," he commands with a hard handclap as he watches his friend approach the plate.

We all seem to hold our breath as Joel Cougar steps up to the plate and takes his stance. The first pitch is a little high, and the batter doesn't swing. Ball one. The next pitch clips the inside corner. Strike. "Come on, Cougar!" Sawyer bellows at his good friend.

The third pitch is low, but is apparently right where the batter likes it. He swings hard, the sound of the bat smacking the ball filling the suite through the speakers. It sails high over the center fielder's head and falls into the bleachers. Home run!

"Yes! That's what I'm talking about," Sawyer cheers with the rest of the guys, walking around and throwing out high fives like party favors. Even though the Rangers are still down by two, the home run by Joel seems to lighten the mood of everyone in the room, especially the groom.

"Hey, guys," Sawyer says, dropping into the chair beside me. "Having fun?"

"We are," I answer, glancing over and noticing Sawyer's eyes are already a little glassy and heavy-lidded. He's definitely well on his way to buzzed.

"Sorry about my language. I can get a little worked up," he says, taking another drink of his beer.

"You don't have to apologize to us," Stuart replies.

"But if you think I'm bad, you should see my future wife," Sawyer adds, a big smile breaking out on his face. "She once cussed an ump out for a bad call and almost got herself ejected from the game."

"Really?" I ask, laughing.

"Oh, hell yeah. My Alison has a mouth that would make a sailor blush," he says with a smile. The way he grins lets me know he's probably thinking about something very specific that she has said or done recently.

"I've only known her in the school setting, and there wasn't a lot of cursing going on," my brother-in-law says.

"No, she's pretty straight-laced when it comes to school. Except for that one time under the bleachers," Sawyer replies. The look he gives us lets us know exactly what went down under the bleachers. Or specifically, *who* went down. "Anyway, make sure you get plenty to eat and drink. The guys bought enough booze to get half the bleachers drunk by the seventh inning stretch."

"The only one we're focused on getting drunk is the groom," Levi adds when he joins our group.

"Don't get me so sloppy drunk that I can't perform tonight," Sawyer says with a laugh.

"Not my problem," Ryan tosses in when he comes over to where we're seated. "My job is to get you drunk. Not worry about the status of your dick later tonight."

"As long as I stay away from the hard shit, I'll be fine," Sawyer replies.

"So noted," Ryan says before turning around to Linkin. "Hey, Link! Our man Sawyer needs a shot of something strong!"

"No, he does not," Sawyer hollers.

A moment later, Linkin joins us all with a tray of shot glasses, each one containing amber liquid. "One shot won't give you whiskey dick," Linkin says as he passes around the shot glasses. "It'll be the fifth or sixth one that does it."

"You guys are assholes. I'm not sure I want to be related to you," Sawyer mumbles.

"Yes you do. We're fucking awesome. Besides, you should be thanking us. We could have let Orval plan the party the way he wanted," Levi says, causing us all to glance over to the food table where the family patriarch is talking to Brian and Sawyer's dad.

"Good call," Sawyer concedes.

"A toast," Dean says, pulling everyone's attention in the room. "To Sawyer and AJ. May their marriage be full of laughter and love."

"And plenty of *the sex!*" Orval exclaims from across the room.

"To *the sex!*" we all reply, raising our shot glasses high in the air before throwing back the liquid. It burns like fire as it slides down my throat, immediately warming my stomach.

As we watch the rest of the game, my thoughts drift to a certain brunette with alluring green eyes. We've spent the better part of a week and a half together, flirting and enjoying ourselves. The kiss from last Saturday night hasn't been repeated, but it's not from a lack of wanting. We've just always found ourselves either in a social setting or at work. And it's not like you can steal a kiss via late night FaceChat or text.

"What time are the girls going to Lucky's?" Stuart asks as we watch the Rangers take the field in the bottom of the ninth inning. They've managed to tie it up with a series of base hits, followed by another solo homerun from Joel Cougar in the eighth.

"Anytime," Dean answers after glancing down at his watch. "They were going to have dinner at the Mexican restaurant at six, but should be heading up to Lucky's after."

"Why? You missing your wife already?" I tease my brother-in-law.

"Knock it off or I'll tell you about this thing she does with her tongue," Stuart (the bastard) replies, making bile rise in my throat.

"Don't you dare, asshole," I reply with the shake of my head. "You've been hanging around her too long. You two are perfect for each other."

"I wanna know," Orval says beside me, an ornery look on his face. "My Emmie has learned a few tricks over the years. I might be able to share some secrets with you, boy."

The look on Stuart's face is one of horror. "No, I'm good. I was just teasing Nick, since I sleep with his sister."

Fucker.

"Suit yourself, but if you ever want to know all about *the sex*, you let me know. I've got stories for days..." Orval adds, gazing out at the baseball field. Though, I don't think he actually sees the field at all.

"I'm about ready," Ryan says, coming over and standing beside me.

"Let me guess, you miss your wife too?"

"Hell yes, I do. She's also due soon, and I hate being this far away from her," he says, glancing down at his watch.

"The game's about over," Linkin chimes in, patting his brother-in-law on the shoulder. "Then I'm gonna drive like the wind to get home to my firecracker."

"I'm ready to head out," Levi says, walking over and tossing his empty beer bottle in the trash. "You think the groom is ready?"

We all glance over at Sawyer, who's now visiting with a few of the big wigs from the Rangers front office. They are in town for the game, and once they heard Sawyer was in a suite for his bachelor party, they all headed over to say hello. "Yeah, but we can't leave until Joel and a few of the others come up after the game," Dean adds.

They mentioned in the limo ride to D.C. that since Joel and another teammate were in the wedding, they got permission to stop by the suite after the game. They can't make the trip back to Jupiter Bay with us, since they have another game tomorrow, but they wanted to see Sawyer and at least help him celebrate for a bit.

The game ends and soon the suite fills up with players, coaches, and suits. It seems like most of the team has filed in, all eager to congratulate their former teammate on his upcoming wedding. Of course, many of them take the opportunity to help clean off the food on the tables too.

An hour later, the party finally starts to wind down and everyone who's not riding home in the limo takes their cue to head out. The guys all give last fist bumps and shoulder slaps to Sawyer, who was constantly handed either a fresh beer or a shot of something throughout the entire evening. He's well intoxicated at this point.

The guys all start to make sure everything is in order with the suite before we leave.

"Hey, I almost forgot! I brought brownies," Orval says to me, holding a tray and wearing a too-wide smile.

"No!" Linkin, Levi, Dean, and Ryan all bellow at the same time. Linkin runs at us, swinging his arm and knocking the tray of chocolate brownies onto the floor.

Everyone is silent for a full minute, no one really knowing what to say.

Orval glances down at the mess at his feet before finally speaking. "I bought those."

It takes a second, but the guys bust up laughing, and since I've heard the infamous Viagra brownies story from Meghan, I join in the laughter. We laugh the entire way down the elevator and out to the awaiting limo. Everyone falls into a seat in the car, huge smiles on our faces.

"I miss my Alison Jane. Take me drunk I'm home," Sawyer slurs, which only makes us all crack up laughing once more.

Chapter Nineteen

Meghan

"I think we should do another toast!" Grandma exclaims as she joins our group at the pool table.

"I'm not sure I can do another shot, Grandma. I'm starting to feel all warm and fuzzy, and that's the perfect level of drunkenness for post bachelorette party sex with my sexy, and might I add well-hung, fiancé," AJ proclaims way too loudly, drawing the attention of everyone around us at Lucky's. Since it's early June, tourist season is officially underway, which means the bar is exceptionally crowded tonight.

"One more shot isn't going to hurt, AJ," Grandma says before turning and heading toward the bar.

"Seriously, make her stop with the shots. If I keep this up, I'll pass out before Sawyer and I can get it on," AJ grumbles.

"You could always just puke on his shoes. You know, for ol' time's sake," I tease my sister, who infamously threw up, hitting Sawyer's shoes, the night they met before they could make it up to his hotel room.

"You just had to go there," AJ mumbles, pointing a finger at me.

I smirk in reply and take a sip of my mixed drink. We've been here for almost two hours and are expecting the guys to arrive anytime. Payton said the game ended a while ago and that they were heading our way. I'm actually really excited to see Nick, considering I haven't seen him since we left work (and not together) yesterday.

Nick's sister Natalie comes over and stands beside me. We've actually spent a lot of time together this evening. She sat beside me at dinner, and promptly filled me in on all of Nick's embarrassing childhood stories. I actually really like Natalie, and have enjoyed chatting with her.

My head is starting to feel a bit fuzzy as the guys finally return from their baseball game. I watch as each one hightails it over to where their wife or significant other is. Sawyer practically mauls AJ, and if the look in their eyes is any indication, they'll be doing it in the bathroom before the night is over.

Nick offers a smile as soon as he sees me. He heads my way, making my heart start to pound in my chest. He looks edible in his shorts and polo, the shirt accentuating the muscles in his shoulders.

Those shoulders are my undoing.

"Hey," he says when he approaches.

"Hi," I reply, my own smile plastered across my face.

"Having fun?"

"Yes. I've been chatting it up with your sister," I tell him.

"Shit, do I want to know what kinda lies she's telling you?" he asks, his voice playful.

"She didn't tell me anything!" I proclaim, innocently.

"I doubt it," Nick grumbles.

We stand there for a few minutes, watching everyone else. "Twelve years old and you still had a teddy bear? Really, Nick?" I ask, the bubble of laughter barely concealed.

"I knew it! That witch is getting it," Nick declares, his eyes dancing. "In my defense, it was the one my Grandma had made me and she had just died."

"Oh," I reply, my shoulders sagging as I take in the impact of his words. "Well, now I feel like the witch for teasing you."

"Don't you dare feel bad, Meghan! Our grandma died when he was six!" Natalie bellows, making Nick's ears burn red.

"I hate you," he tells his sister.

"You do not."

"I do. Wait until I tell your husband about the Zack Morris poster you had on your walls that I caught you practicing kissing on!" Nick sasses to his sister. Now it's her face that turns red.

"Shut up, asshole!" she hollers, Stuart looking shocked beside her.

"Zack Morris was your first kiss?" her husband asks.

"I do hate you," she says to her laughing brother, her eyes narrowing into laser beams.

"You love me," Nick replies.

"I'm going to think up every embarrassing thing I can and tell Meghan."

Nick just shrugs his shoulders. "I'm going to grab a drink. You ready?" he asks me.

"Yep. Malibu and pineapple juice," I tell him.

He turns to head up to the bar with Natalie and Stuart following behind. Most of the guys are standing up there, so I know it'll be a bit before he returns with my drink.

"I have news. I found out one of the authors I edited for received a movie deal. She was asked to write the manuscript and asked me to look it over for any major edits. I get to go to New York right after the wedding and meet with her!" Abby exclaims, sharing her big news with our little group.

"Really? That's amazing news! I'm so freaking excited for you," I reply to my sister, giving her a big hug.

"Wait, you told them? I thought you weren't going to tell them tonight," Levi says, coming up behind Abby, wrapping his arms around her, and placing a kiss on her cheek.

The look of alarm that crosses Abby's face tells me something is up. Something big. Something that has nothing to do with her upcoming trip to New York. "What are you talking about?" I ask Levi, whose face goes from wide smile elation to panic.

"What are you talking about?" he asks, Abby looking like she wants to melt into the floor.

"She was telling us about New York, but something tells me that's not what you're talking about. Spill," Payton directs, her big sister voice stern and bossy.

"Not tonight, okay?" Abby asks quietly.

"What's wrong with tonight? We're celebrating my upcoming wedding to Sexy Sawyer Randall. I'm going to be Mrs. Sexy Ass Randall in a matter of weeks, Abs. Doesn't that call for celebration?" AJ says, her eyes squinting a bit as she stares down Abby.

"Of course, it does. That's all we need to focus on tonight," Abby counters, practically begging for a subject change.

Payton is still staring at her. All I can do is sit back and watch, because with our oldest sister on the case, she won't let it rest until she has sniffed out the answer. "Spill."

"No."

"No?" Payton argues. "You can't keep secrets from us."

"Really? You're going to call me out for keeping secrets when you're the biggest secret keeper of us all?" Abby throws back in Payton's face. The moment she does, two things happen. Abby instantly feels guilty, if the look on her face is any indication. And Payton looks like she stepped on a Lego. She goes from shock to anger to pain in a matter of seconds.

"Okay, what the hell is going on here?" I ask, turning to Payton for answers.

"See? It's not so easy, is it?" Abby says to Payton, a smug look on her face.

"Someone just tell us what is going on. If you don't I'm going to stand here all night, glaring at both of you, until you speak. And then I'm going to bitch because my feet are already killing me and my back hurts. I'll end up having this baby in a bar, which is not anywhere close to my top ten destination places to have a baby, okay?" Jaime chimes in, rubbing her back.

"You're having the baby?" I gasp.

"No, but I might if these two don't stop keeping their secrets from us," she counters.

"Fine!" Abby hollers, drawing all of our attention toward her. Levi grabs her hand and brings it to his lips in a show of love and support. We all collectively hold our breath and wait for her to speak.

"Oh, for Pete's shakes, Abbers, just tell them that you're engaged!" Grandma says from out of nowhere. Abby's eyes are bigger than hubcaps as we all take a second to register the news.

"You're engaged?" I ask, my face breaking out into a huge grin.

"Yeah," she mumbles.

"Oh my God!" Jaime exclaims, grabbing our baby sister and pulling her into a hug.

"Congratulations!" AJ screams, jumping up and down and drawing Sawyer's attention.

"What's going on?" he asks, coming over to our group.

"Levi and Abby are getting married," she tells her fiancé.

"You're not mad?" Abby asks as soon as Jaime lets go of her.

"Why on earth would I be mad? This calls for more celebrating!" AJ adds, turning to Sawyer. "We need more shots! Shots for everyone!"

"You've had enough shots, my love," he says, kissing her on the side of the head and whispering something in her ear that makes her giggle and blush.

"Yep, I've definitely had enough shots," she replies.

"I can't believe you didn't tell me," Abby's twin says when she offers her a hug. "And where's your ring?" She grabs Abby's hand, the ring noticeably missing.

"I didn't want to ruin tonight so I left it at home."

"You could never ruin tonight, Abs. If anything, you've only enhanced it," AJ reassures her.

Nick comes over and stands behind me. "What's going on?" he asks.

"Well, it appears that Abby and Levi are engaged, but she didn't want to tell anyone." I answer.

"Why?"

"Because she didn't want to ruin AJ's night or make it about her," I say, casually shrugging my shoulder. It actually doesn't surprise me at all. Abby always takes everyone else's feelings into account, and this is definitely something she would do. It's AJ's night, after all, so she wouldn't want to steal any of the attention.

"Ahh," Nick says, his hand coming up and resting on my hip. The action makes my body start to tingle and warmth flood to the apex of my legs. He looks so damn sexy tonight. When I saw him walk in, it took every ounce of control I could find to act all casual and not go jump on him.

I really want to jump on him.

"Wait, but Abby said Payton was the biggest secret keeper of them all," Lexi chimes in, leaving the insinuation out there.

"She's right. Someone else has a secret," AJ adds. Everyone turns their attention to Payton. Dean comes over looking a little bit like a perp in an interrogation room, under the harsh lights.

"This is AJ's night," Payton counters.

"Nope, you're not getting out of this one," AJ replies.

"And unless you're jumping on a plane and getting remarried without telling any of us, we know it's not that," Lexi says, referring to the time they hopped on a plane, flew to Vegas, got hitched on the strip, and flew home without any one of us being the wiser.

Payton just stares us down, determined to not say anything. We're at a standoff, a battle of wills, and between Payton and Lexi, I'm not sure either of them will ever give in. "Oh, come on," Jaime argues, but it gets no response from the oldest Summer sister.

"Just tell them the bun is finally baking in the oven, Payters," Grandma says, waving her drink around and sloshing it over the side.

Everyone stands completely still. No one moves. No one breathes.

"You're pregnant?" I whisper, afraid that she'll deny the claims. We all know how much Payton wants a baby, but with her PCOS, the likelihood of that happening is very slim. They've been going through rounds of Clomid, but the results weren't successful. I know they've been talking about trying in vitro and have even checked out an adoption agency, but I didn't think they had decided on anything.

Payton looks over at Dean, whose eyes seem to light up. When she looks back at us, her own green eyes are filled with tears. "I'm pregnant."

Chaos ensues next. I'm pulled into a hug by someone of my size, squeezed to death by someone with a big belly, as we all scream and cry together. My heart is so full for the happiness and love each of my sisters have in their lives. We have three babies on the way, two that should arrive within the next month, and two weddings on the horizon.

"Wait," Jaime says, wiping tears from her cheeks as she looks at Payton. "You took a shot."

"It was water," Grandma says, somehow managing to wiggle herself into the middle of our group hug. Payton gives her a look. "I overheard her order it," Grandma adds with a shrug.

"Overheard," Payton snips with an eye roll.

"It was a total accident," Grandma insists. "And besides, Abby heard too!"

Abby blushes. "It was an accident for me. I was coming up behind you to order another drink. I saw Grandma crouching behind a guy who was standing next to you, and before I could ask her what she was doing, you placed the shot order."

"I was not...crouching, I was...inspecting. Did you know Devin Montgomery has developed into a fine specimen of man-being?" Grandma says, her eyes lighting up with delight. "I thought about setting him up with Meggy Pie, but seeing that she can't keep her eyes off the dentist all night, I decided to just let their sexual attraction play out. I wish I had popcorn. This one is proving to be way more exciting," she says, and *all* eyes fall on me. And Nick, who clears his throat behind me.

"Anyway, so congratulations to you all," I say quickly, trying to (unsuccessfully) draw the attention away from me.

"Can I just say that I'm very proud and happy to be your dad?" My dad stands off to the side, a wide smile on his face. "Weddings and grandbabies, my heart is overflowing." His eyes fill with unshed tears. "I wish your mother could be here to join in the celebration. She truly would have been on cloud nine tonight. And even though the Summer name is slowly dying one by one, I've never been more honored to be a Summer as I am now."

My eyes fill with tears, not only at his touching words, but also at the fact that our last name is slowly disappearing. After Abby and Levi get married, I'll be the final Summer. For years I thought I'd be a Harrison by now, but sometimes fate doesn't work out the way you plan. Fate is a cruel bitch, isn't she? She sneaks in when you least expect it and robs you blind, stripping away your hopes and dreams and forcing you to rebuild from the ground up.

Nick grips my hip, giving it a gentle squeeze of support. It's as if he always knows when I need a friend the most, and he never disappoints at offering me a shoulder to cry on or a hand to hold. He stands close enough now that I can feel his body heat against my back. Maybe it's the bit of alcohol I've consumed, or maybe the fact that I feel connected to him in a way I haven't felt in so very long, but I wouldn't mind if I felt that heat...everywhere.

Preferably without clothes.

While his hard body is pressing me into the mattress.

Is it hot in here?

"I don't want to take any of the credit here, but I'm pretty sure it was the book that ensured proper egg fertilization," Grandma says loudly, pulling me away from my despondent thoughts.

"Are you really going to try to take credit for our baby?" Payton asks, her mouth gaping open.

"Well, I'm not saying I was there, watching in the corner and whispering words of encouragement, but I did buy the book, you know. And I know you tried chapter seven."

"We did n-" Payton starts.

"Chapter seven wasn't nearly as good as chapter ten," Dean interrupts with a shrug and a wink aimed directly at the elderly woman in the group.

"Oh, don't I know it," she replies with her own wink and smile. "Let's celebrate! Oh, I wish I had something sweet," Grandma adds, glancing around as if on the hunt for something to satisfy her sweet tooth.

"I *had* brownies," Grandpa says, turning and glaring at Linkin.

"What's that look for?" I whisper to Nick, who snickers behind me.

"I'll tell you later."

* * *

When the party winds down and everyone is heading out, I gravitate toward the man over with my dad. I've found them together, quietly talking a few times since their arrival at Lucky's, which makes me both nervous and happy. What could they possibly be talking about?

Reaching the duo, I offer a smile as all talking halts. "What are you two talking about?"

"The weather," Dad replies with a grin. "I'm going to take Sawyer and AJ home. Are you guys okay?"

"We're good," Nick answers. "I stopped drinking a while ago. I'll make sure Meghan gets home safely." The way he says it warms my blood and causes dirty images to parade through my mind.

"Good," Dad replies, slapping Nick on the back. "Good to see you again, Nick." Then he steps forward and kisses me on the cheek. "Love you, Meg."

"Love you, Dad."

Lacey Black

When he collects the future Mr. and Mrs. and escorts them to the front door, Nick steps closer, his hand touching the small of my back. His fingers dip low, grazing over my ass and lighting a fire deep in my belly. Yearning starts to spread through my body, and I know I'm ready to see what happens tonight.

I already know what I *hope* happens tonight.

"Ready?"

"Ready," I answer as he leads me out the front door. "Do you have your car?"

"No, I had planned to drive you home in yours."

"Then how will you get home?" I ask when we reach my car. I turn to face him, leaning back against the passenger door.

"I may have to take your car," he answers.

"Or…" I whisper, resting my hands against his chest and slowly sliding down until they're resting on his abdomen. The slight buzz I had earlier is completely gone, replaced with a different kind of buzz.

"Or…" he trails off. His Adam's apple bobs as he swallows, and I can tell he wants to say something, but maybe doesn't quite know if he should.

I should help him.

"Or, I could go back to your place with you, and you can take me home tomorrow," I suggest, my fingers flexing against his six-pack.

Wrapping his arm around my waist and pulling me into his body, his eyes seem to darken. "That sounds like an amazing idea."

"A great one."

216

"The fucking best."

I hold my breath, hoping that he'll kiss me, but he doesn't. Instead, he opens the passenger door and helps me inside, before practically running around the front of the car to the driver's side. When he slides into the seat, Nick hits his knees on the bottom of the steering column. He's not that much taller than me, but I like to make sure I have complete control in my car with my seat close to the wheel.

The drive to Nick's house is charged – sexually. He's holding my hand and making slow circles on my palm with his pointer finger. The touch makes my heart beat faster and my underwear useless. I never knew one little graze like that could pack such a punch to the libido.

When we pull into his driveway a few minutes later, he opens the garage door. As soon as the car is shut off and the door closing, Nick jumps out and meets me at the passenger door. Stepping out onto the concrete, I'm immediately pulled into his arms.

"I've been thinking about kissing you for a week."

"I've been wanting you to kiss me for a week," I confess, a bit breathlessly, as his mouth moves to claim mine.

The kiss isn't gentle, nor slow. It's consuming and powerful. He takes the lead, threading his hands through my hair and gripping my head. My head tilts, allowing him the perfect angle to plunder my mouth with his tongue. My own hands reach around and grip the back of his shirt, holding on tight and refusing to let go. I can feel his very hard cock pressed against my stomach, practically begging to be taken out of his shorts.

And my word, do I want to.

After a few minutes, he rips his lips from mine. "I'm sorry. I'm not sure what came over me," he pants against my lips.

"I kinda like what came over you, actually. I was thinking," I start, gazing up into his lust-hazed eyes.

"What?"

"Maybe we can continue this inside." Deep breath. "With less clothes."

His eyes turn to lava, and his breathing hitches. "Are you sure?"

"I'm pretty sure I've never been so certain about anything in my life," I reply honestly.

Nick watches me for a few moments, as if reading me like a book, before he brings his hands down to cup my ass, picking me up and bringing me into his body. My legs wrap around him as he slowly makes his way into the house, his lips kissing a blazing path down my neck as we go. I hear the door shut behind us, but pay no attention to anything other than the feel of him against me, his lips on my skin.

When we reach his bedroom, we fall together onto the mattress, my arms wrapping tightly around him as his lips meet mine. His hand moves down to my shirt, slowly pushing it upward and grazing his fingers across my abdomen. His touch is like fire dancing across my skin and seeping into my pores. It's too much, and not enough, all at the same time.

His hands slide up and wrap around my heavy breasts. My nipples are hard as he gently glides a finger over each one, making me cry out. It feels so good.

"Does it?" he whispers, kissing along my jaw. At first, I don't realize what he's talking about, but then it hits me. I must have said it aloud.

"Yes. So fucking good," I gasp as he does it again. This time, he pinches each nipple through the material of my bra, and I almost come off the bed. It's been so long since I've felt this raw, this alive.

"Can I remove your shirt?" he asks, his eyes connecting with mine.

"I'd be a little sad if you didn't," I reply with a hint of a smile.

I help him shed my shirt, but I don't stop there. I go ahead and unsnap my shorts, letting him know that they should go as well. His eyes are glued to my waist as I shimmy the denim down my legs and toss them aside. In one swift (and probably well practiced) move, his shirt is over his head and discarded.

I almost swallow my tongue.

This man is a work of art. He's hard and toned and makes me want to trace each and every ridge of his incredible body with my tongue. Yes, definitely my tongue. And maybe my lips. Absolutely my fingers.

I watch as he unfastens his shorts, the fly hanging open and the material riding low on his hips. There's no mistaking the material of his boxer briefs stretched tautly over the head of his cock. I can actually see it through the opening of his pants, and the prospect makes my mouth water even more.

Lying back on his bed in just my bra and panties, he pushes his shorts down his tree-trunk legs, letting them fall to the floor. My eyes are riveted on his incredible physique, taking in the perfection and committing it to memory.

Nick climbs over me, covering my body with his own and pressing me into the bed. The weight of his body only seems to add fuel to an already raging inferno inside me. My legs wrap around his waist, his hard cock pressed firmly into the place I need him the most. I can feel the wetness through my panties as he gently slides up and down, teasing my clit and making me see stars.

His lips find mine once more as he continues to tease and torture me. My hands grasp his back, reveling in the strong definition of his muscles. With each squeeze of my hands, he seems to come that much more undone. His hips go from a gentle glide to a thrust. "You're driving me crazy," he whispers, panting against my lips.

"I want you so badly," I confess, sliding my hands down and grabbing his ass.

His eyes meet mine. "Are you sure?"

"Yes."

Nick sits up on his haunches and unsnaps my bra. My breasts tingle and burn with desire as he gapes openly. His hands move down my body until they reach the wet panties covering me. With his fingers hooked under the lace, he slowly (and I'm talking painfully slow) glides them down my thighs. He hops up and slips them the rest of the way down my legs before throwing them somewhere in the room. Then his hands reach for the waistband of his boxer briefs and he pushes them down his body.

I'm pretty sure I actually gasp when I finally catch sight of the magnificent cock that has been torturing me for the last several minutes. It's large, straight, and hard as steel. I'm overcome with the desire to wrap my hands around it, glide my tongue along it, and feel it thrust inside me.

He reaches into the nightstand and grabs a condom. I watch as he rips the small foil package and covers his impressive erection. Warmth floods my pussy so much that I can feel it. I should be embarrassed by how wet I am – how turned on I am – but I'm not. Instead, I focus on the man who has made me into this sex-crazed feline, hell-bent on riding his cock like a prized rodeo cowboy.

When he joins me back on the bed, he doesn't lie on top of me like I expect. Nick sits between my legs and gazes hungrily at the apex of my legs. With gentle fingers, he pushes two fingers through my folds, gliding them over my pulsing clit. I quickly realize that I'm three seconds away from exploding like a bomb, which would be the definition of embarrassing.

With a single finger, he slowly slides it into my pussy. I feel my body contracting around him, and I fight off the orgasm. I don't want this to end so soon. But when he adds the second finger and swipes his thumb over my clit, I'm unable to hold back. My body detonates as the most intense orgasm sweeps through me. I'm floating on the clouds, blinded by white light, as euphoria washes over me.

As soon as my body starts to loosen, I feel him remove his fingers and move over me into position. "I'm sorry," I whisper, closing my eyes.

"Why are you sorry?" he asks, going completely still above me.

"I've already gotten off. I wanted to wait until we could do that…together." My cheeks burn with mortification.

"You think you're done, sweetheart? We're just getting started," he whispers sweetly, coming down to place a kiss on my lips. "I'm nowhere near done with you."

And then he lines up his cock at my entrance, his eyes locked on mine, and slowly pushes inside me. It stretches as he enters my body, almost to the point of pain. With just one thrust, he fills me so completely that I'm not sure where he ends and I begin.

"Are you okay?" he asks, his eyes searching my face for an answer.

"So okay," I gasp as he flexes his hips before stilling completely.

Nick reaches for my cheek, brushing a lone tear off my skin that I didn't even realize had escaped. I'm crying? Why am I crying? There's no crying in…sex!

But this isn't just sex. I know it. He knows it. This is something greater. This is the coming together of two friends as lovers. This is me ripping off the scab, revealing the deep wound beneath. This is him cradling that wound in his hands and vowing to help it heal.

This is the moment I let go of the past and take a step toward the unknown future.

"Please, keep going," I beg, my body gripping his erection like a vice.

"Jesus, don't do that or this'll be over in about two seconds," he grunts, closing his eyes and digging deep for his control. But frankly, I kinda like the idea of seeing out-of-control Nick. I bet he's just as sexy as in-control Nick.

Let's test that theory.

I place my hand over his pounding heart and slowly slide it up to his shoulders. His shoulders are freaking killer. He's starting to sweat a bit, probably because he's trying to keep hold of any piece of power he can over his body. That's not going to work for me. When I wrap my hand around the back of his neck, I rock my hips and give my internal muscles a squeeze.

"Fuck," he groans, a shiver sweeping through his entire body.

"That's the plan," I whisper brazenly.

His eyes clash with mine once more, and I know that thread has snapped. The control is gone. The beast is unleashed.

Nick pulls back and thrusts hard. Not hard enough to hurt, but with enough force to scoot me toward the headboard. Reaching up with my other hand, I grab on and hold on tight. His moves are stealthy, determined, and direct, and with each one, I feel myself climbing higher and higher toward the sky. I've never orgasmed back-to-back before, but at this rate, I'll be ready to explode in no time.

He moves his hand to cup my breast, working and tweaking my nipple. The sensation is almost overwhelming when you add in the friction of his pelvic thrusts, and the fact that with each one he hits that magical place deep inside of me that makes me want to come out of my skin. I can't believe how alive I feel.

I can feel my body start to tighten around him, and he must know the end is drawing near. His lips claim mine, hungrily and possessively, as he tilts my hips upward, making his cock feel even bigger and deeper. I can't breathe. I close my eyes and just feel.

And it feels amazing.

I grip his back and nip at his bottom lip as another orgasm sweeps through me. This one is much more intense than the first as release washes over me, one name slipping from my lips as the moment consumes me.

Nick.

He reaches his own release, swallowing my moans of pleasure with his mouth and burying himself to the root inside me. We're both left gasping for air and boneless as he falls on top of me, pressing me firmly into the mattress. I run my hands over his sweaty back, loving the weight of his body.

The magnitude of the moment hits me all at once, and before I know it, I can feel the unmistakable burn of hot tears on my cheek.

Don't cry. Don't cry. Don't cry.

But there's no stopping them.

They're unleashed.

Chapter Twenty

Nick

I hear her sob. My eyes fly open and my heart breaks when I see those fucking tears lining those luminous green eyes. Panic starts to set in that I fucked this up. She wasn't ready, and I practically mauled her the moment we got to my house. I thought I had given her enough time to consider everything of what was about to happen, but maybe I didn't. Maybe I pushed her or rushed her or...

Fuck.

I try to push myself up, since I'm lying on top of her, smashing her into the mattress, but the moment I try to move, she wraps her arms and legs tighter around me and squeezes. I'm still buried inside of her, and I'll be damned if my cock doesn't decide it's ready for another round. Hot tears press against my neck, and I almost choke on my own emotions.

"Meg?" I whisper, touching the top of her head gently and stroking her hair. "I'm sorry, honey. I...I was too rough. It was too soon. I didn't mean to hurt you," I say in rapid-fire succession. God, I'm the worst human being on the planet. The thought of hurting her makes me want to rip out my own heart and toss it into the trash.

She gazes up at me, those fucking tear-filled eyes seeing straight into my soul, and says, adamantly shaking her head, "No, Nick. You did nothing wrong, I swear. I'm just emotional." She sniffles. "I'm so sorry for crying like this, but what we just did, that was...amazing."

My heart starts to pound, but for an entirely different reason. Not out of fear, but out of elation. "It was, wasn't it?" I ask, which results in that fucking smile that I love so much.

She runs her hand over my forehead and down the side of my face. "I wasn't crying because of...you know. In fact, I didn't even...that didn't cross my mind."

Taking a deep breath, I decide to address the elephant in the room. No, not the best for pillow talk, especially while I'm still inside her, but I need her to know where I stand. "Honey, you can say his name. I would never hold it against you or be upset because you're acknowledging the man you loved and lost."

Meghan takes a deep breath and gives me a small smile, laced with sadness. "Thank you. That means more than you'll ever know. But I also need you to know that what just happened, between you and me, that was just us. No one else was part of it."

I roll to my side, slipping my already raring-to-go cock from her body, and pulling her so she's lying against my chest. "Thank you for trusting me."

She looks up, her eyes full of honesty and hope. "There's no one else I trust more than you."

We lie together for several minutes with her leg thrown over mine and her arm resting on my chest, just breathing in the magnitude of the moment. She's no longer just my friend. She's the woman I'm insanely attracted to, the one who makes me laugh and feel more content than I ever have. I don't know where this is headed exactly, but I know where I would like it to go.

And it involves a hell of a lot more of Meghan Summer naked.

"I should get up for a second," she says, wiggling out of my arms.

"I'll go get you something to clean up with," I offer, kissing her on the forehead and pulling my arm out from under her.

"No, that's okay. I, umm, have to use the restroom. I have a funky bladder and if I don't use the restroom after sex, I could get an infection." Her cheeks turn an adorable shade of red and she shrugs her shoulders. "It's not very sexy, I know, but that's real life. Abby always reads these sexy stories about women who just roll over, spoon with their significant other, and go to sleep after sex. That rarely happens, actually. Most women have to use the restroom or risk getting a bladder infection."

I can't help but smile at her blabbering. It's cute as hell. It's also a bit of information I didn't know. I mean, I knew Collette would get up and use the bathroom, but I never knew the logistics or reasoning behind it. Makes sense, honestly, and I'm slightly ashamed that it never occurred to me to find out more.

"Well, don't let me keep you," I tell her, watching while she gets up off the bed.

"I'll be right back, and then, we can talk about what to do about that hard-on." She drops the sheet, exposing the perfect globes of her amazing ass and heads to the bathroom. Before she steps over the threshold, she glances back over her shoulder, offering me a killer smile and a wink.

I'm pretty sure I just lost a piece of my heart to Meghan Summer.

* * *

I wake with a warm, naked body pressed tightly against my side and a smooth hand wrapped around my very hard cock. I hold completely still, pretending to sleep, as Meghan slides her palm up and down my shaft. She's going slowly, but it's enough to already drive me wild. Even after having her twice last night, my need for her is never ending.

Which may work out pretty fucking well, since she seems pretty insatiable.

Last night was amazing. Even with the tears. After we cleaned up a bit from the first round of sex, we both fell fast asleep, her tucked against my side and wrapped in my arms. Around two in the morning, she turned to her side, taking me with her. The position lined my already hardening cock up with her delectable little ass.

The next thing I knew, I was reaching for a condom and sliding into her warm pussy from behind. Fucking heaven.

Now, here we are, waking up with the sun and gearing up for another round of incredible sex.

"I know you're awake," she purrs beside my ear.

"Part of me is."

"I'm rather enjoying this part of you. Not that any of your other parts haven't been amazing, but this particular one is spectacular," she coos, sliding her hand down to the base of my cock and gently twisting. "Like that?" she whispers, slowly moving her hand up to the head of my dick. Unable to say words, I moan my reply. "I do believe it's time for me to get up close and very personal with this rather impressive cock."

I swear to God I almost come right there.

But thank fuck I don't, because what happens next is nothing short of remarkable.

Holding my cock in her hand, Meghan positions herself between my legs. Her eyes are locked on mine as she slowly lowers her head, swirling her tongue over the head of my dick.

I see stars.

Without any encouragement, she lowers her mouth over my erection, licking around the head and stroking her tongue down the pulsing vein running down my cock. "Jesus," I grumble, trying to hold completely still.

Her mouth is warm and wet, and she applies just enough suction to ensure my blood pressure reaches stroke level. Meghan slowly glides farther down my dick, swallowing it practically to the base. I've never enjoyed a blowjob so much or been ready to explode in such a short amount of time as I am right now.

She continues to move up and down, circling the head with her tongue and burying my cock down her throat. When she cups my balls in her palm, I almost lose it. "Fuck," I groan, drawing out that one word.

"You like?" she asks when she comes back up, licking the tip and sucking off the pre-cum.

"I'm not sure I'm going to survive this," I pant, grabbing a handful of her long brown hair and holding it out of her face.

"Now, that would be a shame. I'm not nearly done with you yet," she teases right before she goes all the way down on me. I let her play for a few more minutes, but with each pump of her hand and lick with that amazing mouth, my control is slipping.

Quickly.

Finally, I can't take it anymore. While this would surely end in spectacular fashion, that's not how I want to come. I need to be inside her, lose myself once more in her tight pussy, with her coming right along with me.

"Come here," I say, reaching down and grabbing her armpits. I gently pull her up, her mouth popping off my cock loudly.

"I wasn't finished," she pouts, straddling my hips and rubbing her pussy against my erection.

"I'm not finished either," I tell her, cupping her breasts in my hands and toying with her hard nipples. Moving my hand to her neck, I pull her forward, planting my lips against hers.

She tries to pull back. "I haven't brushed my teeth."

"I don't care," I say as my lips meet hers, hungrily.

My cock twitches against the wetness between her legs, and I'm completely out of patience. Reaching for the nightstand drawer, I start to pull it open, but she stops my hand. "I got it," she says, grabbing a condom. She rips it open with her teeth, making my cock jump for joy, and scoots back a bit. With delicate fingers, she holds my shaft and slides the protection until I'm completely sheathed.

Then, without saying a word, she straddles my hips again, holds my cock to her entrance, and slowly sits down, impaling herself on me. Our joint moans fill the room as she holds completely still, allowing herself time to adjust. She must be sore, considering this is the third time we've had sex in the last nine hours.

Slowly, she starts to move. Up and down, gradually increasing her speed. My hands flex on her hips as she starts to bounce, rocking and grinding her hips. I try to hold perfectly still, letting her take what she needs, but the more she moves, the harder it is to remain still.

Finally, I can't *not* move anymore. I thrust my hips upward, earning a loud gasp and a long moan. "Do that again," I tell her as I continue to tilt my hips and press them upward.

"Do what?" she asks, breathlessly.

"Tighten your sweet pussy around my cock."

"Like this?" she asks, and does just that. Words seem to evaporate. I'm lost in a sea of raw need and inhabited desire.

"Just like that," I demand. Then, I watch her ride me, her perfect breasts bouncing as she takes my cock over and over again.

This. This feeling that I have with her. I'll never get enough of it. I'll always want more.

"I'm so close," she whimpers, rocking and grinding against me.

"Don't stop until you come, honey."

"I won't," she pants, her inner thighs tightening on my outer thighs. I can tell she's almost there, which is good, considering the death grip on my shaft has me about to come hard myself.

Then, I feel her let go. She rides me hard, pivoting her hips and grinding her clit against me. When I hear my name spill from her lips, I follow her over the edge, coming with force and a string of non-coherent words. As soon as we're both boneless, she falls on my chest, our lungs both begging for oxygen. I wrap my arms around her, hugging her into my chest and loving the way she fits so perfectly there.

After a few more minutes, Meghan starts to wiggle. I recall what she said last night about using the restroom after sex, so I let her go take care of business, while happily watching her ass as she goes. I remove the condom and wrap it in a Kleenex, tossing it in the garbage can over by my dresser. When she's all finished a few minutes later, she rejoins me in bed.

"I hope you don't mind, but I used one of your spare toothbrushes."

"I don't mind at all," I tell her, wrapping my arm around her shoulder and pulling her into my embrace. "I happen to know where I can get a few extras to keep at my place."

"So, you steal from work?"

"I do. Floss, too, but don't tell the boss."

I can feel her smile against my chest. "Your secret is safe with me."

We lie together for a while, our collective breathing and the occasional passing car the only sound in the room. I wonder if she fell back asleep. It wouldn't surprise me, considering how little sleep we actually got last night. But even now, I can't seem to calm my mind enough to fall back asleep.

I just spent the night with Meghan.

We had the most amazing sex I've ever had.

And she's not freaking out or running away, like I might have expected. I guess that just proves how strong this woman really is. She's had a major life-changing event happen, and is willing to take a few steps forward, albeit very slow and deliberate steps. The point is that she's trying. She's willing to step out of her comfort zone and give this whole dating thing a try again. The fact that she wants me by her side, along for the ride, only makes it that much sweeter.

"So, I was thinking," she starts, drawing little circles over my chest. "My family is going to Payton and Dean's for breakfast. I'm pretty sure everyone will be there. Well, maybe not Levi since he sometimes works weekends, but everyone else should be." A big pause. I'm not sure she's breathing. "Do you think you'd like to join us? I mean, if you don't have anything else going on this morning."

Pulling her tightly against me, I reply, "I'd love to go have breakfast with you. And if your family is there, then that's fine too. I had a great time with them yesterday."

"They're completely nuts, but I guess if you don't mind them, I'd like you to join us."

"Then, there's no place I'd rather be," I answer honestly, bending down and kissing her forehead. "What time is breakfast?"

"Ten."

"Then we have about two hours before we need to get up and shower. Why don't you catch a few more minutes of sleep, and then we'll get ready to go."

"Okay," she whispers, settling her cheek against my chest. There's nothing in the world better than the feel of her in my arms. That's a heady revelation, but one I'm not about to dive into right now.

Instead, as exhaustion settles in, we both curl into each other and slowly drift off to sleep.

Chapter Twenty-One

Meghan

"I did a thing." My words are barely a whisper as I pin my cell phone between my cheek and shoulder, my hands twisting the engagement ring on my hand. I'm hiding in Nick's bathroom, pretending to shower.

"Is that what we're calling it? A thing?" my sister AJ retorts on the other end.

"No, silly, I definitely did *that* thing. Three times, actually."

She's silent on the other end of the line for several long seconds before she finally woops with excitement. "Atta girl! Three times?"

"Yes, three amazing, perfect times. But that's not what I called about," I say, gripping my towel around my chest.

"What other thing did you do? Because if it were up to me, I'd say forget that thing and go back into the bedroom and do the other thing."

"Okay, stop saying thing. It's getting weird," I tell her, glancing at my reflection in the mirror. I look a bit tired, but thoroughly screwed. (In the good way.) My hair is mussed into a horrible rat's nest, my lips are swollen and pink, and my cheeks have that freshly fucked glow.

"Well, tell me what you did," she encourages through the phone.

"I invited him to breakfast at Payton's. With the family. All of them."

There's a pause. "Okay, I don't understand. You invited him to come eat with us. That's a bad thing? Wait, hasn't he been there before?"

"Well, yes, actually he has, but that was before we had sex three times and I let him do dirty things to me with his tongue," I growl at my sister.

"Really? Tell me more about these magical tongue things he did," she encourages.

"You're incorrigible, Grandma. Can we focus on the problem at hand?" I huff, pacing the small bathroom.

"I don't see the problem at all," AJ replies. "You were friends before. Now, you're friends who have seen each other naked. What's the big deal?"

"You should see me, Alison. I look like I was up all night having sex! I can't go to breakfast like this. Grandma is like a dog with a bone when it comes to anything sexual. You don't think she'll smell him on my skin, even after I've showered?"

"Good point. She'll definitely know."

"So that's it? She'll know. That's the best you've got for me?" I ask, my mouth gaping open as realization sets in. There's no getting out of this.

"That's it, sunshine. But don't worry, I'll have that freshly fucked glow myself, so maybe she'll focus on me rather than you," AJ offers, laughing.

"That'll never happen. You and the hot baseball player have been going at it like bunnies for a while now. You're old news."

"And you'll be the front page headline! I'm so excited for you!"

Grumbling, I reply, "Yeah, thanks. Anyway, if you could create a diversion when she starts to ask questions about why I'm all rosy and smell like a man, that'd be great."

AJ laughs. "A diversion? Like what?"

"I don't know. Announce you're pregnant or something?"

"Ain't happening," she says, with a hint of a smile in her voice. "Not because we aren't practicing, but because we're not ready for that yet. We both want kids, but we'd at least like to get down the aisle first."

"Then come up with something else. I'm counting on you, Alison Jane. Don't let me down."

"Fine," she sighs. "When Grandma starts asking why you look like you had *the sex* all night long, and why Nick has that thoroughly sexed grin on his face, I'll create a diversion."

"Thank you," I say, breathing a sigh of relief.

"You owe me."

"We'll take this one off your tab."

"Deal. Now, let's get back to what he did with his tongue…"

* * *

"Nick, good to see you again," my dad says the moment we step into my oldest sister's house.

"You too, sir," Nick replies, sticking out his hand for a quick shake.

"Just Brian, please," he responds, shaking Nick's offered hand. When his eyes turn to me, they're soft and smiling. "Meggy," he says, pulling me into a tight hug and pressing a kiss on my temple. "Good to see you smiling," he adds with a whisper for only me.

I swear I blush the color of a tomato.

"Is Meggy Pie here?" I hear hollered from the living room, moments before my grandma enters the foyer.

"Oh, Dr. Adams!" she exclaims, completely bypassing me and going to where Nick stands. When she gives him a hug, I swear I can see an evil smile on her grandmotherly face and her hand snakes up his arm, giving his bicep a little squeeze.

"Good morning, Emma. I hope it's okay I crashed your breakfast," Nick says, my grandma's frail arms still wrapped around him like a spider monkey.

Still. There.

And she's smiling.

Still.

"My dear, Doc, did you know breakfast is my favorite meal? It's the sausage. I can never get enough of the sausage. The more, the merrier." Suddenly, I see Nick jump and I know exactly what just happened. "Don't you just love sausage, Meggy Pie?" Grandma asks, glancing over her shoulder with that evil 'I just had a handful of his ass and what are you going to do about it' grin.

The woman is the devil incarnate.

"Okay, knock it off or he'll run from the house screaming," I say to the old woman, looking to retrieve my date from my grandma's clutches and make a hasty retreat into the living room.

When we step around the corner, we find much of our family already here. Jaime and Ryan are seated on the loveseat, and she looks as miserable as ever. Ryan sits with his arm around her shoulders, rubbing gentle circles on her upper back, while his other hand rests on her huge belly.

"How ya feeling, Jaime?"

"Like a beached whale," she mumbles, her head falling back on his arm.

"You look stunning," he whispers loud enough for everyone to hear and kisses her shoulder.

"You have to say that. You want sex again someday, but I have to admit it's not that appealing right now."

"You're the most incredible woman I know," he replies to her grumblings, and is rewarded with a smile from my second oldest sister. Even though she looks miserable, and probably feels ten times worse, the way he dotes on her and compliments her always seems to make her smile again.

"Hey, Nick," Linkin says as he comes into the living room, from the kitchen, one of the twins sitting on his hip.

"Hi," Nick responds, keeping his hands in his pockets but smiling at one of my little nephews. "I hate to ask, but which one is this?"

I move and take the baby from his dad and kiss his forehead. (The baby's, not Linkin's.) "This handsome little man is Hemi," I reply before Linkin has a chance.

"And the other is attached to his mom's boob, like always. He definitely takes after his daddy," Linkin says with a grin as he watches me pepper the little guy's face with raspberry kisses. The result makes my nephew squeal and my heart soar with love.

"Quit talking about my boobs at breakfast. It's impolite," Lexi chastises as she enters the living room, Hudson happily cooing on her hip. Linkin takes him right away since Lexi has a hard time keeping the wiggle worm in place, considering her huge pregnant belly.

"Hey, Meg. Hey, Nick," Lexi says as she walks by and drops onto the couch beside Abby and Levi.

"Hi," we both reply in unison. I'm waiting for the onslaught of questions about Nick's appearance today, but they never come. Instead, everyone seems to focus on the pending arrival of more babies and the upcoming weddings.

"How is that going to work, anyway? When the new baby arrives?" I ask my sister.

"These two are about to get the boot. I'm not feeding three babies come next month. We started introducing the bottle, and so far the transition is going well."

Linkin steps over to Nick, and quickly engages him in conversation. It warms my heart that they've embraced him as easily as they have. It's not easy for me, and I'm sure it's difficult for them, as well. Josh was a huge part of this family for several years, and I know my family grieved him, as I did.

Not wanting to get choked up now, I hand Hemi to my sister and make a quick break for it, heading into the kitchen. Dean and Payton are there, with Brielle sitting on a barstool, coloring with Grandpa. "Good morning," I say, giving my grandpa a kiss on his cheek as I walk by.

"Good morning, Meggy. Did I hear the good doc's voice this morning?" he asks, his eyes lighting just a little.

"Umm, yes. I invited Nick to join us this morning. I hope that's okay," I say, grabbing a bottle of water from the fridge.

"Okay? Of course, it's okay! Nick was rooting for the Rangers yesterday, so we will keep him," Grandpa exclaims before going right back to his coloring.

The thought of *keeping* Nick makes my heart beat like a snare drum in my chest. "Good morning, sunshine," I say to my niece, who glances up only long enough to give me a big, toothless grin, before going right back to her coloring.

"She's coloring a cat for the fridge," Dean offers, flipping a griddle full of pancakes.

"And a beautiful cat it is," I reply, gently tugging on her long braid.

"How are you this morning?" I ask my newly-pregnant older sister.

"Feeling like I could sleep for three days straight and it would still not be enough," she mutters as she finishes dicing the fresh fruit and placing it in a large bowl.

"Growing a baby will do that to you," I answer, though I have no first-hand knowledge of the fact.

"I'm trying not to complain, really. I'm just so blessed to actually be pregnant, without all of those shots and hormones, but this baby is already whooping my butt," Payton adds with a tired smile.

"I'm going to be a big sister!" Brielle announces to the room.

"I know! I'm so excited. You're going to be the best big sister ever," I tell my niece, kissing her on the top of the head.

"Sorry, we're late! We got…distracted," AJ says as she joins us in the kitchen.

"Distracted," I snort.

She gives me a pointed look. "Yes, *distracted.* You know, like a *distraction?*" she says, her eyebrows raising as if to remind me of our earlier discussion.

"I've heard the term," I reply with a grin.

"Time to eat," Payton hollers. "Bri, can you pick up your coloring stuff so we have room to eat, please?"

"Sure, Mom," the little girl says, making my heart stop and then skip a beat. The sound of Bri calling Payton Mom will forever make my heart happy. Payton too, if the tears that well in her eyes as she gives her daughter a smile is any indication.

Everyone files into the kitchen, grabbing a plate and filling it with food. Nick and I jump in, and it's the first time I realize how famished I truly am. I load my plate up with scrambled eggs, fruit, and a pancake. Then I throw a few strips of bacon on top, just to be sure I don't go hungry. Nick glances down at my plate and gives me a smirk. It's like he's suddenly recalling *exactly* why I'm starving this morning.

I can't help the smile on my face.

I follow Jaime and AJ into the living room, where a large table is set up. Jaime sits down and winces, unable to mask her discomfort. It makes me hope this baby girl or boy comes sooner, rather than later.

"So, how was your night?" Jaime asks.

"It was fine," I reply, stuffing a strip of bacon into my mouth.

"Just...fine?" she asks, giving me one of those smiles that lets me know she suspects something a bit more than *fine* happened last night.

"Oh, don't be shy, Meggy Pie. She definitely has that glow, doesn't she, Orvie?"

"She does, my love," Grandpa replies, sitting down beside Grandma and patting her on the hand.

"So? What was it? A night filled with hiding the pickle or a morning packed with stuffing the flounder?" Grandma asks, her beady little eyes pointed directly at me. Of course, I can also feel the eyes of everyone else in the room. I can hear their snickers too.

Instead of answering, I glance at AJ, who's shoving food into her mouth like there's no tomorrow. I glare at her, silently reminding her of her one job this morning. *The distraction.* I notice Jaime stand up, but keep my eyes focused on my traitor sister. She's smirking behind her mouthful of bacon and eggs, silently letting me know I'm on my own.

Before I can reply, Brielle enters the room. "Aunt Jaime peed her pants!"

We all stop and glance at the little girl, who's pointing and smiling at Jaime. Then we turn our attention to Jaime, whose pants are clearly wet as she stands there, wide-eyed and full of shock.

"Shit!" Ryan exclaims, jumping up and hustling around the table to his wife. "Your water broke?" There's a mixture of panic with the excitement in his voice.

"I'm pretty sure I didn't pee," she replies to her husband.

"I'll go get the truck," he exclaims, tearing out of the house like his ass were on fire.

Everyone else gathers around Jaime, trying to keep her calm and collected. Lexi comes out of the kitchen, a plate of food in one hand and a baby in the other. "This does *not* mean you get to have the name Henry!" she proclaims, quickly trying to stuff food into her mouth and keep the rest of the plate away from the reaching hands of her son.

"Whatever, Lexi. First one in labor gets the name," Jaime says breathlessly.

Ryan flies back inside, leaving the front door open. He comes over to Jaime and takes her in his arms and placing a hard, loud kiss square on her lips. "This is it. We're about to meet our son or daughter, and I just want you to know that you've made me the happiest I've ever been. This life would be nothing without you." His words trail off at the end (I'm pretty sure he's super emotional). That would actually suit this family well, considering most of us are now crying as we watch their private exchange.

She places her palm on his cheek. "I love you," she whispers moments before a contraction takes hold. Jaime cringes, but keeps her eyes locked on Ryan's. "Okay, that wasn't so bad," she says with a huff and a giggle.

"You ain't seen nothing yet," Lexi chimes in, earning a stern look from, well, all of us. It doesn't faze her though. Lexi just rolls her eyes and takes another bite of food.

We all watch and wait as Ryan slowly ushers Jaime from the house and toward the waiting truck. "I'm right behind you," Dad says to Ryan after helping make sure he and Jaime are set.

"We going?" Payton asks, glancing around at all of our stunned faces.

"I know I am," Grandma says, pushing past Grandpa to grab her plate. "We'll take these to go," she says picking up her paper plate and plastic utensils. The moment the sisters started to pair up was the moment that a standard set of dinner plates and silverware were no longer enough.

Suddenly, we're all scrambling to pick up our plates and to cover the remaining food. I grab my plate and Nick's and turn toward him. "Do you want to go with one of your sisters? I can head home so I'm not in the way," he says.

"No way! This is the best part. Something major always happens," I tell him, handing him the plates so I can grab my purse. "Last time Lexi and Linkin got married and Grandma got kicked out of the delivery room! There's no way we're missing that," I add as we follow suit with everyone else and file out the door.

"I'm not getting kicked out this time, Meggy Pie! I've been taking online classes. I'm practically a doctor," Grandma says, hightailing it to her car, climbs into the driver's seat, and tears out of the driveway.

"Do you think I could have a ride?" That's when I turn and notice Grandpa standing beside me, watching his wife drive away like a bat out of hell.

"Grandpa!" I bellow, bursting into laughter. "I can't believe she left you," I add, walking with him toward Nick's car. Nick helps me in in the back seat, while Grandpa slides in the front passenger seat. He hands me my plate of food, before we jump in line and head to the hospital, eating a few bites of food along the way.

When we arrive at the hospital, our group makes their way up the elevators and to the maternity ward. We all usher into the large room, while Jaime is pushed to the counter in a wheelchair. Ryan gives the front desk their information, while we all get comfy.

"Do you think it'll be a while?" Abby asks, sitting down in a chair beside me.

"Probably. It's her first baby. It could take forever," AJ replies, getting comfy on the opposite side of the room.

"I think we should head home, babe. The boys don't need to be here for the wait." Linkin says to Lexi, as he sets the twins' car seats down on the table.

Lexi stands by the doorway and rubs her lower back. "Yeah, you're probably right. I haven't been feeling so well today," she says, rocking on her feet as if she's uncomfortable.

"Do you want something to drink? I thought about walking down to the vending machine," Dean asks.

"I'll go with you," Levi says, standing up and following Dean to the entryway.

"Shit," Lexi gasps, glancing down at the floor.

We all look down, including Levi and Dean, who stand right beside her, a look of horror on their faces. "Alexis Renee, why did you pee on the floor?" Grandma asks as she enters the room.

"I don't think it's pee," she gasps, her wide eyes searching out her husband.

"Really?" he asks, slowly walking over to where she stands, his entire demeanor calm and collected.

"Are you kidding me, right now? You're doing this so you can have the name, aren't you?" Jaime growls from her wheelchair.

"Yes, I made my water break five weeks before my due date so that I can have the name," Lexi argues sarcastically.

"I wouldn't put it past you," Jaime refutes, crossing her arms over her chest.

"Well, you know what they say, the second baby always comes quicker than the first. You could be here for *days* in labor, while I might pop this baby out in forty-five minutes," Lexi counters, mimicking Jaime's stance and crossing her arms over her chest.

"Girls, do we have to do this now?" Abby says, walking over to where Lexi stands in a puddle of amniotic fluid.

"I'm calling my mom to come get the boys," Linkin says, turning and making eye contact with me.

"I got them. Go make your call," I reply.

Jaime is wheeled off to her room, with Ryan and Grandma both hot on her heels, while a second nurse comes to get Lexi with a second chair. "Come with me. We'll get you in a gown and hooked up to a monitor," she says before wheeling our youngest sister off to a room.

Everyone is left stunned by the turn of events, and the fact that we now have two sisters in labor. Before I can turn to Nick and apologize for the crazy family I just so happened to be born into, I hear a wail. I quickly get up and glance down at the two small humans sitting in the car seats on the table.

"Hey, buddy, are you upset?" I ask, unstrapping Hudson and slowly pulling him from the seat. As soon as I have the little man in my arms, his brother decides to let me know just how much he doesn't like being strapped in the seat either.

Quickly, I turn and place Hudson in Nick's arms and spin back around to grab his smaller twin brother. I blow kisses and make faces while I unlock the harness and pull Hemi into my arms. The little guy reaches up and grabs my lips, giggling as I try to blow kisses against his tiny hand.

"How's my little man doing?" I ask Hemi, giving him a raspberry kiss on the neck and making him giggle. He reaches up and grabs a big handful of hair, pulling it hard and laughing. "That's not very nice. I'm supposed to be your favorite aunt, remember? We talked about this."

When I glance over at Nick, my heart starts to tap dance in my chest. He's standing statue-still, staring down at the baby in his arms as if it were a bomb. Hudson is looking up at him with a bit of a stink-eye, almost like he's trying to figure out who's holding him.

"You okay?" I ask Nick, reaching forward and running my finger across Hudson's jaw and making him squeal.

"Uhh, yeah. I've just," Nick starts and glances around. Dropping his voice, he continues, "I've never held a baby."

"What? You've never held a baby?" I gasp, too loudly and drawing everyone's attention. Hudson seems just as shocked by this revelation and takes that opportunity to slap Nick on the cheek with his wet, slobbery hand.

"Thanks for broadcasting," Nick says when he hears chuckles.

"I'm sorry," I giggle. "Do you want me to have Abby grab him?"

"No, I think we've come to an understanding. He keeps all of his fluids inside his body and I'll hold him for a bit."

Again, I can't help but laugh. "Let me know how that works out for you, buddy," I sass Nick as I place more kisses on Hemi's face. I could kiss these babies all day long. When I glance back up, Nick is watching, a subtle smile on his handsome face. "What?"

He catches me off guard by stepping forward into my personal space. I close my eyes as he slowly bends down and kisses me on the lips. It's a quick, no-tongue kiss, but still packs a powerful punch. "You're so beautiful," he whispers, his lips still grazing against mine.

"Are we going to have to talk about the birds and the bees? You know how these two cuties got here, right? I could do a demonstration," Grandma offers as she returns from Jaime's room, her face practically pressed between Nick's and my face.

Rolling my eyes, I glance her way. "Butt out," I tease my grandma.

"If you two would like to go practice for a bit, you just let me know. There's a storage room down the hall that wasn't locked last time we were here, and I'd be happy to watch the boys for a bit." Of course, she practically yells this so that the entire waiting room hears.

"We're okay," I mumble, my face similar to that of a strawberry.

"Actually," Nick starts, leaving the insinuation door wide open, a wide grin on his face as he waggles his eyebrows.

"Doc, I think I like you," Grandma says with a laugh, wrapping her arms around him for a hug. She makes it look like she's only doing it to shower the baby with attention, but the moment I see Nick jump, I know that's not the case.

"Leave his ass alone," I chastise my elderly grandma.

When she turns back my way, her eyes are wide with delight and she wears a devilish grin on her face. "That was an accident. I was hugging the baby."

"Hey everyone, she's definitely in labor," Linkin says as he rushes into the waiting room. "They hooked her up to a fetal monitor, and the baby looks good. Heart rate's strong and running one-fifty. Doc is on her way, and the nurse says it shouldn't be too long. My mom is coming to grab the boys, and she offered to take Bri with her too." Linkin glances at Dean and Payton before coming over and kissing both of his boys on the crowns of their heads.

"We've got them until she gets here," I assure him, rocking little Hemi in my arms. When we glance over at Nick, he's struggling to keep hold of Hudson, who looks like he wants to get down and crawl.

"Not yet, buddy. You can get down and move when you get to Grandma's house," Linkin says to the boy in Nick's arms.

"I'll just go keep Lexi Lou company until you're ready to go back in," Grandma offers. Before Linkin can even formulate a reply, Grandma is already hustling out of the room and toward our youngest sister.

"She shouldn't be left alone with an emotional, pregnant Lexi," Dad says, turning and following in her wake, making Grandpa snort.

"I'm going to regret letting her go in there, aren't I?" Linkin says, taking Hudson from Nick.

"Definitely," Abby chimes in.

About ten minutes later, Linkin's mom, Karen, along with Linkin's ten-year-old twin brothers, Jackson and Jefferson, enter the waiting room at a high rate of speed. "How is she?"

"She's doing well, but I don't want to leave her in there too much longer, Mom."

"How about I pop in and say hello for a minute, and then I'll come out and take the boys home with me," Karen says. "I'm more than happy to take Brielle with me for a while so you both can stay here," she adds to Payton and Dean.

"That would be appreciated," Dean says.

Payton looks over at her daughter. "Do you want to go with Karen and the boys and play with them this afternoon?"

"Can we have a tea party?" Brielle asks the older twin boys.

"Can we bring our swords?" one of the twins (I can't tell them apart) asks, giving Brielle a look.

"Sure," Brielle says, shrugging her shoulders.

"Okay, but do we have to drink tea? I think tea tastes like rotten feet," the other twin adds.

"Yeah, I want root beer!" a boy hollers.

While the kids all discuss different beverage options, Karen heads to Lexi's room to say hello. Grandma comes out of Lexi's room and heads across the hall to Jaime's. It doesn't take long before Ryan practically runs from the room, looking a little frustrated.

"She kicked me out. That old woman just walked in and told me to leave."

"She tried that shit with me last time, and I had to get stern with her," Linkin adds with a smile.

"Don't let her be the boss of you," Nick says, earning a laugh from Linkin.

"You're the man, Elson," Levi chimes in as he joins the group after handing Abby a bottle of water.

"Fuck off," Ryan mumbles, quiet enough that none of the kids should hear. He rubs his forehead and glances around the room. "Are you all staying?"

"I think so. At least for a while," I answer, still holding Hemi.

"Is that okay?" Abby asks.

"Of course. Just as long as you can help distract the old woman and keep her occupied so she doesn't come in and assist the doc," Ryan says, rubbing his hands over the back of his neck.

"Good luck with that," Levi replies with a laugh.

"Ryan? Your wife is asking for you," the nurse says, standing in the waiting room doorway.

"Gotta go." Ryan says, slapping Linkin on the back and bolting for his wife's delivery room.

"She's getting closer," Karen says as she enters the room. "Her contractions are only four minutes apart now. You should probably head back in."

"Okay," Linkin says to his mom, placing a kiss on Hudson's forehead and squeezing him tight. "I gotta go, buddy. It's time for you to become a big brother." He walks over to where I stand with

Hemi and does the same thing. "Mommy and Daddy love you, boys," he says as he helps his mom put the twins in their car seats.

"We'll be fine. Go be with Lexi and don't worry about us," Karen says as she hugs her son and pulls him down for a kiss on his scruffy cheek.

"I'll call you as soon as I know," Linkin tells his mom before kissing both boys again and heading off to Lexi's room.

"We'll help you take them down," Dean says, grabbing one of the carriers off the table. Levi quickly takes the other, while Karen rounds up Brielle and her twin sons, who just so happen to be killing each other in the hallway (with fake swords).

Sawyer and Nick follow, grabbing diaper bags and a bag for Brielle as they head out. "Good thing she has a minivan," I mumble to AJ.

"No shit."

Taking a seat next to my sister, I exhale loudly. "Well, we might as well get comfy. We might be here a while."

Chapter Twenty-Two

Nick

"So neither of them get the name Henry?" I ask sleepily, smiling into the phone in my hand.

"Nope! Isn't that hilarious? They've been arguing for months about who gets to name their son Henry, and they both had girls!" Considering it's about two in the morning, she sounds like she's wired to stay up all night long.

At seven o'clock last night, she sent me home to get a bit of my Sunday chores done. Even though I was perfectly content sitting in that waiting room with Meghan and her family, I conceded since my pile of laundry was overflowing and my dirty dishes were ready for the washer. So, I spent the evening catching up on my chores and wishing I were at the hospital with everyone else. That feeling of longing to be with her got worse as darkness fell and I was off to bed.

Alone.

"Everyone is doing fine?" I ask with a yawn.

"They're all perfect. Lexi had Stella right after you left, after only an hour of pushing, while Jaime just delivered little Amelia almost an hour ago. Everyone is completely over the moon for these two babies, including their daddies. Ryan won't let anyone else hold her yet, and when I left, Linkin was curled up to Lexi's side in the hospital bed while she fed the baby. Grandma tried to worm her way into Jaime's room for the delivery, but was pushed out. No one wants an eighty-two-year-old woman looking on while you're trying to push a watermelon out of a grapefruit."

I can't help it; I cringe. "I'm glad everyone is doing well," I tell her. After a few passing seconds, I add, "I miss you."

"I miss you too." Her confession puts a smile on my face.

"My bed is lonely tonight."

"Mine too. If it wasn't so late, I'd come over."

"Your car is still here," I remind her.

"Oh yeah. That'll make getting to work difficult," she says with a loud yawn.

"I'll come get you. I'll even bring fancy coffee."

"That would be amazing. I can't believe I have to get up in like four hours. I'm not even tired," she says with another yawn.

"That's the adrenaline, but I think it's starting to wear off."

"It is," she concedes. "I'm suddenly really tired."

"I'll let you go to sleep, honey. I'll be there at seven thirty, okay?"

"Thank you," she says softly, the sound going straight to my cock. Not good, considering I'm home alone tonight.

"Good night, Meggy Pie."

"Good night, Nicholas Adams, D.D.S."

I hang up, chuckling, and set my phone down on the nightstand. I reach for the pillow, and I'm not talking about mine. I'm referring to the one that cradled Meghan's head just twenty-four short hours ago. Like a weirdo, I inhale, the scent of her shampoo filling my senses and not helping my hard-on any.

It's definitely going to be a long five hours until I see her again.

* * *

"I have a surprise for you," I tell Meghan as I enter her room.

"A surprise?" she asks, turning and offering me a full-watt smile.

Meghan is wrapping up her day, even though it's only one o'clock. Since Tuesdays are our late appointments nights, we try not to schedule many afternoon appointments on Mondays, except post-weekend emergencies. Today we are lucky and our last patient was at noon. Patty and Erika left a few minutes ago, which means it's just me and my dental hygienist left in the empty building.

Alone.

And to say I'm craving her is an understatement.

"I brought lunch," I tell her, pulling the bag out from behind my back.

Her eyes twinkle as she says, "I'm starving."

"Me too," I reply. But not for food.

Unable to resist any longer, I set the bag on the chair and pull her into my arms. She goes willingly, wrapping her hands around my waist and holding on tight. When she's finally against me, I grasp the sides of her face with my hands and lower my lips to hers. Her breathing hitches moments before I feel her against me. She tastes like honey and cinnamon, like sexy woman. I coax her mouth open with my tongue and dive inside. I can feel her fingers dig into my lower back, and the burn only fuels my already raging fire for her. I'm hard as stone, ready to devour her with my mouth, my hands, my cock.

But it'll have to wait.

First lunch.

Then, if I'm a good boy, sex.

It practically takes an act of Congress to pry my lips from hers, but I do it. Her eyes are all glossy and her lips are pink and swollen (a look I fucking love on her), so I place one more chaste kiss on her lips and begrudgingly pull away. "That'll tide me over for a few minutes. First, we eat," I tell her, reaching for the bag and pulling out the contents.

There are two deli sandwiches that I had sent over, plus a few homemade sides. I take the containers out and set them on the counter. The deli included plastic utensils with my order, so I shoved the two forks in the salads and called it lunch.

"This looks good," she says as I hand her a ham and cheese on wheat – hold the mayo.

"I took a chance that you didn't have lunch plans," I tell her, unwrapping my own sandwich and taking a bite.

"No, not today. I'm going to the hospital around three to see the babies. They're both supposed to be released later, so I wanted to go see them both together before they head home."

"They're sending them home today? They just had babies. Is that safe?" I ask, completely shocked by this news. I mean, I know I'm a smart man and have had my share of schooling to become a dentist, but I've never really been around babies. Never deliveries. So I'm a little shocked that mere hours after delivery, they send them home.

"It's completely safe, as long as the deliveries were normal. I know if a woman has a C-section, she'll be in the hospital a little longer, but with most vaginal deliveries, a woman is usually released the next day."

"Wow, that just seems so soon," I reply, taking the fork from the macaroni salad and offering her a bite.

Her lips wrap around the fork, making my cock twitch in my trousers. "That's delicious," she replies, licking away the trace of salad from the corner of her mouth. "It does seem soon, but I've learned that most parents just want to get home where they can rest more comfortably in their own space," she adds.

"Makes sense. Hospitals are definitely not everyone's cup of tea," I reply and watch as her eyes darken and slowly turn misty. Something tells me she was remembering the exact reason why she's not a fan of hospitals.

"Anyway," I start, trying to pull her attention away from whatever memory she's trapped in, "if you're interested, I thought we could spend a little time together this afternoon." Now, I'm not so sure my plan is the best deal – especially since she's probably thinking about Josh right now.

She gives me her full attention and a smile. The storm clouds seem to dissipate, even if for a little while. "Sounds great," she says between bites. "And if you want, you can go with me to the hospital to see the babies?" It comes out a question, like she's a bit uncertain that I'd want to go with her.

"Absolutely. I'd love to go meet your new nieces," I tell her, placing a soft kiss on the tip of her nose.

I'm rewarded with another grin before she reaches into the container of fruit and grabs a grape. Instead of bringing it to her own mouth, she moves it to mine. Our eyes connect as I slowly move toward the fruit she holds. The fruit is sweet, but not nearly as delicious as the fingers I wrap my lips around. Those sexy green eyes widen as my tongue swirls around the tips of her fingers before sucking the fruit from her grasp and pulling back to chew.

As soon as I swallow, I move. She's in my arms, my lips claiming hers in a bruising kiss. I'm starving, but not for the food. I need her. My body craves her touch.

Forgetting lunch, I devour her mouth with my own, savoring the hearty taste of fruit and Meghan. Sliding my hands up her sides, feeling the burn of her hot skin as I push her scrubs out of the way. She tugs on my dress shirt and undershirt, stripping them from my waistband, and scores her nails against my side. Shivers rack my body and my cock swells unbelievably hard. So hard I'm afraid I might suffer some sort of permanent damage if I don't rectify this situation.

Now.

"Jesus, I can't believe how bad I want you," I groan as I push her top over her head and toss it somewhere into the room. Her breasts are wrapped in lace, a delicate pink color that reminds me of those rosebud little nipples inside.

Instead of feasting on that particular prize, I focus on her neck. The smooth, creamy, slender column of her delectable neck. My tongue teases and my teeth nip just enough to cause her to gasp in pleasure. The sound is like a tornado to my soul, reckless and wild, yet surprisingly soothing.

"This is crazy," she says as her hands slide down and grip my ass.

"Definitely crazy."

"We shouldn't do this here," she adds, her slender fingers finding my belt and working on the closure.

"Definitely not," I reply, continuing to shower open-mouthed kisses down her neck and collarbone.

The sound of my belt unbuckling, followed by the unmistakable release of zipper teeth has me on edge and gritting my teeth. Jesus, I'm ready to explode and she hasn't even touched me yet. She pushes my pants down, my boxer briefs stretched tightly across my throbbing cock.

"It feels kinda good to be bad," she whispers just as her hand slips into my underwear and wraps around my cock. When she slowly strokes from root to tip, my eyes cross and all ability to breathe ceases to exist.

"Sooooo good," I groan, forgetting all about her neck. I have to place my hands on the counter just to keep myself upright.

Suddenly, she drops to her knees and grabs the waist of my boxer briefs. With one quick swoop, she pulls them down to my ankles, my hard cock practically slapping her in the face. The tip is wet, my body taut with need and alive with desire. She gazes up at me, her own yearning written all over her face, and slowly brings her mouth to where I need her most.

"Fuck," I groan as her lips wrap around my shaft. She sucks, hard and fast, bringing my entire cock into her warm mouth. I can't breathe. There's not enough air in the room, in the building, in the world.

Meghan places her hands on my ass and with nothing but her sweet mouth, starts to work me over like a fucking porn star. I've never experienced anything like this before in my life, and considering how amazing our weekend was, that's saying something.

I focus on my breathing, which becomes increasingly difficult, as she bobs up and down, using only her mouth and wicked tongue. She takes me straight from horny to crazy in about ten seconds. Any other time, I might be a little embarrassed by how quickly I'm about to come, but not today. Not with her.

It's because I want her so fucking much.

"I'm going to come," I warn her, gazing down and watching as she takes my cock in and out of her mouth. Her eyes connect with mine and she doesn't let go. Instead, it only fuels her further. She practically swallows me, my dick disappearing into her mouth and the head of my cock sliding down her throat. I lose it. Yes, I come harder than I've ever come before, but it's more than that. It's that moment that I realize I'm in jeopardy of losing so much more.

My heart.

Her name is a sweet song spilling from my lips as she swallows and gently licks my shaft. Another shiver sweeps through my body as she pops off my cock and smiles up at me. And I swear to God I almost tell her that I love her. No, it's not one of those lust-fueled, I just got off confessions.

It's real.

I'm not on the verge of falling for her.

I fucking have.

Years of friendship have transformed into something real and deep and meaningful.

And that scares the ever-loving shit out of me, because she's not there.

She's not ready.

And she may never be.

On the verge of a full-on panic gripping hold, I push all thoughts of that crazy L word from my mind and focus solely on the woman on her knees before me. She's smiling up at me with that ornery, satisfied grin, and I can't help but smile back. She makes it so easy.

Needing somewhere else to focus my attention, I reach down and pull her to stand, my mouth greedy and hungry. Completely ignoring my own pants, I push hers down, revealing the sexiest little scrap of lace panties I've ever seen. "What is this, Miss Summer? You've been hiding these in scrubs all morning?" I ask, running my thumb over the coarse, wet material.

"Surprise," she whispers, gasping as my thumb traces the slit between her legs.

"You seem full of surprises today." Gently spinning her around, I help her sit down on the dental chair. I pull slip-on shoes off her feet, followed quickly by her pants. "You know," I say, gliding my palms up the insides of her thighs and gently spreading them as I go. "I didn't get to finish my lunch."

"No?" she inhales, her eyes following my every move.

"Nope. And I'm so fucking famished," I tell her moments before I bend down and graze my tongue over the lace between her legs. I hear another gulp for air as I continue to swirl my tongue over the soaked material.

Making sure the armrest and other obstacles are out of my way, I step on the foot pedal to raise her up. There's a hint of laughter in her eyes as she slowly moves upward until she can go no more. It's still not quite high enough, but it'll do. With my hands on her thighs, I bend down and lick hard, sliding my tongue between her folds. The scrap of panties is slightly restricting, but also more erotic.

"Hands behind your head," I instruct. There's no hesitation, only lust in her eyes, as she reaches over her head and grabs the headrest. "Now, hold on tight, honey."

My mouth waters as I push aside her panties and slide my tongue into her pussy. Meghan spreads her legs as far as she can, giving me the perfect glimpse of her sweetness. With a firm tongue, I flick her clit before sucking it into my mouth. Keeping the lace to the side, my hands slide beneath her ass, raising and tilting her toward my mouth.

Then I devour.

I lick and suck every part of her, gliding two fingers into her pussy. She's tight, already gripping my digits, but begging for more. My cock is already hard and ready, but before I give in to that particular need to feel my dick engulfed in her tight, wetness, I want to make her come with my mouth. Her hips start to gyrate, moving in rhythm against the friction of my tongue. The sweetest moans of pleasure fill the air as I thrust two fingers inside her and suck hard on her clit. It pulses in my mouth, an indication that she's getting so close. I can't wait to taste her release on my tongue and feel it around my fingers.

It doesn't take long and she's there. Her body tenses, her pussy gripping my fingers like a vise, as she screams my name over and over again, her body riding the ultimate wave of pleasure. I could do this all day, every day, and never tire of it. Watching her come is my newest favorite pastime. My favorite addiction.

When she's left boneless and sated in the chair, I maneuver it down and help her stand. "I've never done that here," I tell her, kissing her lips and unsnapping her bra.

"No?" she gasps when my fingers connect with her hard nipples.

I shake my head. "Know what else I've never done, but have been thinking about nonstop for the last week?"

She shakes her head, shivering against me.

Grabbing her in my arms, I bring her to my chest and start walking. "Fucking you against my desk."

Chapter Twenty-Three

Meghan

"You've been making babies!" Grandma exclaims loudly in the middle of Jaime's room, drawing everyone's attention, including the nurse.

"What?" I gasp, too embarrassed to meet anyone's eyes as Nick and I enter the room. But I feel them. Every single pair of eyes is watching, judging, and probably laughing that I'm the target of Grandma's sexual comments.

"I can feel it, Meggy Pie. And smell it. You smell like man. And sex. Like Abby does," Grandma proclaims, glancing at poor Abby and offering her an evil little smile. This woman is the devil, plain and simple.

"I didn't...we didn't..." Abby stammers, her face as red as a tomato.

"Yes we did," Levi mumbles, wrapping his arms around her and pulling her back against him. She's still blushing, but she giggles as he kisses her neck and whispers something in her ear.

"I just walked in the room. Why are you bothering me already?" I ask the ornery old woman who's cooing down at baby Amelia.

"Sex looks good on you," Grandma shrugs.

"Can we stop talking about sex in front of my daughter? She'll never have it. Ever," Ryan says hovering over where Grandpa sits in the chair with the baby in his arms.

"Oh, Ryan, don't be silly. Of course, she'll have *the sex!*" Grandma bellows.

"That'll be hard since she's never allowed to date," Ryan grumbles, placing a kiss on Jaime's forehead.

"Never underestimate the levels of sneakiness a girl will go to for sex," Grandma reassures Ryan, who suddenly looks a little nauseous. "Anyway, we'll let Meghan and the hot dentist visit for a bit. We'll just buzz across the hall and see Lexi Lou and the stripper."

Grandpa stands up and walks toward me, Ryan looking like his brain is about to explode with each step Grandpa takes with his baby girl. He seems to visibly relax as Grandpa places my newest niece in my arms. Her face is wrinkled, even in sleep, and I instantly fall in love.

"She's perfect," I whisper to no one in particular.

"She is," Jaime agrees, smiling up at her husband.

"I think she looks a lot like Ryan," Abby says beside me, reaching for Amelia's tiny little hand.

"Definitely," I add, tracing a finger where dark little peach fuzz sticks out wildly from beneath the little cap. My niece purses her lips and makes a little sucking motion.

"I'm ready to get out of here," Jaime grumbles, sitting on the edge of the bed and stretching.

"Soon, love," Ryan reassures her, sitting beside her on the bed and wrapping his arm around her shoulder. Jaime sinks into him easily, closing her eyes and breathing him in.

"We're going to head out," Abby says, heading over to our sister and giving her and Ryan each a hug. "Congratulations again, you two. She's a beautiful little girl."

"She is. She's amazing like her mother," Ryan says, placing a kiss on his wife's lips.

"Are you heading over to see Lexi?" I ask as Abby gathers up her bag.

"We already did, and there's no way I'm going back now that Grandma is there," Abby says as they head out the door. "We'll stop by and see you in a few days," she hollers to Jaime as she follows Levi into the hall.

"How's everything with you two?" Jaime asks when Nick and I are the last ones in the room.

"Good," I reply, not giving anything away.

"You two seem to be...spending a lot of time together," she hedges, clearly looking to get a little more details out of us.

"I love spending time with your sister," Nick says, reaching down and taking Amelia's tiny little hand in his much bigger one.

"She is pretty great," Jaime replies with a huge grin.

"She is," Nick agrees, returning her smile.

"I am still here, ya know," I mumble, feeling my cheeks turn heated as they talk about me.

"We know," he says, placing a kiss on the side of my head and making my blush turn even darker. The show of affection makes me blush and feel a little self-conscious, but when I glance up at my sister, she's merely smiling at us, which makes me smile.

We visit for a bit until the nurse comes in with discharge papers. Dad also arrives, ready to help Jaime and Ryan home with their new daughter. After giving him a quick hug and promising to come over and see the baby once Jaime and Ryan get settled, we head across the hall to Lexi's room.

As soon as we step over the threshold, I immediately feel like we're invading on a private moment. Lexi and Linkin are both sitting on the bed, baby Stella cradled in her mom's arms. Linkin has Hemi in his arms, while Hudson crawls between them, his small hand reaching for his new sister.

"You have to be gentle with the baby," Linkin instructs softly as Hudson grabs the blanket Stella is swaddled within. I can't help but smile adoringly at the moment, which is actually broken the moment Hudson swings and hits his new baby sister in the leg. Stella startles and instantly starts to scream, Hudson quickly turning to look at his dad with big innocent eyes.

"Yeah, you did that, buddy. You have to be nice to your sister," Linkin grumbles, taking Hudson in his arms and setting Hemi down between he and Lexi.

"Not sure this was a good idea," Lexi says as Hemi now reaches for his sister. But instead of hitting her, Hemi gently rubs his sister's leg and starts to babble baby talk. Stella immediately calms down and falls back asleep, while Hemi crawls onto his mom's lap and lays his head next to his sister's.

My heart soars.

"Do you see that, little man? That's how you're supposed to treat your sister," Linkin says to Hudson who seems more interested in chewing on a plastic set of keys than trying to make nice with his new sister.

Lexi glances up and gives us a smile. "This might be more challenging than I thought."

"They'll get used to her. They've had you two all to themselves, and now they have to learn to share," I tell my youngest sister as we come over and sit in the empty chairs. "I thought the grandparents would be here."

"I made them leave," Linkin says, blowing kisses on Hudson's neck and making him giggle.

"He did not. They started to give each other the do-me eyes and said something about a broom closet," Lexi says with an eye roll.

"Do I want to know what's happening right now in the broom closet?" Nick whispers over my shoulder.

"Not unless you want nightmares," I confirm.

"Someday we'll tell you stories, Nick," Lexi says as she stands up with baby Stella. "Here, Miss Stella. Meet your auntie Meggy." She kisses the baby's cheek before placing her in my waiting arms.

She's tiny, but not nearly as small as her brothers when they were born. She fusses for a moment before settling into the crook of my arm and falling back asleep. Something inside of me starts to yearn, something that I wrote off as a life goal. But holding all of these babies? I'll be honest, it makes me hungry to be a mother.

And sad that the one person who I pictured in this moment isn't here.

Then I just start to feel guilty because the man who is here has been nothing but supportive as I deal with my crazy issues.

"So, I have to admit, I was a little surprised that you chose the name Stella. I don't remember it being on the list," I say to my sister as she picks up one of the boys and changes his diaper.

"It wasn't on the list," Lexi says as she removes the wet diaper and replaces it with a fresh one.

"What was on the list?" Nick asks, staying right by my side, his large fingers gently touching the baby's cheek.

"Henry for Henry Ford and Shelby for one of my favorite cars," Linkin says, moving to change Hudson's diaper right beside my sister.

"Shelby GT 500? Nice," Nick agrees with a smile. Linkin glances his way and raises his knuckles for a bump.

Guys.

"I didn't want Shelby. I wanted Stella. And since we named our boys after his *other* favorite cars, I decided I wanted this one to be feminine and classic." Lexi smiles down at her happy son and sweeps him into her arms.

"You should have gone with Nova," Nick says casually, but there's no mistaking the way Linkin tenses.

"Nova? That's fucking brilliant. Babe, why didn't we name her Nova?" he asks his wife.

"Because if you ever want to use your dipstick again, you were going to let your wife name your daughter Stella," Lexi says without even looking his way.

"Ahhh. Yeah, we decided on Stella, man," Linkin says to Nick with a wink. "But there's always next time."

"No, no. There is no more next time. You're getting fixed," Lexi says.

"The hell I am! No one is coming near my balls with a scalpel, babe. That's a no-sharp instrument zone."

"Stop being such a man. It's quicker and easier for you to get fixed than me."

"Neither one of us are getting fixed. Not yet. I'm not done reproducing with you," he says and waggles his eyebrows at her.

"You are for the next six weeks, buster. Remember what happened the last time?" she sasses, clearly talking about the time they only waited four weeks to engage in sex after the boys were born. She was pregnant right away.

"Oh, I remember. I remember you did this one thing with your –"

"Stop! For the love of God, please stop talking," I beg. "You're going to scar these beautiful children."

"Thank God they don't remember anything right now. Mommy is a bit of a dirty, horny, potty mouth," Linkin tells Hudson as he picks him up and holds him against his broad chest. My heart soars for my sister – for all of them, actually. They all have wonderful men in their lives and their families are growing rapidly.

"And Daddy is a raunchy, sex-fiend who thinks he's going to die if his penis isn't played with daily," Lexi says to Hemi in a baby-talk voice.

"You love my penis. Admit it," Linkin teases, giving his wife a wolfish grin.

"I will do no such thing. Your penis makes me pregnant," Lexi sasses, holding her face stern as she tries not to laugh, a face that makes Linkin laugh.

"Things just got weird," Nick whispers in my ear.

"Definitely," I reply, turning back and facing my sister, who's looking at her husband like she wants to swallow him alive. "Anyway, we're going to head out and grab some supper, where people aren't talking about penises."

"Well, we're glad you stopped by to meet our angel," Lexi says, giving Hemi to her husband and coming over to take Stella into her arms, cradling her closer to her chest.

"It was good to see you guys," Nick says to my sister and her husband. Linkin gives him a head nod, since his hands are full of kids, and walks over to his wife and daughter. Before I slip out of the door, I watch (slightly mesmerized) as Linkin bends down and gently kisses his new baby girl's forehead before placing a tender kiss on his wife's lips.

My heart starts to pound as I watch their exchange.

Their family.

The dream of my own family someday was ripped away, my heart stomped on and pulverized with five-inch stiletto heels. That picture perfect future I once saw so vividly is now dark and full of uncertainty. I hurt, ache actually, for Josh. His touch, his laugh, his love. I want that back. I want *him* back.

But that'll never happen.

He's not coming back.

Then I feel Nick's hand on my lower back, and just his touch offers so much strength and comfort. It honestly makes me feel like

I *can* do this, even though I have no idea what is on the horizon. Maybe – just maybe – with him by my side, it won't be so scary to think about the "next."

We're both quiet as we make our way down the hall and toward the exit. After turning the corner and heading to the elevator, a door on the left opens quickly, and my grandparents spill out.

"Oh, Meggy! Here, this storage closet is open for business," she says, making my brain bleed.

"Grandma! You're at a hospital," I chastise, giving her my best stern look.

"Oh, knock it off. We may be in a hospital, but we're in the maternity ward. You know, where the babies are born? You do know where babies come from, right? Do I need to get out the diagram again?" she asks.

"No, no, not necessary."

"Diagram?" Nick asks, his eyes lighting with humor.

"Yes, it was quite detailed. Orvie stayed up two nights making sure that diagram was anatomically correct. Not all penises are the same size, you know," she says to Nick.

"I've heard," he chuckles.

"It's okay if you're on the small side, Nicholas," she says, her eyes dropping to Nick's crotch. "But something tells me you don't have that problem, do you?"

Nick chokes on air. "No, ma'am. I don't have that problem at all," he replies, laughter laced in his voice.

"I didn't think so. You look like a man who's packing a decent sized meat-club. I have an eye for these things, you know." Grandma nods repeatedly.

"I bet you do."

"Come on, Emmie. Let's grab a bite to eat. I'm starving," Grandpa says, taking my Grandma by the hand.

"Engaging in *the sex* always makes him hungry," Grandma whispers as she turns his way. "Let's head home to eat dinner. Brian is going to Jaime's for a while. I bet we have plenty of time for another pickle tickle."

A gasp slips from my mouth and I swear my jaw hits the ground. You'd think I was used to their sexual banter, but I'm not. I'm never prepared.

"I'll take a pill," Grandpa assures with a kiss on her forehead as they shuffle off to the elevator.

We stand there for a few more moments and watch them step onto the car. "Are we catching the elevator?" Nick asks.

"Nope, we'll wait for the next one. I don't trust them not to start rubbing…things."

"Good point."

Together, we stand there and wait as the door to the elevator closes, sending my grandparents down to the ground floor. After we wait a few more minutes, I finally walk over and push the button for the car. Inside, neither of us speaks as we start to move downward two floors.

Nick reaches for my hand, wrapping his large, warm hand around mine and bringing it to his lips. "I was thinking, maybe you'd like to come over tonight. I can make dinner," he suggests.

"I like dinner," I reply casually.

"I suspected as much. Then maybe afterward, we can watch a movie or some television."

"What do you know, I like movies."

"Good to know. Then I thought we could wrap up our sleepover with a pickle tickle," he says, his hazel eyes lighting up like a Christmas tree.

"What a coincidence. I really, *really* like pickle tickles," I state boldly as I wrap my arms around his chest and plaster my body against his. He's hard against my lower stomach, as he grips my ass and grinds against me. At the rate we're going, we'll be lucky to make it to dinner.

"Me too, Meggy Pie. Me too."

Chapter Twenty-Four

Nick

We're walking side-by-side, her eyes lighting up in that way I haven't seen in so very long. When she smiles, her entire face illuminates and I feel almost invincible. Like I can do anything – *will* do anything – for this woman.

Suddenly, we're walking down an alley.

Where are we?

Meghan is still talking and smiling, but something feels…off to me.

Suddenly, she's pulling away. I try to hang on to her hand, but it's no use. I just can't keep my grip on her.

She spins around, looking, searching for me. "Nick?" she panics, the whites of her eyes visible, even in the darkness.

"I'm here," I reassure her, trying frantically to find her hand once more.

Our eyes connect, and all feels right again. But suddenly, she looks fearful once more. "Josh? Josh? No, Josh! Don't leave!" she hollers into the darkness, my heart breaking from her angst, her tears.

I glance around and spy the familiar light in my room, and suddenly realize where I am. The sheet is tugged against my naked body. Meghan is there, thrashing in her sleep, calling out for the man who is no longer here.

"Josh!"

Taking her in my arms, I pull her close, trying to gently wake her from her dreams. I swear you can hear my heart pounding in my chest for miles. "Shhhhh," I whisper, placing a tender kiss on her temple. "You're having a dream," I tell her, feeling the moment she wakes with a start.

"Nick?" she asks, gasping for air.

"It's me, honey. I'm here." My heart cracks open, bleeding a little bit for her – and for me. But I try to push aside the hurt I feel at her calling out someone else's name, and focus on helping her breathe deep and calm down.

She's silent for what feels like an hour, even though in reality, it's only a couple of minutes. Her gasps slowly even out, but her hold on me doesn't loosen. Her hands are around my arms, her body tucked against mine. Every so often she snuggles in closer, like she just can't get close enough.

"I have dreams," she finally says in the darkness. I try to remain relaxed, but I know my body tenses. I can't help it.

"Do you want to talk about them?" I ask, gently rubbing her hair and swiping it away from her sweaty forehead.

She takes a deep breath. "I've never talked about them."

Releasing my own breath, I kiss her temple. "It's okay. You don't have to."

She lies beside me for several long seconds before speaking again. "It's always the same dream. Most nights. I've had it since he died."

Again, I remain quiet, not really sure if she's ready to tell me about it. Honestly, not really sure I'm ready to hear it.

"It's the hospital. Every night, I'm right back in the hospital, where my dad is walking me down the hallway and into the ER." I feel the tears fall on my arm and chest before I hear the sniffle. "He's lying on the gurney. There's so much blood and he's so swollen that I can hardly recognize him." She chokes on her sob, gripping my arms so tight I'm sure I'll have bruised nail marks from her hold, but I don't care.

I pull her even closer, her arms wrapping around my body. She's shaking, but I'm not sure if it's from the crying or the memories.

"He was in and out of consciousness, but when I walked in, he held out his hand. There was so much defeat in his eyes. He slowly brought it to his lips, which were cracked open, and he said... he..." She pulls away and looks directly into my eyes. "He said I was the love of his life." Her bottom lip trembles, and all I want to do is hold her until the pain stops. I want to take every ounce of hurt she feels and carry it as if it were my own.

She takes a deep breath. "He said I was the love of his life, but...that he wasn't mine." Her voice drops almost to the point I can't hear her.

"He knew he was going to die, didn't he?" she asks, begging for me to answer.

"I don't know, honey. Maybe. He wanted you to know that if he didn't survive the accident, that you were the best part of his life. That you were the one he loved most in this world." I can't help it, tears well up in my own eyes.

"He knew and was telling me goodbye. He made me promise him that I'd live. It was the hardest promise I've ever made."

I nod, not really able to say words. She falls back onto my chest and cries.

"I didn't go visit him Sunday. I always go on Sunday afternoons to the cemetery, but I missed it."

"Because of the babies coming."

"Yeah. But do you know what? I didn't even realize it until now that I didn't go. It was like…life just moved forward without me even noticing. Does that make me a horrible person?"

"Hell no, it doesn't. It means you're moving forward, one step at a time. They always say there's no timeline for grief and we all process and deal with it in different ways."

"Yeah," she says, exhaling against my chest.

"Did I ever tell you that I talked to him right before he died?" I ask softly, this particular memory coming back to me suddenly. I'm not sure if I'm right in telling her or not, but there's no going back now.

I feel her shake her head against my chest as she pushes up once more, her eyes meeting mine. "You didn't."

"It was that Friday; the day before the accident. I remember because he came to the office to take you to lunch. You were wrapping up with a patient, so he hung around, by the back room. I saw him there and went over to say hello. We chatted about the severe storms that were supposed to be coming in that weekend and it was one of your sisters' nights.

"I don't even remember how we got on the subject, but he thanked me for giving you a steady job and being a good boss and friend. I tried to brush him off when he stepped forward, kinda close so that no one could hear." I swallow over the lump that has formed in my throat, but I keep my eyes trained on her misty ones.

"He made me promise him that I'd always be there for you. At first I thought it was a little odd and maybe a touch dramatic, but now? I don't know. Maybe he was just making sure you had a big enough circle of friends to help catch you if you fall."

She sniffles, and keeps her eyes trained on mine. "He was a good person. The best."

I nod in agreement. "He was. And he loved you completely."

"I loved him too," she whispers.

"And that's okay, honey. You're allowed to still love him. I just want you to keep that heart open, okay? Share it with anyone and everyone. You're an amazing woman, and you deserve the world."

The tears fall once more, but I can see the smile on her lips moments before they meet mine. The kiss is slow and gentle. I let her set the pace this time. Her sweet lips coax mine open, and her tongue slides inside my mouth, tasting and tempting me. I slide my hands around and grab her ass as she climbs on top of me, straddling my waist. My cock is already rigid and ready to play, but I keep control over myself and hold as still as possible.

Her hands explore my chest, my sides, my hips. She slides her pussy against my cock, leaving a trail of wetness behind. I can't help it. I groan.

Meghan kisses me again, this one more urgent and a bit frantic, like she can't get close enough or...well, just enough. I know the feeling all too well. My hands come up to her head, threading into her long hair. The kiss becomes one of necessity, like air or sleep. It's vital to our survival.

"Make love to me, Nick," she whispers tenderly against my lips.

Who am I to deny her?

Reaching for my nightstand drawer, she stops my hand. "I'm clean. I promise. You're the only one I've been with since…Josh."

My heart pounds in my chest. "I'm clean too."

"I trust you."

She raises up, shifting her hips until she's directly above my cock. Taking it in her hand, she slowly starts to lower herself on my dick, stealing my breath and my sanity. "Fuck," I moan, trying to bite back the desire threatening to take over, as my cock is completely engulfed in her warm, wet heat.

Meghan gasps when she's fully seated, her eyes wide and she looks down at me. My body is begging me to move, but I hold out. I don't move until she's ready. And when she moves? Holy shit, does she move. She slowly moves up before sliding back down. It's a torturously slow pace, but the feelings that transpire punch me square in the gut. Her eyes are so trusting, so alive, so free.

"You feel so good," she whispers as she keeps up her agonizingly deliberate pace.

My body is tense, taut like an electric wire, as she seductively moves and grinds on me. "You're killing me," I mumble, moving my hands from her hips to her hands, holding them to give her leverage.

She starts to move with a bit more urgency now. Up and down, rocking her hips and grinding against my pelvis. I can feel her starting to tighten around me, gripping my cock firmly. Meghan becomes more vocal as she takes what she wants, and the view – the sound – is spectacular.

When she finally lets go, all I can do is lie there and watch. Lie there and fall deeper in love with her. It's euphoric and addictive, and I haven't even gotten off yet.

Instead of letting myself go with her, I roll her over and position myself between her thighs. "My turn," I growl just before burying myself to the hilt. She pulses around me, driving me wild, and digs her nails into my back.

"Yes," she moans, tilting her hips upward and giving me perfect access.

My pace is a bit faster than hers as I chase my release. Needing to touch her, I take her hands in my own, I hold them above her head, our fingers linked. Her breasts bounce with each thrust as I feel that familiar tingle at the base of my spine. I'm so close, and when my eyes connect with hers, I can tell she is too.

I'm determined now.

She's coming again.

I tilt my pelvis and thrust hard, grinding against her. She tightens around me a second time, gripping me from within. My eyes connect with hers and I feel it. I feel it clear down to my soul. She's the one I'm supposed to love. She's my forever everything.

And maybe, just maybe, I'm meant to be hers.

I hold her gaze as she lets go for a second time, riding out the waves of pleasure that filter across her face. My own release is imminent, there's no stopping it. Her name spills from my lips as my orgasm rips through my body, but I never take my eyes off hers. I can't. I'm lost in a trance. I'm lost in her.

My limbs start to shake and practically give out on me, and I cover her body with my own. We're both warm and sweaty, but I could get used to the way she feels against my skin for the rest of my life.

I want to say something, but this moment doesn't call for words. We just expressed ourselves with our bodies. No, she may not be in love with me, but she trusts me to cherish and protect her, and honestly, that's about all I can ask for right now.

Someday, maybe we'll be more – maybe I'll be able to tell her how much I love her.

But right now? I'm not taking the risk of sending her running the other way. She's here – in my arms – and that's right where I want her. So if that other stuff has to wait until she's ready, then it's a damn good thing I'm a patient man.

She's worth the wait.

Chapter Twenty-Five

Meghan

The summer begins to fly by. We visit the beach, which happens to be one of our favorite hangouts, for sunset dinners and walks on the sandy shore. He holds my hand and alternates between kisses on my knuckles and those on my temple. (Those are my favorite.) It's been perfect. Spending my time with Nick has been perfect. We alternate time between his place and mine, and often travel to work together. If anyone at the office notices, they don't say. We don't flaunt our relationship, but we're not exactly hiding it either. Why would I want to hide him? He's caring, generous, and pretty damn good with *the sex*.

That makes me giggle.

"What are you laughing at?" Lexi asks from across the altar. We're decorating the church for AJ and Sawyer's wedding tomorrow afternoon.

"I don't know what you're talking about," I reply to my youngest sister.

"Whatevs. You have that pleasantly sexed glaze in your eyes," she sasses with a big grin.

"Let me see. I know all of the just-had-sex signs," Grandma says, pushing her way to where I stand. She looks me over from head to toe before declaring, "Yep. She just had *the sex*."

"Knock it off," I chastise, rolling my eyes.

"No, I totally see it. You're practically glowing!" Grandma exclaims.

"First off, I'm pretty sure you're not supposed to talk about *the sex* while standing in a church, and second, I'm not glowing. I'm sweating. AJ picked the hottest freaking month of the year to get married, Grandma."

"That's because my groom is smokin'," AJ replies with a grin.

"I don't see how that has anything to do with the fact that I'm going to have swoob marks on my dress during your wedding photos," Jaime replies, pointing to her enormous boobs.

"Those puppies practically need license plates, Jaimers. They're as big as Buicks," Payton teases as she hangs floral pieces from the pews.

"Right? And Ryan can't keep his hands off them! But I think they're annoying. They're either leaking milk all the time or gathering boob sweat underneath," Jaime grumbles.

"We all have boob sweat, Jaime," Lexi counters.

"Yes, but your boobs barely grew with this baby. Mine went up two bra sizes. Two!" she exclaims loudly. "And my husband is constantly horny and grabbing them!"

Suddenly, a throat clears behind us. We all turn to see the red-faced pastor of the church looking down at the ground. "Well, I was just checking in on you. It looks like you're doing well with the decorating. If you need anything, please don't hesitate to ask. I'll be hiding – I mean working in my office," he says hurriedly before turning and practically sprinting from the sanctuary.

"Way to go, Jaime. You scared away my pastor with your huge boobs," AJ rebukes.

"See? Even a straight man of the cloth is afraid," Jaime whines.

"But not Ryan. He thinks you're sexy," Abby reminds her, helping Payton hang the last of the silk flowers.

"That's because he hasn't had sex in almost six weeks," Jaime says.

"You're waiting? Like the full six weeks?" Lexi asks, her eyes wide.

"Hell yes, I am. I don't want to get knocked up like you did!"

Lexi narrows her eyes at our sister. "We're using condoms this time."

"So you're not waiting the six weeks?" Jaime asks, dumbfounded by this revelation.

"Hell no. Have you seen how sexy my husband is, Jaime? I can barely wait two weeks, let alone six," Lexi replies with a wicked grin.

"You dirty slut," Payton adds, shaking her head.

"Yep," Lexi says before busting out laughing.

Jaime still stands there, her beautiful daughter sleeping in the carrier next to her. "I'm having sex. Weddings make everyone horny. He's so getting some tomorrow night," Jaime says, glancing down at Amelia. "You're going to have to be extra good tomorrow night, Princess. Mommy and Daddy need to spend about thirty minutes alone."

"Thirty minutes? And neither one of you have had sex in six weeks? Try five minutes," I tease, making my sisters laugh.

"Oh, there has been other stuff," Jaime rebuffs.

"I love the other stuff. Grandpa is a pro," Grandma chimes in, making all of our faces turn from laughter to sour.

We all work silently for a few minutes, adding the final touches to the church. It didn't require much decoration. A few candles here, some flowers there, and it was good to go.

"Oh, I almost forgot," I start, turning and grabbing everyone's attention. "You all know Dad is bringing a date to the wedding, right?" I ask gently, gauging their reactions.

AJ quickly nods her head. "He came over a few weeks back and asked Sawyer and I if we were okay with him bringing someone to the wedding."

When I glance at the others, they seem shocked. "He is?" Abby asks, not really looking upset, but just surprised.

"He is. He told me too, a few weeks back. I told him we all wanted him happy and if he was dating someone, well, we support that," I add.

"Definitely," Payton says as she sits down on the first pew. She places a hand on her still-flat stomach. "I'm really happy for him."

"Me too," Abby says, sitting next to Payton.

"It's a big step," I say, voicing everyone's feelings aloud.

"It is. But I don't want him to be alone forever," Jaime says, tears welling in her eyes. "Mom wouldn't want that either."

"No, she wouldn't," Lexi says, walking over to where I stand. We all seem to congregate at the first pew.

"It's time," AJ whispers, as tears blur my vision. Everyone nods their heads.

After several seconds, Grandma walks over and joins us. "If it makes you feel any better, she's a lovely woman," she offers with her own sad smile.

"You've met her?" Payton asks, wiping a stray tear from her cheek.

"Yes," Grandma says with a warm smile. "He brought her over for dinner last week."

"Wow, really?" Abby asks.

"Yes, really. He told Orvie and I about her a few weeks back, and I offered to cook dinner. We had an enjoyable evening. She really is a lovely woman, and I think my Trisha would have like her too. I really believe that." I see a few tears slip from Grandma's eyes, and I wrap an arm around her.

"He has been alone for too long," she continues. "It's time for him to enjoy someone who makes him feel alive again. We want him to be happy." She glances my way when she says it, letting me know she's also talking to me. I give her a smile, letting her know I'm working on it too.

"He has been," Jaime says, clearing her throat. "I'm actually really excited to meet her."

"Me too," Abby says.

"Me three," AJ adds.

"If she makes him happy, then I'm happy," I reply.

"Agreed. It's time," Payton offers.

Lexi exhales. "It's going to be weird, but I want him happy," she says honestly.

"It will be, at first," Grandma adds as she steps into the center of the circle. "This was a very big step, and don't think he did it lightly. Deep down, he worries you'll think he's replacing your mother."

"I don't think that," I tell her.

"None of us do," Payton assures.

We all step forward, surrounding Grandma in the middle, and wrap our arms around one another. We form a circle of love, friendship, and support.

"He has six amazing, supportive daughters, who only want the best for him. He knows that. Your dad has put you all first since your mom got sick and passed, but now it's his time," Grandma says, wrapping her arms around us all.

"It is," Payton adds. "And I can't wait to meet her."

"Me either." And I didn't realize how much I want to meet her until this moment. Until I've talked to my sisters, and know that my grandparents have met and like her. Now, I'm ready.

* * *

"Can I have everyone's attention?" Sawyer says, standing in front of the room, his future wife by his side, wearing a short white dress and a big smile. I can't help but grin at the picture of perfection they make as a couple, and in less than twenty-four hours, will make as man and wife.

"AJ and I wanted to take the opportunity to thank you all for coming this evening. Both of our families, many of which traveled quite a ways to be with us this weekend. My former teammates, who'll be heading out early Sunday morning to catch up with the team for a Sunday night game. Her sisters who spent the day decorating the church and reception hall for tomorrow's wedding."

He glances down at my sister with nothing but love and adoration in his eyes. "The night I met this beautiful woman was the night my life changed forever. And I'm not just talking about the fact she vomited on my shoes," Sawyer says, making the room fill with laughter. "I was hooked on her smile, on her grace, on her sass, and her beautiful heart. I'm a better man just by knowing her and hope to be the best husband and provider for her and someday our eventual family." He turns to face her, my sister's eyes filling with tears. "Thank you for making me the happiest bastard on the planet tonight. Thank you for loving me and walking through this life by my side. I love you, Alison Jane," he whispers moments before she throws herself into his arms and kisses him soundly on the lips.

The entire room erupts into applause. I clap from my seat, dropping my head onto Nick's shoulder. He's wearing a pair of black Dockers with a sage green button-down shirt and black tie. His sleeves are rolled up to his forearms, in that sexy way that men do. Every time I glance his way, I practically drool on my chin just taking in his gorgeous appearance tonight.

And don't get me started on tomorrow. He's wearing a suit, which is basically the equivalent to catnip for women.

My body is already on fire at the thought.

We just finished eating, which was a delicious surf and turf dinner. Sawyer's family tried to take care of dinner tonight, but Sawyer wouldn't have it. AJ told us that they paid for the rehearsal dinner at his first wedding, which is tradition, and he refused to let them foot the bill the second time around. AJ and Sawyer picked The Seaside Restaurant for tonight's festivities, and had rented out the entire upper deck, which sports an amazing view of the Bay.

"It's been a while since I've been here," Nick says, glancing around at the lanterns hanging from the deck and the pergola-style overhang.

"Me either," I reply, following his gaze and finding AJ and Sawyer dancing under the lights on the far end of the deck. He holds her possessively and protectively against his large frame, slipping his fingers into the long waves of her hair.

Not too far away, Dean holds Bri in his arm and wraps the other around Payton, where it comes to rest on her belly. She looks up at him and gives him a blinding smile that could probably be visible from space. Payton reaches down and links her fingers in Dean's, covering her lower abdomen. Brielle laughs at something her dad says before dropping her hand down and placing it on top of theirs on Payton's belly.

Lexi holds baby Stella, while Linkin has a twin in each arm. He bends down and kisses his five-week-old daughter on the top of her head before offering his lips to his wife. She smiles against his, mumbling something that's probably dirty. He laughs, offers her a wink, and goes back to playing with Hudson and Hemi. Yet, he never leaves Lexi's side.

Levi pulls Abby into his arms and twirls her around on the dance floor. Her laughter filters above the conversations around us as she wraps her arms around his neck, her feet lifting off the ground. Levi pulls her close and they gently sway to the beat of the song. When I see his lips moving near her ear, I know he's singing to her. The smile on her face is her tell.

Ryan sits at the table across from us, holding baby Amelia. He has one hand on her tiny back and the other propping up her butt. She's out – mouth hanging open and sawing logs. Jaime sits beside them, one hand on Ryan's forearm and the other running soft circles over the top of their daughter's head. She gazes into Ryan's eyes, their entire world wrapped up in each other and their child.

I don't even realize I'm crying until Nick swipes a tear from my cheek. The pad of his thumb is warm against my skin, and I find myself leaning into his touch just a little bit more.

"Come on, honey. Let's go for a walk," he says, standing up and offering me his hand. I take it without hesitation, and together, we head toward the beach.

Chapter Twenty-Six

Nick

The evening is about perfect. The weather, the dinner, the ambiance. It's all setting the stage for an epic, memorable night. I can feel it in my bones.

I take her hand in mine and lead her down the stairs to the beach. Music wafts from the deck above as we walk toward the water. The wind blows her hair, making my fingers twitch to touch it. She's wearing a dark blue dress that hits just below her knees and dips dangerously low at her chest. When she opened the door tonight, I almost swallowed my tongue. Not to mention almost begged her to follow me inside so I could make her scream three ways to Sunday.

"It's a beautiful night," she says, gazing out as the waves crash on the shore.

"Stunning," I reply, though I'm not referring to the night, as much as I am the woman.

"Tonight was perfect. I can't wait for tomorrow."

"It should be a beautiful day," I add, keeping her hand tucked in mine.

"You're sure you don't mind sitting with the guys behind my dad and grandparents?" she asks.

"I'll sit where ever you want me to sit," I tell her, bringing her hand to my lips. "Just as long as I get to dance with you afterward."

She stops and turns to gaze up at me. Her eyes are smiling, along with her seductive pink lips. Lips that I crave more than air itself. As the breeze gently blows her air, I take her in my arms, my lips finally meeting hers. There's a fire within that kiss, an unbridled passion that erupts whenever she's near. My tongue teases and tastes her, my arms feeling complete as they wrap around and draw her body near.

The kiss is almost magical. Yeah, I said it. Standing there, on the beach, with the water washing over my shoes and tickling her bare feet, I let go of everything and just…feel. Feel the wind, feel the water, feel her body, and feel her lips. And most importantly, feel the happiness and love that only she delivers. I've been in love before – once with a college girlfriend, and years later with Collette. But this? This is…

Magical.

Suddenly, I need to tell her. This overwhelming desire to share everything with her fills my being. It's not just the night or the kiss. It's the fact that I love this woman more than I've ever loved anyone – that I see her so completely standing by my side, much the way Sawyer referred to AJ tonight. I see her so vividly that the idea of her *not* being there only makes my heart ache and my soul cry.

That prospect steals my breath almost as much as this very kiss does.

Pulling back, I stare down at Meghan. Her lips are wet and bee-stung and her eyes sparkling. "Wow," she whispers, a soft smiling teasing her lips.

"It's you," I reply, running my hand along her hairline and pushing those little fly-aways from her forehead.

"What's me?" she asks, her arms resting comfortably on my hips.

"Everything. Everything is you." I know I should stop, but I can't. I *can't*. I have two months worth of feelings for this woman that are suddenly bubbling to the surface, dying to get out. So, I take a deep breath and start.

"I've always respected and enjoyed you. First, as my employee and friend, and now as the woman I'm in a relationship with. This thing between us," I continue, waving my hand between her chest and mine, "has transpired into something I wasn't expecting. I wasn't expecting...you."

Her eyes glisten, but I don't stop talking. "I wasn't expecting to need you as much as I do or love you as much as I do. I wasn't expecting to...fall in love with you." Those tears in her eyes fall, and that smile drops from her face. "I love you, Meghan."

There.

Said it.

The weight on my chest lifts and my heart starts to calm.

I've told her how I feel, how much she means to me.

What I wasn't expecting was her reply.

"You can't love me," she says, those tears ripping though my chest and stabbing at my heart. "Please don't love me, Nick. People who love me die."

What?

"Wait, what?"

"You can't love me!" she says, louder and with more conviction. "Loving me is bad, very bad. And I don't want that for you, Nick," she adds, stepping back out of my arms.

"Meghan," I start, at a loss for words suddenly.

"No!" she demands, adamantly shaking her head. "You don't love me!" she insists, those fucking tears ripping me to shreds.

"I do," I assure, taking a step toward her and reaching for her hand.

But she pulls away, shaking. "People who love me die. I'm tainted. I don't want that for you, Nick. You deserve to love someone who's capable of loving you back."

"You're not capable?" I ask gently, taking another small step in her direction.

"No. I'm not able to love. I loved once and he left. I killed him," she whispers, her eyes turning dark and hard.

"Honey, you didn't do that. You had nothing to do with what happened to Josh," I reassure.

She growls, frustrated, and turns away. "Everything was fine, Nick. Everything was great. Why did you have to say it?"

Her back is to me, but I still feel the weight of her words. "Because it's true. I said it because I'm in love with you. Have been for weeks now, if not much longer."

She shakes her head. Turning and facing me, she looks me straight in the eye. "Then this is over."

My heart pounds in my chest so loud I'm sure they can hear it at the party over the music and laughter. Over the happiness. "Meghan, just because my feelings for you are the way they are doesn't mean we have to stop seeing each other. In fact, it doesn't mean anything has to change at all," I softly declare.

"Everything has changed," she states, her eyes hard with tears. "If you love me, something will happen. Something bad, and I can't, Nick. I can't...go through that again. It hurts too much, and if I lost you, I don't think I'd survive it."

This time, her slow tears turn into agonizing sobs. I move toward her, wrapping my arms around her and drawing her close. She's shaking and crying, her tears quickly soaking through my dress shirt. I keep one hand on her back and the other I run down the back of her head, trying to convey as much comfort and support as humanly possible through just a touch.

She's been hurt so badly already – and I'm the stupid idiot who didn't think about that before declaring his undying love. The last man she loved is no longer here, and the thought of someone else loving her is terrifying.

I get it.

But it doesn't stop my feelings.

Suddenly, she pushes back and swipes harshly at her cheeks. "No, it's over. I don't love you, Nick. I can't."

Before I can even open my mouth to reply, she turns and runs up the beach, leaving me standing at the shore. I watch her go until she disappears around the side of the restaurant. What the fuck just happened? One minute I'm confessing my love and spilling my feelings, and the next she's breaking everything off and running away.

I'm the biggest fucking idiot on the planet.

Not for loving her. No, there's nothing wrong with loving that woman. She owns my heart already, even after only a few months. But for just blurting it out the way I did, without even thinking about how it would make her feel.

My feet start to move through the sand as I run toward the party. I fly up the stairs and begin frantically searching for Meghan. Jaime and Payton each give me a look, one that lets me know they can tell something's wrong, but I don't go to them. I don't have time. I need to find Meghan.

Before it's too late.

Chapter Twenty-Seven

Meghan

"I need your keys," I say quickly, trying not to let on that something's so very wrong, but of course, Dad doesn't buy it.

"Why? What's wrong?" he asks, pulling them from his pocket.

"Nothing. I just need to leave for a second."

"A second?" he asks, clearly taking in my tear-stained face and my frantic breathing.

"Maybe longer. Can you get a ride home?" I ask.

"Of course, but are you okay? Did something happen?"

"Something…did. I can't talk about it. I need to go."

"Is it Nick? Did he do something?" he asks as he places the keys in my hand.

I take a deep breath. "He didn't do anything. He's just…wrong."

Dad gives me a once-over. "Okay. The key to the house is there too, if you need it. I'll catch a ride with Grandma and Grandpa," he says, wrapping his hand around mine. "Everything's going to be okay, Meggy. I promise." He pulls me into his arms and gives me a hug. I want to stay, and I almost do. Wrapped in his arms gives off that same false sense of security I get when Nick does it. I feel safe and secure.

But it's a lie.

"I'll get your car back to you," I tell him, pulling away.

"I'm not worried about the car. I'm worried about you."

"I'll be fine." Deep breath. "I'll be fine." I'm not sure if I'm trying to convince him…or myself.

Probably both.

But Dad sees through it. If anyone can see past the hurt and fake front, it's him.

I glance back at the water's edge, but don't see anything – or anyone. "Go. I'll make sure he's okay," Dad offers. "And when you're ready, he'll be waiting."

Blinking back the tears, I reply, "I don't think he will."

Dad places a kiss on my forehead. "Trust me, honey. He'll be waiting."

When I look at his eyes, I see his love – that unmistakable, unbreakable love that only a father has for his daughter.

Except, that's not true.

I've seen that look before.

Twice.

And one's dead because of me.

I quickly squeeze Dad's hand and turn to the door. I move quickly, without making eye contact with anyone, and head toward the parking lot. Inside his car, I'm wrapped in comfort and memories. I stick the key in the ignition, and slowly pull out of the parking spot. As I move onto the road, I can't help but glance to the water. Will he come after me? But I don't see him.

It's probably for the best.

I drive without a destination, yet know exactly where I'm headed. I pass the cemetery where my fiancé now rests and head out of town. When I reach the quiet country road, I turn off, and for the first time, wonder if I'm making a mistake.

It's late.

They're probably in bed sleeping.

But I keep driving, ignoring my conscience that tells me I should call first.

I pull off the road and into their driveway. There are several lights still on, so I know I haven't woken them up. As I shut off the car and open the door, a petite figure steps out through the front door and onto the porch. "Meghan?" she asks, her voice exactly the same as I remember.

Shutting the car door, I take a step toward the woman I once considered my *other* mom. "Hi, Mrs. Harrison," I whisper, my voice suddenly shaky and filled with emotions.

Josh's mom takes a step forward, and then another. She comes down the stairs and stands before me, tears welling in the eyes that look so much like her son's. Her late son's. Without saying a word, she wraps her arms around me, enveloping me in warmth and familiarity. As soon as she does, it's like the dam breaks. The tears and the pain just burst from my soul.

"Come inside," she offers soothingly, placing her hand on my lower back and guiding me up the stairs.

When I step inside the house I haven't been to for more than two years, I'm assaulted with memories. Christmas dinners, birthday celebrations, random afternoon visits. I glance at the couch that Josh and I used to sit on together and notice it's different. The brown leather one that was so worn and comfortable is now replaced with a brighter blue piece that fits the ambiance of the room. The recliner that Josh's dad used to sit in to watch the Sunday afternoon football game is now beige and on the opposite side of the room.

"You changed the room," I say aloud, mostly to myself.

"I did. It was time. That old stuff was the furniture we bought when Josh was little. The chair would recline well enough, but it took an act of Congress to get the stupid thing back down again," she replies with a smile.

The old photograph on the mantle catches my attention. I've seen it before. So many times. Josh's photo from graduation. He's smiling brightly that same smile that I remember so well, wearing a black cap and gown with a green and yellow sash around his neck. I don't even realize I've approached the photo until I'm there, touching it. I run a finger down his face, remembering how familiar that particular face once was.

But when I close my eyes, it's not Josh's face I see.

And that makes me feel like the worst person on the planet. I should be locked up with the murderers on death row. Instead of picturing Josh, I picture…Nick.

Guilt riddles my entire body, weighing it down with a thousand bags of sand.

I glance over at the other photos. There's one of Josh and his parents at their anniversary dinner a few years back. I took that photo. There's one of a young Josh riding his bike and offering a big toothless grin for the camera.

There's one of him and me. I remember the day so vividly. We were at Lucky's after a sisters' night. My eyes are bright (probably from too much alcohol) and our arms wrapped around each other. I'm smiling for the camera, but not Josh. He's looking and smiling at me. I reach out and touch that photo too, as if somehow it'll help me touch the memory. Touch him.

"He sent me that picture the day after you took it."

"He did?" I ask, turning back to the woman behind me. She's smiling, but there's so much sadness in the gesture. It's that reminder that I'm not the only one who lost him on that cold, rainy February night.

Mrs. Harrison nods and looks at the photo. "He did. It was one of the last ones taken before…" her words drop off, but I know what she was about to say. Before the accident. Before he died.

Slowly nodding my head, I turn away from the photo, away from the painful memories, and face her. "I'm sorry I haven't been by to see you much." Guilt fills my soul once more as I think about this wonderful couple who lost their son, but essentially lost me too. I came over a couple of times after the accident, but stopped because it was too painful to be here without him.

"Oh, don't be sorry, sweet girl. I know it was probably very difficult for you," she says, pointing to the couch, while she takes a seat next to me. "Why do you think I don't come over to the house?"

Her question rings loudly with me. "I had a hard time going home those first few nights," I confess. "But when I did, I just felt…closer to him. Then, for a while, I stayed there because I was waiting for him to come home. Like he'd walk through the door and laugh, telling me he wasn't really gone."

The tears are falling in earnest before I realize it. "After the first few months…" It's hard to swallow. "I realized he wasn't coming home, and it made it hard to be there. So I started joining groups and doing activities that would keep me busy. Things that would keep me away from the house. I haven't cleaned it out yet," I confess, my voice barely over a whisper. "It's all still there, waiting for him to come home. But he's not coming home."

It was the first time I really spoke that aloud, even though everyone probably already knew it.

"I slept in his room for the first six months after he passed," Mrs. Harrison admits, taking my hand in hers. "So I understand, probably better than most."

Nodding, I look down at our hands. "I'm sorry."

"For what, dear?" she asks.

"It was my fault. Everything. The accident. His…you know, it was my fault," I state, sagging into the couch.

"What on earth are you talking about? Nothing that happened to Josh was your fault," she insists, her pretty features seeming genuinely perplexed.

"But he was coming to see me. I was the reason he was out on the road that night," I recall.

"Josh was on that road because he wanted to be. He wanted to be with you. He would have followed you anywhere," she assures with a soft voice, void of any anger.

"Exactly!" I declare, my hands starting to shake. "He was on that road because of *me*."

"He was on that road because he loved you. Nothing is guaranteed, sweet girl. Not life, not forever, not even love. Love is the ultimate risk, and when you love someone, you risk everything. He knew that risk, and took it because he loved you. He loved you until the day he died, and when he died, he went knowing that he lived a happy life. Do you know why?" I can't breathe, let alone answer, so I shake my head. "Because he loved you, and when he died, he died with your love. You gave him the ultimate gift, sweetheart. He loved and was loved. That's all I ever wanted for him. We don't blame you, Meghan. We never did and never will. It was an accident. It took me many months and countless hours of therapy, but I know that now. It was his time, and even though I'd rather him be here with us, I know he's in good hands, waiting for me when my time is up, as he will be for you. What happened to Josh was not in your control any more than it was mine. Believe that, sweet girl. It wasn't your fault."

I break down hard, feeling a sense of relief wash over me. I've carried this incredible weight around for the last two plus years. I've blamed myself, and thought for sure everyone else did too, but to hear Mrs. Harrison not only admit that she doesn't hold me responsible, but that she appreciates the love I gave to her son, well, that's an incredible gift in itself.

"I loved him too. I will always love him," I tell her.

"I know," she replies, wiping her own tears before swiping the ones on my cheek, and giving me that smile. The motherly one I always appreciated when I was dating her son. "I know," she repeats with the slightest of head nods. "Okay," she says, clearing her throat and patting my hands. "Now tell me about the man."

If I wasn't surprised before, I damn sure am now. I glance her way, my eyes feeling like they're going to bug out of my head. I have no idea what to say, but my mind immediately goes to Nick, and the way I left him earlier.

"Don't act so surprised," Mrs. Harrison says with a chuckle. "It's a small town. People talk," she adds, shrugging her shoulders. "Tell me about him."

Suddenly, I'm as uncomfortable as a hooker in church. "Well, uh, what do you want to know?"

"Well, how about his name?"

"Nick. His name is Nick Adams."

"The dentist!" she exclaims, surprisingly happy by this revelation. "Not mine, but I've heard of him. You work for him, right?" she asks, returning to her serious state.

"Yes, but this thing between us, it's new." I don't know why I say it, other than to reassure her that what Nick and I have came way after Josh.

"Oh, I know, silly. I remember how you and Josh used to look at each other. Do you feel that way about Nick?" she asks. Why the hell must she ask the hard questions?

I don't have to think about it, because deep down, I already know my answer. I know how I feel for him. I've just been too scared to see it. "Yes, I think I do."

She smiles again, and this one isn't sad. It's hopeful and full of joy. "Good. I'm really happy to hear that, Meghan. I don't want you going through this life in the motions. I want to see you live, and yes, even love."

"But it almost feels…wrong. Like I'm letting go of Josh and replacing him with someone else."

Mrs. Harrison nods. "I get that, but what you need to know is that the heart has room for more than one love, Meg. Your heart can love one person, as well as another. One love is in your past, but that doesn't mean you won't carry him with you for the rest of your life. Loving another isn't a replacement. It's a privilege. To find two great loves in your lifetime is something wonderful, Meghan.

"I know I'm speaking for my son when I say...love. If you want to do his memory justice, then live your life and love. If you find happiness with this Nick, then grab onto it and don't let go. Because we have no guarantees in this life, sweetheart. Tomorrow isn't a promise, so hang on to today with both hands."

"Thank you," I choke out over the massive ball of emotions lodged firmly in my throat. "You have no idea how much I needed this."

She pats my hands again and says, "I think I did. I did because I needed this too. I've missed you," she confesses. "You were the daughter I never had."

"And you were like a mother to me. Thank you for that," I tell her sincerely.

We cry together for a few more minutes, before we hear footsteps on the stairs. Josh's dad comes into view, looking like the spitting image of his son. My heart starts to pound as he approaches, and I quickly stand up. "Meghan," he says softly with a smile. "How are you, honey?"

We end up talking for the next thirty minutes, and when I glance at the clock, I realize how late it's getting. "I should get going."

John and Angie walk me to the front door. "Please don't hesitate to stop by anytime, sweet girl. We've missed you," Angie says, wrapping me in a warm hug.

"Yes, please do. I'd happily warm up the barbecue for dinner," John says as his arms engulf me in a big, warm hug.

"Thank you. I will, I promise," I reply as I head through the front door, feeling much lighter than I did when I arrived.

"Oh, and Meghan?" Mrs. Harrison asks, stepping into her husband's arm and standing at his side. "Bring your Nick by sometime. We'd love to meet him."

I stand there, slightly dumbfounded, for probably too long. "Really?" My voice sounds hoarse, even to my own ears.

"Absolutely! I can show him how to barbecue a brisket," John adds with a smile. A smile that was his son's.

Angie nods in agreement. "Yes, we'd be honored to meet the man our Meghan has fallen in love with," she adds with a wink.

My heart starts to soar, and I can't stop the smile that spreads across my face. "I will. Thank you."

And I truly mean it.

Before I walk away, I do the one thing I know is necessary to finally move on: I take the ring off my finger. "Here," I whisper, holding the cherished piece of white gold in my hand, the moonlight reflecting off the diamond.

Angie glances down, her eyes filling with tears once more. "No."

"Yes," I insist. "It was your mother's ring. It should stay in the family."

She shakes her head, and slowly reaches for the ring Josh gave me – the one he asked his mother for when he was going to propose. "You are family," Angie insists.

"I know," I reply with a sad smile, "but I don't need it anymore."

They both seem to understand that this is a big moment for me. She takes the ring, gripping it tightly in her palm, and offers me another smile. We exchange hugs once more before I slowly make my way toward the car.

I wave before slipping inside. Suddenly, I'm overcome with the need to see Nick, to explain why I ran, and what I discovered along the way. What I was too scared to face, yet realized it with the one woman I never would have expected.

I need to see Nick.

But, I have one quick stop to make first.

Chapter Twenty-Eight

Nick

"I bet you're surprised to see me here," I say aloud, the breeze gently blowing warm July air. "I'm pretty damn surprised myself, if I'm being honest."

I glance down at the marble stone, the moonlight reflecting off the name.

Joshua David Harrison

"I know we weren't exactly friends, but I always knew you were a good guy. You've left some pretty big shoes to fill, and I'm not really sure I'll ever be able to step inside them. Not that I'm trying, though. I'm not really sure what I'm trying to do, honestly," I say to the stone, crouching down and touching the grass with my fingers. "I guess what I'm trying to say is that I fell in love with her, but you probably already knew that." I feel the wind pick up and blow my tie. "I fell so fucking hard I'm not sure I'll ever remember what it feels like to *not* love her."

I glance up and let the breeze just wash over my face. "But I fucked it up. I told her tonight, and she wasn't ready to hear it. She seems to think she's unlovable for some reason, but you and I both know that's far from the truth. If anyone knows how easy it is to love that woman, it's you.

"So I guess that's why I'm here. I thought maybe you should hear it from me, in person. But now I just feel silly because I'm here, talking to you, instead of continuing my search for her.

"Her dad told me she took his car. He also assured me that she'll be fine. I hope to God he's right because I'm not sure what I'd do if something happened to her. She has quickly become my everything."

Looking down at his name and the two dates below it, I take a deep breath and exhale slowly. "I'm scared she'll think I don't love her as much as you did." The words are out of my mouth before I have time to consider their meaning. I've never really thought about it before, but that doesn't make them any less true. "I'm terrified that I'll never be enough for her because you've shown her just how amazing life can be with someone you love.

"I'm not asking her to stop loving you. In fact, what I'm asking of her is the opposite. I'm asking for a little room in that big, beautiful heart of hers, you know? I want to share it with her, and you, because you were a part of her life for so many years. You were her future. But if given the chance, I want to be a part of that future, and show her that there's so much yet to live for. That she's worthy. I want to show her how much I love her, if she finds me worthy too."

Headlights reflect off of the trees and stones, drawing my attention to the drive that winds through the cemetery. I watch as the car draws near, eventually stopping behind mine. I recognize it immediately, and the sense of relief that washes over me is almost staggering.

Standing up, I turn and watch her exit the car. The headlights turn off after she walks a few feet in my direction. As she approaches, I see her smile. It's small and tentative, but it's there nonetheless, and I feel its power clear down to my toes.

"Hi," Meghan says as she approaches me.

"Hey." I have no idea what to say.

"I'm a little surprised to see you here," she confesses, glancing down at the stone beside me.

"I'm sure you weren't the only one," I suggest, making her laugh. She shrugs her shoulders and offers me a slightly bigger smile.

"I'm glad you're here, actually," she says stepping up beside me and facing Josh's headstone.

"You are?"

"I am," she replies, reaching for my hand and intertwining her fingers with mine. "I have something to say. To both of you."

Swallowing hard, I nod. "Okay."

She steps right up to the stone, but doesn't let go of my hand, forcing me to take a step closer with her. "Hey, Josh," she says, softly, reaching down with her left hand and touching the top of his stone. "I see you've met Nick," she adds, glancing over her shoulder and giving me a smile.

"Technically, we already knew each other."

"You did," she says with a nod. When she turns serious, I decide to keep my mouth shut and follow her lead. "I went to see your mom and dad tonight. It's been a while, which I'm sure you know too. The thought of seeing them without you has been almost unbearable, so I stayed away. Funny thing is your mom said pretty much the same thing to me.

"I told her how I've blamed myself for your accident," she says, and my entire body tenses. "And before you get all pissy with me and start to argue, I know now that it wasn't my fault. I think I've always known, but needed to focus all of my energy on something, on someone, so I chose me. But you know your mom, she wasn't having it," she adds with a chuckle.

"She let me have it and said a lot of stuff that made sense. We actually had a really nice talk. I needed it. I needed her." I hear her take a deep breath before she continues.

"We also talked about Nick," she says, which has me tensing all over again. She talked to Josh's mom about me? "She told me how happy she was that I had found someone who was able to look past my pain and hurt, someone who makes me smile and laugh again, someone who loves me. You can imagine how uncomfortable it got right then, but you know your mom. She wasn't letting me go without digging for the details.

"But do you know what? She made me realize so much too, Josh. She made me realize that I was in love with him too, but so terrified of getting hurt again that I pushed him away."

Wait. She loves me?

Meghan glances at me for a moment, tears swimming in her eyes, before turning back to the stone. "She reminded me that loving someone is the greatest gift in life, and I'd be doing myself a huge injustice if I didn't live. That I'd be doing your memory an even bigger injustice by not living the life you wanted for me. She told me you would want me to live, and yes, love again.

"Hearing her say those words brought it back to me. That night. When you told me I was the love of your life, but that you were not mine. You begged me to live.

"Well, I think you were wrong. You were the love of my life – my first love. But maybe you're not my last. Maybe I'm meant to love someone else," she says, squeezing my hand so hard I begin to lose circulation to my fingers. But I don't care. I don't move. I barely breathe.

"There is enough room in my heart for two. There's you, Josh. My first love. The man who taught me just how truly wonderful love can be," she says, before glancing at me. "And then there's Nick. My last love. The man I'm supposed to spend the rest of my days with." She chuckles, sniffling her nose and frantically wiping at tears with her left hand.

I turn her to face me.

"That is, if I didn't already fuck it up when I ran away from him," she says, her green eyes so bright in the moonlight.

"You didn't fuck it up. Actually, I was here telling Josh how badly I fucked it up," I say, catching a few tears with the pads of my thumbs.

"No," she says, anxiously shaking her head. "You spoke the truth, right?"

I nod.

"Then you didn't fuck anything up. I did," she insists.

"No, honey, you didn't. You were scared. I know that. But you don't have to be afraid anymore. You don't have to run from me. I want to help you. I want to stand with you when times get tough. I want to be your friend and your lover, who carries the burden when it gets too much. I want to be by your side," I tell her, wrapping my arm around her back and pulling her close.

"I want that too, and do you know why?" she asks, gazing up at me with big, wide eyes.

"Why?"

"Because I love you." I've never heard sweeter words in my life than having this woman in my arms, staring into my eyes, and saying them directly to me for the first time.

"I love you too," I reply, dipping my head down and kissing her soft lips. I link my fingers with hers and notice the change right away.

Pulling my lips from hers, I glance down and notice her left hand. Or more accurately, the fact that her hand is now ringless. "You took it off?" I ask, my heart pounding against my breastbone.

"Yeah," she says softly. "It was time. When I was visiting with Josh's mom, I realized that the only way to fully move forward was to let go of the past."

"I'm so proud of you," I tell her before taking her lips in another searing kiss.

Realization sets in all too quickly, and I slowly pull back. It's as if we both know it at the same time. She gives me a sad smile before turning and facing Josh's stone.

"Thank you, Josh, for loving me. I'll never forget you," she whispers, closing her eyes and tilting her head up to the sky. "I'll always love you."

Just then, a light breeze picks up again. Her hair gently blows against my face, and I see her smile. I feel her smile, all the way down to the bottom of my heart. My heart that beats just for her.

When she's ready, we turn and walk toward the cars. Our hands are still linked as I walk her to the car parked behind mine. My hand immediately goes to her face, brushing the hair from her forehead and tracing the gentle curve of her jaw. "What do you think?"

"I think I'm ready to go."

"Do you want to go to my place?" I ask, not wanting to assume we'll be going anywhere together, but damn sure hoping.

"Actually, I was kinda hoping we'd go to my place. I have a few things to put away." I can see her resolve reflecting in her eyes.

"Are you sure? We don't have to do this tonight," I offer.

"No, I'm sure. I'm ready," she says with conviction, giving me a decisive nod.

"I'll follow you," I reply, pulling her into my chest and placing a kiss on her forehead.

"Actually, I'll follow you," she sasses as she opens the driver's door.

"I'll meet you there," I tell her before turning and heading to my own vehicle.

Before I climb in, I glance back at her. She has one foot inside the car, but she's facing Josh's final resting place. I almost turn and go back to her when she says, "Goodbye, Josh."

She offers a smile before sliding down into the car and starting the engine. I do the same, and together, we slowly make our way out of the cemetery.

Toward her house.

Toward our future.

* * *

We step through her front door, the light above the sink, as well as the moonlight filtering through the big picture window. She releases my hand and drops her purse on the table before awarding me with one of her killer smiles.

I don't say anything. I can tell she has something on her mind, a resolve in her posture and determination in her eyes that tells me to just stand aside and watch.

Meghan reaches for the shoes sitting beside the door. She takes them in her hands and seems to gaze lovingly down at the pair of runners before bringing them to her chest in a hug. She smiles a small, sad grin as she opens the closet door and sets them inside. She slowly closes the door, her green eyes on mine.

I'm not sure if I should say anything or not, but I know how big this moment is.

No words are spoken as she reaches for me, offering so much more than just her hand. She's offering me her heart, the greatest gift ever.

I will forever cherish it.

And her.

Chapter Twenty-Nine

Meghan

"Hey," he says, giving me that smile that I've always loved.

"Hey, yourself," I reply as he jumps up out of the chair and approaches.

"I've been waiting," he adds, giving me a knowing look.

"Yeah, well, sometimes I'm a little slow on the uptake," I sass, laughing.

"No kidding. You're as bad as your sisters sometimes, you know?" he teases and comes over to where I'm sitting. "I'm going to miss you."

My eyes and throat start to burn. "I'm going to miss you too."

"But you don't need me anymore, sweetheart. You have someone else now."

I drop my chin to my chest and nod.

"I really like him," he says, drawing my eyes back to his. "I've always liked him. That's why I know you're going to be in great hands, Meggy."

"He is pretty wonderful. But so were you."

"Ehh, I was only wonderful because of you. You made me the man I was."

"Don't sell yourself short. You were the only one who could put up with me and my crazy family," I reply, making him laugh.

Lacey Black

"They are pretty nutty. I enjoy dropping in on them from time to time and seeing what they're all up to. They all have a pretty good life," he says with that familiar smile as he reaches for my hand.

"They do. I'm proud of all of them."

"And I'm proud of you, Meggy. For finally taking the steps you needed to take. I know it wasn't easy. Hell, it wasn't easy, nor fun to watch. But you got there, just like I knew you would. And I owe a big chunk of the gratitude to Nick for that. He helped you see just how amazing you are, and just how big your heart is."

"It wasn't easy," I tell him honestly.

"No, it wasn't. Life isn't easy, Meggy. But love makes it worth it. Like I told you that night... Live, Meg. Live and love, because that's who you are and why you were put here."

We're both silent for several seconds. I memorize his features, the way his eyes light up when he smiles, and the way his hand feels in mine.

"I gave the ring back to your mom," I tell him.

"I know. She cried after you left, but she'll be okay. You're both going to be okay," he says, offering me a sad smile. "It was hard watching you take it off."

"It was hard to take it off," I confess, my fingers automatically going to the place that ring has sat for the last couple of years. "But it was time."

"It was," he agrees.

"I'm going to miss you so much," I say, silently crying once more.

318

"I'm going to miss you too. I promise to check in on you every once in a while too."

"I'd like that," I tell him honestly.

"You were my forever love, Meggy. But now I leave you in Nick's hands. He'll help guide you and love you through the rest of your life. And someday, we'll meet again. I promise."

"I look forward to it," I say as we both stand up. "I will always love you, Josh."

"And I will always love you, Meghan. Be free, sweet girl. Be free and love."

"I will," I state, shedding more tears as he moves forward, placing a gentle kiss on my cheek.

"Goodbye," he says as he turns and walks away.

"Goodbye," I reply, watching him go.

When I wake with a start, I know he's gone. The house feels different now. Even though I realize Josh will always be with me, I know that the rest of this journey through life isn't with him by my side.

But I'm not alone. I have my family. I have friends.

And I have Nick.

For how long? No one knows.

But if I'm lucky, I'll get to spend the rest of my life beside him, loving him.

Angie was right. There's room for two in my heart. Josh's love was my past, and Nick's is my future. One doesn't trump the other, they just co-exist.

I feel Nick's arm wrap around me, pulling me into his chest. His heart is beating steadily beneath my fingertips as I softly caress the light dusting of dark hair on his chest.

"You okay?" he whispers.

Snuggling in close, I recall my dream. Not the one I've been plagued with since the night Josh died, but the one I had tonight. The one where we said goodbye. The one where I let him go.

"Yes," I answer honestly, smiling upward. Because I know that I *will* be okay.

I'll be okay because of this man I have at my side, as well as the one who watches over me.

I'll be okay because I'm a strong woman who has survived heartache and come out only slightly scathed and yet smiling on the other side.

I'll be okay because I know how to love, and how to accept it in return.

That's what I'll carry with me forever.

My forever.

Chapter Thirty

Nick

She is stunning in that red dress, but all I can think about is getting that damn thing off her.

Meghan chats with her family, slowly sipping a glass of champagne. Her smiles are lighter, carefree even. She seems much more at ease than I've ever seen, at least since she lost her fiancé.

But tonight is a night of celebrating.

Earlier, I sat in the pew with Dean, Ryan, Levi, and Linkin, as well as a few babies, while Sawyer and AJ exchanged vows. It was an emotional ceremony for many, but for me? Well, I just couldn't stop staring at the sexy bridesmaid in the middle. She kinda owns my heart.

Now, everyone is hanging out, drinking and laughing, and I find myself hanging back and just watching them interact. They're a close family, sure, but they're more than that. They're friends too, and their love for each other is evident.

"Happy to see you here," I hear behind me. I turn to find Meghan's Dad, Brian, standing there.

"I'm pretty happy to be here myself," I tell him honestly, taking a sip of my Sprite.

"I take it everything worked itself out last night?" he asks.

Nodding, I reply with a smile, "It did."

"Glad to hear. I really like you Nick. You're a good guy," he adds, grabbing my shoulder and giving it a gentle squeeze.

I offer him a smile, not really knowing what to say. I feel like there's so much more he's not saying, but implying with his simple statements. "Thank you, sir."

"Don't let her push you away," he says, turning and looking at his group of daughters.

I follow his gaze and smile when I see Meghan kissing her tiny niece Amelia on the cheek. The baby is once again in her father's arm, where the big guy seems to prefer her to be. She must sense my gaze and glances over. When she sees me watching, she says something to her group and starts to make her way toward me.

"Hey," she says when she reaches me. She quickly wraps her arms around my chest and steps in close. She smells like vanilla and champagne.

"Hey yourself," I reply, placing a kiss on her forehead.

"Hi, Daddy," Meghan says, offering her father a warm smile.

"Hi, sweetheart. Having fun?"

"The best," she answers just as a pretty blonde walks up and stands at Brian's side. "I still can't believe you're the woman my dad has been seeing," Meghan adds, offering her a smile.

"Sometimes I can't believe it myself," Cindy says, glancing up at Brian. "He's a pretty amazing man."

Brian wraps his arm around Cindy's shoulder and gives her a little hug. "She's the amazing one," he says.

Meghan was completely surprised when she saw Cindy at the wedding this afternoon. When she asked what she was doing there, Brian intervened and said she was the woman he had been seeing. Meghan appeared a bit shocked at first, but quickly recovered, wrapping the woman she considered a friend in her arms and hugging her tightly. She whispered something into Cindy's ear that made her tear up, but I don't know what was said.

"Dance with me?" I ask the beautiful woman in my arms.

"Always," she replies with a grin.

I lead her to the dance floor, where Sawyer and AJ, as well as Dean and Payton, are already dancing to a slow song. The familiar melody speaks of love and forever, which is pretty damn fitting for this night. Not only are we celebrating the love of Meghan's sister, but in a way, we're celebrating the love I now share with Meghan. Last night, I took a chance, and while it may have been a little hairy during that time I couldn't find her, it worked out for the best. Now I get to spend my days with this amazing woman, sharing our love and enjoying our time together.

Maybe someday, I'll get to add the word forever.

I can't wait for that day.

Meghan fits against me like a puzzle piece. We gently sway to the music, my arms around her waist and her head against my shoulder. We continue to move in time to the beat, and I secretly wish this song would never end. There's no other place I want to be.

The dance floor starts to fill up. First, Brian and Cindy share a dance, and then the rest of her sisters. Brielle comes out and jumps into her dad's arms, and together, the three of them dance to the song and share a few laughs. Levi holds Abby close, her hand in his. He toys with the engagement ring on her finger and kisses the top of her head. Jaime and Ryan take to the floor next. Their sleeping daughter is still in his arms, and as he brings his wife against his chest, they form a protective cocoon around the sleeping infant. Lexi and Linkin have Stella, while their twin boys left about a half hour ago to go home with Linkin's mom.

Finally, Emma and Orval join us on the floor. He pulls his wife into his arms, and they move in time, their hips swaying to the music. He holds her so tenderly, so lovingly, that a lump forms in my throat.

I want that.

I want sixty years with the woman in my arms.

Years of love and laughter and inappropriate sexual innuendos.

Orval glances my way and gives me a grin. "Hey, Doc," he whispers just over the music. "There are a few pieces of cake left in the back. I made it special just for tonight," he adds with a wink.

Special cake?

Suddenly, I see Sawyer move uncomfortably, adjusting not only AJ in his arms, but his black tuxedo pants as well. Linkin moves a bit, juggling his daughter and his wife as he tries to get comfortable. Levi stops completely and glances down. Dean gives his daughter to his wife and tries to discreetly adjust his own pants.

And me? I'm stuck watching it all like a train wreck. You know the one where you should definitely look away, but you can't seem to do it?

Abruptly, all of the guys turn and face the ornery old man. There's no mistaking the *problem* they're all trying to conceal and the looks of panic on their faces. They all go from wide-eyed shock to outrage in a matter of seconds. Even Brian looks a bit uncomfortable in this situation, but I don't dare laugh.

And Grandpa just smiles, gazing adoringly down at his bride of sixty-some years.

My heart starts to pound in my chest as I look down at the woman I love. "Thank you," I say, pulling her flush against my body, my own groin stirring in my pants, though not for the same reason as everyone else.

"For what?" she asks, stopping her dance and looking into my eyes.

"For taking the chance. For letting me love you."

She gives me that smile. The one I hope to see on her face for the rest of my life. "Loving you is the easy part."

"Loving you is pretty damn easy, too, honey. I'm just glad you realized it. But know that if you wouldn't have, if last night had ended much differently, I wouldn't have given up on you. I wouldn't have given up on us. Because you and I? We're forever."

Her eyes fill with unshed tears, and even though I know these are the good ones, it still makes me unhappy to see them in her eyes. I never want to see those fucking tears again. She's cried too much, and I make a silent vow to never put them there again, for as long as I live.

I'm about to tell her when the moment is shattered like a glass on ceramic tile. Even the music seems to stop and all eyes turn in one man's direction. Tension (and erections) fill the dance floor as all of the guys stand there and gaze at the only smiling man still dancing with his wife.

"Orval!"

Epilogue

Meghan

1 year later

It's a Summer sister tradition that on the first Saturday of each month, the six of us get together. We take turns picking the location or activity, anything from margaritas and a movie to wine and painting classes at the small gallery uptown. One thing, though, is as certain as the sun rising over the Chesapeake Bay every morning: there will be alcohol involved.

Always.

The landscape of our monthly sisters' night has changed a bit over the years as our family continues to grow, but we still get together every month. Tonight, we went to dinner at one of those little hotdog stands down by the touristy spots along the Bay. AJ is craving cheese fries like no one's business. You know the ones that they make right there in front of you by peeling and slicing the potato with their fancy little machine, dropping the shreds of spuds into a fryer basket, and then dipping it into the big pit of grease? Not to mention the fact that she's practically drooling as they cover it with cheese – three extra pumps, as per her request. She's been extra munchie since finding out she's pregnant. At only three months along, she's eating like she's feeding eight babies, not one. At least, we think it's only one.

I take a drink of my beer and set it down on the picnic table. Besides AJ, the only other one not drinking is Payton, who is still breastfeeding baby Noah. He's almost four months now, and has his mom wrapped around his tiny finger.

The rest of us all decided to have a drink with dinner from the alcohol vendor just up the beach. Hot dogs (minus AJ who isn't allowed to have one) and beer, with our toes in the sand. It's a pretty great combination, if you ask me.

The bright orange sun is starting to set behind us, but it's a beautiful sight the way it reflects off the water. "I'm so glad we still do this, even though our lives have been all sorts of crazy lately," I say, finishing off my hotdog and dragging a French fry through my ketchup.

"Agreed. I hope we always do this. Every month," Jaime adds.

"Even when we're dealing with snotty noses and cranky nappers," Lexi contributes.

"All the more reason to make sure we never skip them," Payton says, glancing at her watch for the nth time in the last hour.

I toss my empty wrapper onto the tray and add, "Of course, it helps that we have amazing men at home to help."

"Amen," Jaime says and the same time Lexi replies, "Truth!"

Right now, all of the guys and the kids are gathered at AJ and Sawyer's beachfront house, waiting for us to return. They decided to grill out in a "Guys' Night" while we're out. They started this a few months back, which allows us girls to all still go out and enjoy a bit of free time away, but gives them all a chance to hang out together too. Plus, no one has to find a babysitter. We just have to make sure someone remains the designated driver, but that's been pretty easy since we've had someone knocked up for much of the last two years.

I'm not there. Not knocked up in any way, shape, or form. Not that it isn't on the horizon…someday. Just not now. Not yet.

Over the last year, a lot has changed. I finally packed away all of Josh's belongings. His mom came over and helped, which was a blessing in disguise. We cried together and were able to decide what to part with and what to save. I kept a small box of keepsakes – things he had given me or items that would always remind me of him, like his favorite coffee cup. All of his clothes we donated, including that pair of worn running shoes that I finally put away in the closet that night Nick and I met up at the cemetery, and when it was all said and done, I couldn't believe how much better I felt.

It was a step in the right direction to help me move forward.

Nick was there too. He never pushed me, but silently stood by my side and offered me as much support as possible. He was a godsend, and never complained when I would break down in tears.

After a few months of alternating back and forth between his place and mine, we decided to take the next step and try living together. Both of our houses were cute and more than acceptable, but both also hold memories of our pasts. So, after much talking and consideration, we decided to sell our houses and buy a different one.

Together.

And we got a cat! Not that we really had a choice, considering my grandparents dropped it off on our second day in the new place. They say it showed up at the house the night before, and they knew we'd give the young, male, tan and brown kitten a good home. He even came with a name, courtesy of Grandpa. Rooster.

Yep, he named our cat Rooster, and now all the guys snicker and mutter something about Nick's little cock running around the house.

"How many dirty diapers do you think they talked Dean into changing?" Abby asks, grinning from ear to ear, referring to the fact that Dean seems to be the only one who doesn't gag and make a big production out of cleaning poop off a bare baby bottom.

"All of them," Jaime replies. "Amelia loves green beans, but they make her poop look like she ate grass and really runny. Ryan turns this weird shade of green and thinks he's going to throw up every time he has to change her diaper."

"Linkin once paid me a hundred bucks to not have to change one of Hemi's diapers. It was seeping out the top and leg holes," Lexi says, sticking her final French fry in her mouth.

"I can't wait," AJ adds. "Sawyer is going to be the best daddy."

I nod. "He will be."

"How about you, Abs? Any baby-popping plans yet?" Payton asks one of the twins.

"We just got married two months ago. Can we enjoy the honeymoon phase for a bit?" Abby asks, her cheeks flushing a light shade of pink.

"Ohhh, we enjoyed the honeymoon phase a bit too much. That's why we're in this predicament," AJ contributes with a bit of laughter and a rub of her still-flat belly.

"I think Jaime and Ryan will be pregnant by Halloween. He couldn't keep his hands off her while she was pregnant," Payton adds, glancing back down at her watch before finishing off her bottle of water.

"Agreed," everyone chimes in.

"I don't think so. We're enjoying our little family of three right now. I'm in no hurry." Jaime finishes off her beer bottle and tosses it in the trashcan.

"Are we about ready?" Payton asks, standing up and grabbing our piles of trash.

"What's the rush? You're in such a hurry, and you've checked your watch every two seconds since we got here," I state as I grab the rest of my own garbage and throw it in the can.

"No rush," she insists, her purse strap thrown over her shoulder.

"She's anxious to get back to her family," Lexi insists with a nervous laugh.

"Yep, I am," our oldest sister urges. "Let's go."

They're all walking a bit faster than expected as we make our way from the beach walkway to the parking lot. Everyone is laughing and carrying on, sharing stories of things their kids did or something that happened at work. It's comfortable. Familiar.

Payton drives Lexi's SUV, which comfortably seats all six of us, once we took the car seats out. The trip to AJ's place is short, since she seems to take the turns at forty and disobeys every traffic law on that twenty-mile stretch of shore roadway. I'm actually a little relieved when we finally pull into AJ and Sawyer's driveway.

"Let me out of this car," I grumble, waiting for Jaime to open the door so I can climb out of the third row.

"Oh, don't be dramatic. It wasn't that bad," Payton retorts, throwing the keys to our baby sister.

I follow as we make our way through the front door. The first thing I notice is the sound. There's laughter and growling, clearly the house has been overrun with monsters.

"Hurry, hurry!" Brielle exclaims, running from the living room with Hemi and Hudson hot on her heels.

"Daddy Monster is coming!" Hudson proclaims.

"Huh-we, huh-we," Hemi mimics with a wide grin, running straight into the entryway and hiding behind our legs.

"Rahrrrr!" Linkin growls, his hands raised high above his head as he stomps into the foyer in search of his boys. When he spies his wife, he changes course and stalks toward her. "Rahrrrr, Mama," he says, wiggling his eyebrows suggestively and pulling her into his chest.

"You're nuts," she says, laughing as he mauls her where she stands.

The boys start laughing and cheering. "Get her, Daddy!"

"Eat Mommy!"

As we make our way into the living room, we find the rest of the gang in there. Dean is rocking baby Noah in the recliner, who's sawing logs, even though it's as loud as a sports arena in this place. Ryan is sitting on the floor watching Amclia bang on pots and pans from the kitchen cabinets with a wooden spoon. Levi is chatting with Sawyer, glancing back and forth between the chaos in the room and the baseball game on the television.

And Nick?

He's nowhere to be found.

"Hey, where's Nick?" I ask, glancing around at my brothers-in-law, waiting for one of them to answer my question. When none of them do, I decide to check the kitchen, where I find a couple of open cabinet doors and a pile of dirty dishes from their little "guys' night."

"Do you want a drink?" AJ asks as she joins me in the kitchen.

"No, I was looking for Nick. Did anyone see where he went?" I ask, starting to get concerned. Maybe he wasn't feeling well and went home. Maybe there was a dental emergency at the office, and he was needed. I hope that's not the case because I haven't checked my phone the entire time, and I'd feel guilty if I missed his message and he had to take care of the patient on his own.

"Oh, uh, Sawyer said he went for a walk. You should check the beach," AJ suggests with a bright, almost fake, toothy smile.

Why is she acting weird?

Choosing not to dive into one of the many reasons why one of my siblings is acting strange, I head to the back door. It's standing open, so it doesn't take much for me to slip through the screen door and step out onto the deck.

Their party lights are on, probably left on from when they were out here cooking. As I head toward the stairs that lead down to the beach, I can hear music off in the distance. When I reach the sand and take off my sandals, I realize the music is closer than I originally thought. I head in the direction of the sappy country song, trying to figure out where it's coming from.

It takes me about a hundred yards to find it.

Or more specifically, to find Nick.

He's standing along the shore, a blanket at his feet and a smile on his face. The combination of waves crashing on the beach and the sentimental love song playing on the radio makes for a pretty great ambiance.

"What are you doing?" I ask, smiling as I approach him.

"Waiting for you." His hair is slightly tussled as the warm breeze filters off the salty Bay.

"For me? Why are you out here and not at the house with everyone else?" I ask, finally reaching his side.

"Because I didn't want an audience," he says matter-of-factly.

I stop in front of him, glancing up at his serious face. "For what? Is everything okay?" I ask, starting to get a bit worried. Even under the darkened sky, I can tell he's slightly flushed and seems a bit sweaty. Maybe I wasn't far off on the whole not feeling good bit.

"Everything is fine. Perfect, actually. Well, almost," he says, stumbling on his words and chuckling dryly.

"Nick?" I ask, stepping into his space and touching my palm over his forehead. Maybe he has a fever.

As soon as my hand touches his skin, I can sense his relief and feel him relax. "What's wrong?"

"Nothing, honey. I promise," he says, seeming to find his confidence. "I have something I wanted to say to you."

"Okay," I whisper quietly, my entire body suddenly on guard.

"You know I love you, right?" he asks, his eyes brightening under the moonlight.

"Yes," I reply with a smile.

"Good, because there's no one else I imagine spending the rest of my life with. We both have a bit of baggage that we carry, but I want you to know that I'll always be here to help shoulder that burden. You were once engaged, and that didn't exactly go as planned," he says softly, taking my hands in his own. The tears well in my eyes, but I can't look away from the hazel ones in front of me.

"I know how much it hurt to lose Josh, and I know how far you've come since it happened. But everything that happened, everything in your life and in mine, led us to each other, to this place. It was ugly for a while, but together, we've found beauty once more. We've found love. We've found forever."

He takes a deep breath and drops to his knee in front of me. A gasp slips from my lips as I watch in shock and awe as he kisses my knuckles and gazes up at me. "Meghan, you're the only one I want to spend the rest of my life with. The only one I want to wake up beside in the morning and fall asleep with every night. You're my forever, honey. Will you marry me?"

I close my eyes, letting his sweet words wash over me, and when I do, I see Josh. I see his smiling face, nodding his approval. I know he's watching over me, encouraging me to *live* as he always said in my dreams. To live for me *and* for him.

When I open my eyes and glance down at Nick, my heart beats wildly in my chest. I know what my answer will be. The *only* answer. "Yes. Yes, Nicholas Adams, D.D.S., I will marry you."

I barely even register the ring being slipped onto my finger before he jumps to his feet and takes me in his arms, spinning me around on the sand and planting a kiss on my lips. It's a kiss of everlasting love and friendship. One of grief and forgiveness. Hope and peace.

It's the kiss that starts my forever.

With Nick.

Another Epilogue

Emma

The kids all took off down to the beach, with Brian and Cindy not too far behind. Orval and I hung back a few moments, happy just to watch them all race to congratulate Nick and Meghan.

"One more wedding," I say as he takes my hand in his.

"Last one," he replies as we make our way to the crowd of family by the shore.

"Maybe not," I add, glancing over to where our son-in-law stands with the woman he loves.

It was difficult at first to see Brian with someone, but that only lasted a second, really. Cindy is a lovely woman, who makes him smile again. We haven't seen him smile in so very long. Not since our Trish died. To see him enjoying life and finding love again, well, that makes me as happy as any woman could be.

As we approach the group, we're immediately pulled into hugs. Meghan is crying, but for once, I don't mind. They're happy tears, and they match the big smile on her joyful face.

"I didn't know you were here," Meghan says.

"We were right behind you. As soon as you slipped out the back door, we came in to wait for the announcement," I confirm to my beautiful granddaughter.

"Pretty confident I was gonna say yes, weren't ya?" she teases, elbowing Nick in the stomach.

"I wasn't going to let you say no," he tells her, pulling her into his broad body and putting the moves on her.

"Hey, knock it off. I'm still her old man. I don't need to see that," Brian teases Nick when they come up for air.

"There'll definitely be plenty of *the sex* tonight," I say, winking at the newly engaged couple. Both seem to blush, which is always my goal. I love getting a rise out of them all.

"Nick, Meghan, I just wanted to congratulate you and wish you a lifetime of happiness and laughter." Orvie brings my hand up to his lips, making my entire body flush with desire. "Once you find that special person you're supposed to spend your life with, well, everything just falls into place."

"To Nick and Meghan," Brian says, holding up a mock drink in salute.

"To Nick and Meghan," everyone hollers before more cheers break out.

"And may you always have good sex," I add, hip bumping my husband and giving him a wink.

As we all slowly make our way back up to the house, everyone jovially carrying on about wedding plans and bridal showers, I think about the website I found earlier today. The one that I spent days researching and hunting for. The woman I was trying to find.

Funny thing is, she wasn't hard to find at all. She was hidden in plain sight all along.

But I won't get into that right now. I intend to keep her a secret until the right time.

Like a wedding.

Stay tuned, folks. This is sure to be…

My Kinda Wedding!

And you don't want to miss what I've got up my sleeve.

Orval won't see it coming.

~ THE END ~

Stay tuned for My Kinda Wedding, A Summer Sisters Novella, coming soon!

Dear Readers,

I can't tell you how much this book means to me. When I originally came up with Meghan's storyline, way back when I was plotting the series and writing My Kinda Kisses, I knew that this book would be the ultimate test. The greatest challenge as a writer. I did something in My Kinda Night that I've never done before, and I swore to you that I would make it right. I would give Meghan her happily ever after. No one deserves it more than her.

I dedicated this book to you – the readers who stuck with me and saw this storyline through. It's been an emotional ride, but so very worth it!

Thank you, from the bottom of my heart, for the incredible outpour of support and love for this series – this crazy and hilarious family. I do have a little something up my sleeve, and I can't wait to share what I have in store next with My Kinda Wedding.

Hang on tight, readers! It's not over!

Love,

Lacey

Acknowledgements

This book wouldn't be what it is without the amazing team I have in my corner!

Sara Eirew – This one. This one's my favorite. ;) Thank you for your wicked talent on each and every cover!

Nazarea, Kelly, and the InkSlinger PR team – Thank you for your tireless promotion and work on each new reveal and release.

Amanda and Jacob – This photo was one of the first ones I found when I was plotting this series, and I fell in love. I knew it was perfect for Meghan and Nick.

Kara Hildebrand – You were officially the first person to read this book, and it was agony waiting to hear from you while you worked on it. (Yes, all 5 days.) I thank you for your love and support, and for talking me off the ledge a time or two. I can't wait to start our next project together!

Sandra Shipman – I get so excited sending you each book, but never more than with this one. Thank you for helping me and making sure I have the appropriate amount of f-bombs. That is such an important part of any Lacey Black book!

Jo Thompson – I told you what I had planned, and you told me you had my back. You cried with me during Night, even though I broke your heart. You told me I could do it when I questioned the storyline. THANK YOU for your help and encouragement. I'm sorry I made you cry. I mean, I'm sorry your allergies gave you fits while reading.

Carey Decevito – I'm so thankful that I've found you on this journey in publishing, and thank you for all your love, help, and support!

Brenda Wright of Formatting Done Wright – As always, the BEST formatter ever. Thank you!

Holly Collins – Thank you for always cheering me on and encouraging me. I'm sorry I made you cry too when you read this. We can blame the pregnancy, right? Love you!

Lacey's Ladies – Ladies, you all keep me going. You keep me sane and make me laugh daily. Thank you for your constant love and support, and for sticking by my side when I killed off your favorite character!

My husband and two kids – I love you. So much.

Every single blogger who helped with the cover reveal or shared the release – THANK YOU!

And last but not least, the readers - THANK YOU for purchasing this book! Thank you for loving this series.

About the Author

Lacey Black is a Midwestern girl with a passion for reading, writing, and shopping. She carries her e-reader with her everywhere she goes so she never misses an opportunity to read a few pages. Always looking for a happily ever after, Lacey is passionate about contemporary romance novels and enjoys it further when you mix in a little suspense. She resides in a small town in Illinois with her husband, two children, and a chocolate lab. Lacey loves watching NASCAR races, shooting guns, and should only consume one mixed drink because she's a lightweight.

Email: laceyblackwrites@gmail.com
Facebook: https://www.facebook.com/authorlaceyblack
Twitter: https://twitter.com/AuthLaceyBlack
Blog: https://laceyblack.wordpress.com

Made in the USA
Middletown, DE
17 July 2023

35123618R00195